Cora untied the ribbon, lifted the lid and gasped.

Swathed in tissue lay a gown done in the cerulean silk she'd admired at Madame Dumont's. Tears of gratitude smarted in her eyes. Had Aunt Benedicta ordered the gown?

The moment Cora drew the gown from the box, she knew that wasn't the case. This gown was beyond what her aunt could afford. This gown wasn't practical. It was...magical. "Elise, come see this."

"Oh, where did that come from?" Elise breathed in awe, a fingertip daring to stroke the silk. "It's lovely. You would look breathtaking in it with your dark hair."

"I don't know. It's not ours." Cora sighed wistfully. Best not to get too attached. She began putting it back in the box.

"No, you don't! We are not putting the dress back until you try it on," Elise called over her shoulder.

"I suppose it couldn't hurt. But don't get your hopes up. It's not likely to fit since it's not mine." Cora let Elise help her out of her clothes and into her new things.

"Now, you may look." Elise led her to the pier glass and for a moment all Cora could do was stare. Was that truly her staring back?

T0197896

Author Note

When is the last time you did something for yourself? It's probably been a while. It certainly has been for my heroine, Cora Graylin. She's a damsel in distress until she finds herself a damsel with a dress—a dress that can change everything for her. Cora's and Declan's journeys are about the pursuit of happiness while balancing their personal wants with the needs of those who count on them. They are both individuals who take family and duty seriously. The story is also a bit of a reverse fairy tale that starts with a happy-ever-after and unravels from there because nothing worth fighting for ever comes easy. While the backdrop is familiar—London in the Season— I hope you enjoy the little tidbits interspersed about the Season of 1824 and maybe have the chance to learn a little something you didn't know before. Most of all, I hope you can relate to Cora and Declan's story and see your own journey reflected in theirs.

CINDERELLA AT THE DUKE'S BALL

BRONWYN SCOTT

HISTORICAL

If you purchased this book without a cover you should be aware that this book is stolen property. It was reported as "unsold and destroyed" to the publisher, and neither the author nor the publisher has received any payment for this "stripped book."

Harlequin®
HISTORICAL

ISBN-13: 978-1-335-53969-4

Cinderella at the Duke's Ball

Copyright © 2024 by Nikki Poppen

All rights reserved. No part of this book may be used or reproduced in any manner whatsoever without written permission.

Without limiting the author's and publisher's exclusive rights, any unauthorized use of this publication to train generative artificial intelligence (AI) technologies is expressly prohibited.

This is a work of fiction. Names, characters, places and incidents are either the product of the author's imagination or are used fictitiously. Any resemblance to actual persons, living or dead, businesses, companies, events or locales is entirely coincidental.

For questions and comments about the quality of this book, please contact us at CustomerService@Harlequin.com.

TM and ® are trademarks of Harlequin Enterprises ULC.

Harlequin Enterprises ULC
22 Adelaide St. West, 41st Floor
Toronto, Ontario M5H 4E3, Canada
www.Harlequin.com

Printed in U.S.A.

Recycling programs for this product may not exist in your area.

Bronwyn Scott is a communications instructor at Pierce College and the proud mother of three wonderful children—one boy and two girls. When she's not teaching or writing, she enjoys playing the piano, traveling—especially to Florence, Italy—and studying history and foreign languages. Readers can stay in touch via Facebook at Facebook.com/bronwyn.scott.399 or on her blog, bronwynswriting.blogspot.com. She loves to hear from readers.

Books by Bronwyn Scott

Harlequin Historical

"Dancing with the Duke's Heir"
in *Scandal at the Christmas Ball*
The Art of Catching a Duke
The Captain Who Saved Christmas

Enterprising Widows

Liaison with the Champagne Count
Alliance with the Notorious Lord
A Deal with the Rebellious Marquess

Daring Rogues

Miss Claiborne's Illicit Attraction
His Inherited Duchess

The Peveretts of Haberstock Hall

Lord Tresham's Tempting Rival
Saving Her Mysterious Soldier
Miss Peverett's Secret Scandal
The Bluestocking's Whirlwind Liaison
"Dr. Peverett's Christmas Miracle"
in *Under the Mistletoe*

Visit the Author Profile page
at Harlequin.com for more titles.

For Kathy who is a fairy godmother to
so many people and animals in her life.

Chapter One

London,
April 1824

In the Season of 1824, Cora Graylin, twenty years old, and fresh from the sheep-ridden Dorset countryside, knew these truths to be self-evident: that life began with a dress and all subsequent success depended on it being the right dress. Every significant milestone of a woman's life was marked by a dress—a baptismal gown to mark her entrance into the community of the Anglican church, the letting down of her hems to presage her entrance into Society, a dress for presentation at Court to mark her entrance into that Society, a debutante's white ball gown, and, ultimately, the wedding gown that heralded the pinnacle of a woman's achievement—to marry well.

Dresses marked every hour, every second of a woman's life. Morning gowns, afternoon gowns, tea gowns, evening gowns, dressing gowns, night gowns, travelling dresses and riding habits. The list was as endless as the variation on the theme. The dress did more than mark time. The dress was a gatekeeper, determining who one met and who one *could* meet. Every mama and eager young girl—descending on London with hopes of snatching the right husband—believed in the absolute truth that the right dress could even determine the course of a life.

Anyone who doubted this wisdom had only to look at the first appointment in a woman's diary upon arrival. It was not with the patronesses of Almack's, although they ranked a strong second—after all, a dress *had* to be seen in order to be useful—nor with a best friend not visited in a year. No, the first appointment was with the dressmaker.

Beginning in March, the needles of London's twenty thousand dressmakers began to sew feverishly. For the first time in years it was acceptable to travel to the Continent, to borrow fashion from the French, and there were—saints be praised—*men*, a commodity that had been in alarmingly short supply during the long years of the war, to see that fashion. Waists had come down to an almost natural level, skirts had become fuller, and the concept of presenting a fashionable triangle was all the rage.

Appointments were made months in advance and one defaulted on that appointment on pain of social death. The visit to the dressmaker's was the beginning of rounds of shopping, of being seen. And for girls like Cora and her sister, it was the beginning of hope, predicated on the belief that everything could change with a stitch, with the right swath of fabric against the right complexion. A fairy tale to be sure.

A part of her wanted to believe it was true, that such miracles were possible. This part of her had kept her awake most of the night, although her sister's snoring may also have contributed. Cora stifled the tiniest of yawns as she pored over fashion plates at Madame Dumont's. But the thrill of hope—optimistically and stubbornly rippling through her since the onset of this mad adventure—was still undeniably there. All the realism in the world had been unable to subdue it. She indulged that hope for a moment, closing her eyes and letting herself bask in the knowledge that she was in London and she had an appointment with a Bond Street dressmaker—or nearly so, give or take a few blocks.

For the first time in the two years since Mama passed, there was a thread of hope and that was more than she'd had for a long while. With the right dress, who knew what that thread might be woven into if she dared to grasp it? Cora suppressed a longing sigh. The daring was harder than one might think. She'd learned the painful lesson that when one had been deprived of hope before, it was difficult to trust in hope again. Hope was a precious promise for the future. Lost hope was a promise broken, a future denied. But what choice did she have but to believe? She had to try, for her family's sake.

Cora held a swatch up to her sister's cheek. 'Elise, this yellow muslin with the white flowers would look wonderful on you.' Elise had inherited their mother's blonde good looks and their father's warm brown eyes. Cora had no doubts that, with the right gowns and their aunt's connections, Elise would make a fine match. She hoped so. She'd promised Mama she'd take care of the girls and Elise deserved more than the wilds of Dorset. It would be a relief to have one sister settled, one part of her promise kept, even if it meant missing Elise desperately when a husband swept her off to parts unknown.

There was an approving nod from Aunt Benedicta over the yellow fabric. 'You've a good eye, Cora.' Her aunt smiled before returning to the fashion plates. 'The yellow is perfect for Elise. But don't forget about yourself. The blue would bring out your hair.'

'Yes,' Elise added her enthusiasm. 'Choose the blue, Cora. We are here for you, too.' A bit of her initial excitement surged, exerting itself over reality's brief intrusion into this happy occasion. She *would* choose the blue, Cora decided. And the green with the white sprigs as well. She smiled to herself, indulging in a luxurious moment of joy. How wondrous it was to think of having new clothes and in such pretty colours! No more blacks and dull browns.

Being here in London, buying new clothes, was like having her life begin again. It was a heady realisation to wake up to each morning in the townhouse off Curzon Street. Every rumble of a carriage past her window, every hawking cry of a vendor reminded her *she* was in London. This life of leisure, of shopping and paying calls, had taken some getting used to after years of nursing Mama and running the house, seeing to her little sisters' education. Then she had lost Mama, only to realise she'd lost Papa as well, as he had taken Mama's death hard, which meant the parish burdens had fallen into her lap, too.

She'd been so busy in Dorset caring for others, making opportunities for others, that her own chances at a life had slowly slipped away. She was going to have her chance now though. There'd been a rescue from the mundane sameness of her life when she'd least expected it. Aunt Benedicta and Uncle George had been unlooked-for angels, sweeping into Papa's rectory and inviting her and Elise to spend the Season in London with them. She and Elise hadn't believed their good luck. It had seemed unreal, like a fairy tale. But Papa's resistance had seemed real.

He'd argued with his brother, the Baronet, reluctant to let Cora go. Who would run the house? Who would care for the girls? Who would organise the parish? Papa would be helpless without her. With a sinking heart, and desperate to save at least Elise's chance for London, Cora had offered to stay behind. It had taken hard persuading on Aunt Benedicta's part to convince Papa both of them must come.

'Alan,' Aunt B had said, fixing their father with a stern eye, 'there are only two fates for these girls if they stay in Dorset—marriage to farmers or spinsterhood. *And* you have three other girls to marry off in addition. The kind of help you need cannot be found here. The girls must go to London.'

Aunt Benedicta had been relentless in her truths. Elise and Cora were pretty, lively girls who could do better than a Dorset sheep farmer. Better for themselves and better for the family. Who would bring out the younger girls if their older sisters weren't poised to help them? Aunt Benedicta had stopped short of highlighting the genteel poverty Cora's family flirted with all too often, and Papa's own inability to help himself.

As a vicar with a small living, her father wasn't set

up to raise five daughters and provide for them. Dowries and Seasons were beyond him, even more so now that his beloved spouse was gone. Thankfully, Aunt Benedicta's arguments had been enough. They were *here*, poring over fashion plates and selecting from an array of fabrics, which bordered on dizzying after years of loss and deprivations that had made Cora something of an expert in counting pennies and pounds. She knew the cost of a gown down to the trim of its lace and the price of its buttons.

Cora fingered the green muslin she'd selected with its dainty print. Even now, she didn't dare let herself get entirely carried away. It wasn't all furbelows and fairy tales. She was practical enough to understand that. There was work to be done.

'Alan, give them a Season, give them a chance,' Aunt Benedicta had argued. *'Good matches for them will set the other three up.'*

That last argument had resonated strongly with Cora, giving her the fortitude to leave her sisters and Papa. The family was counting on her and Elise. She was twenty, Elise eighteen. Both of them were old enough to marry. The enormity of that made her pause.

Beneath the thrill of dressmakers and debuts was a numbing reality. In the next twelve weeks she was expected to meet and marry a man she would spend the rest of her life with. It cast the words 'until death do us part' in a rather ominous context. There was so little time in which to make such a large commitment. Her family was counting on her—the words came again, a refrain that had become a constant litany in her mind over the last weeks. More than that, *she* was counting on herself.

These next twelve weeks would decide *her* life. If she didn't find a husband in London, she'd return to Dorset and become a spinster by default, her days spent caring for her family, for her father who seemed unlikely to suddenly acquire the skills to care for himself, or the grit to pull himself out of the depression that had plagued him since her mother's death. And caring for the parish in the absence of her father's ability to do more than preach on Sundays and perform ceremonies.

Even without those burdens to detract from marriage, there wasn't anyone who appealed. Aunt Benedicta was right in her arguments. A baronet's nieces needed more than what a sheep farmer could provide. Cora had experienced that first-hand. She knew what was on offer back home—the likes of dour John Arnot with his fifty acres, one hundred head of sheep and three children in need of a mother. He wanted a cook, a housekeeper and governess all rolled into one, whom he didn't have to pay. She wanted something slightly more than what he offered.

Yet, despite the pressure to wed within weeks, she still harboured hope that she might find a man who at least respected her as something more than a servant. She was realistic, though. She did not expect romance. A whirlwind romance was overrated and romantic love had its limits. Love wasn't enough to make a marriage, to conquer problems. She'd seen that with her own parents. She would be happy with a man who had the potential to grow to love her, and she him. Surely, that wasn't too much to ask. Otherwise, it would make for a long fifty years.

The shop assistant assigned to them approached. Aunt Benedicta gave instructions for the muslin day dresses before turning to the girls. 'Now, for some evening wear.'

Ball gowns. The flicker of hope burned a bit brighter at the announcement. Cora's mind couldn't help but quietly sing with cautious joy. They were going to get ball gowns! She felt Elise squeeze her hand, as excited as she was. They exchanged a secret look of joy. The Season was indeed serious business, but there was no denying it was also a fairy tale come to life. Somewhere between the two lay reality.

The shop assistant led them to a clutch of chairs gathered about a low table, upon which was spread copies of fashion magazines accompanied by a tray of lemonade and biscuits. 'Please, enjoy a drink and I'll be back shortly with fabrics.' The assistant left them and Cora sipped at her lemonade, letting her mind contemplate the materials the clerk might be assembling behind the curtain. She imagined silks and satins in primrose, and poppy, maybe a cerulean or hortensia. Oh, what she'd give for a cerulean gown.

Cora was envisaging herself waltzing across a chandelier lit ballroom in a gown of cerulean silk when the bell over the door tinkled. Three women entered, two older, one younger—a blonde Cora's age who was conversation-stoppingly beautiful. The whole trio was turned out in the first stare of fashion, from the tips of their dyed-to-match kid leather boots to the brims of their elegant bonnets. Cora did a quick calculation. The lace on the young woman's gown alone would buy meat for a month.

Aunt Benedicta's posture went ramrod straight, her eyes following the newcomers in measured recognition. 'The Duchess of Colby and her daughter,' she mouthed.

The whisper had scarcely crossed Aunt Benedicta's lips before Madame Dumont herself emerged into the showroom, a parade of assistants behind her, and a maid bearing a tray of iced glasses of champagne. No tepid lemonade for these guests. Madame Dumont made a curtsy. 'Your Grace, it is an honour to have you visit our salon.'

The Duchess of Colby gave a cool, polite smile that suggested she agreed with Madame Dumont's assessment. 'Madame Devereaux recommended you. She is overrun with business at present and time is of the essence.' Cora thought she saw a slight tightening of Madame's smile as if a hidden message had been expressed.

The Duchess nodded towards the beautiful blonde. 'My daughter, Lady Elizabeth Cleeves, requires a ball gown for the Harlow Ball, which as you know is next week.'

Oh... Cora nearly sighed. The Harlow Ball—to which she and Elise had not been invited given they were merely nieces to a baronet, with a respectable but moderate address by Mayfair standards—was all anyone had talked about at Aunt Benedicta's at-homes.

At the mention of the ball, Madame Dumont gave a clap of her hands, sending her assistants scurrying off to gather bolts of cloth. Seven assistants to take care of one duke's daughter. Just one assistant to care for a baronet's two nieces. Cora refused to let the disparity ruin her day. She was still getting ball gowns, after all, and the thought was just as lovely as it had been a few minutes before.

Moments later, the curtain separating the back of the shop from the front was held open by the maid who was now sans champagne tray—the parade of fabrics began. Cora looked on wistfully as shades of azure and daffodil, rose and parma violet were marched towards Lady Elizabeth Cleeves. Cora's curiosity piqued as each bolt passed. What had their assistant chosen for them? Perhaps more of the poppy, or the cerulean? Their assistant came last, bearing bolts of cloth to her chin. Cora fought the urge to rise and go to her aid.

The assistant set the bolts on the low table and Cora looked past her for another assistant. Perhaps the maid had been pressed into service to help, for surely there must be more fabric, because these were all white, every last one of them. Fine white linens and cottons, to be sure, but they were not *colours* and they were not silk. She'd hoped…well that was the problem wasn't it? Hoping.

She'd let her hopes get ahead of her and that had led to an unwarranted disappointment. She never should have hoped on silks and satins to begin with. It was entirely ungrateful of her. It was no small expense to outfit not one but two girls for a Season and her uncle was generously footing the entire bill.

Cora schooled her features, trying not to let her disappointment show, her gaze sneaking one final glance at Lady Elizabeth Cleeves. The woman would look stunning in the cerulean. She would be the belle of the Harlow Ball. Cora could imagine it now—how conversation would halt when she walked into the room, deep sky-blue skirts swirling, gold hair piled high. Men would forget to breathe, women would turn green with envy. The young Harlow Duke would see her and ask her to dance… Cora felt the gentle press of her aunt's hand on hers.

'Lady Elizabeth Cleeves has been out for two Seasons,' her aunt explained. The lady might dare some colour now that her debut was behind her. But this was Cora's first Season and the expectation was white and pearls. A bit of the fairy tale faltered. If it were *her* second Season, Cora, too, might be allowed to venture a little colour, but she'd not get a second Season. It was this or nothing.

'These fabrics are exactly what we need for the events we'll attend.' Aunt Benedicta selected a length of white roses on fine white cotton. 'This would be lovely with bright blue ribbon for trim at the hem and the Brussels lace at the sleeves.' It would be, Cora couldn't argue with that. Nor could she argue with the practicality of it. Should the Season not reap results, the dress was not so highbrow it couldn't be worn again for years to come, or altered and passed down to her sisters when they came of age. Coming of age in Dorset would not require fancy clothes or even new clothes for a girl destined to marry a sheep farmer.

No. She would not let it come to that. Not for her or for her sisters. John Arnot would have to look else-

where for his indentured wife. She would find someone, she would.

But who? Cora let Aunt Benedicta make the selections while her own mind pondered the worrisome question. She knew who she *wouldn't* meet—men who attended the Harlow Ball. Heirs to titles and fortunes. She wouldn't meet the young Duke—young and needing to marry quickly, if the gossip pages could be believed.

It was no secret his mother was eager to see him wed and this ball was to be a culling of Society's best so that he might pick his bride by Season's end. She supposed that was one thing they had in common. They both needed to be wed in twelve weeks. Was he feeling the pressure, too? Did dukes feel pressure? Probably not. Everyone wanted to marry *them*. He simply had to choose. Men had it easier. She sighed.

Her aunt looked in her direction. 'Are you happy with the choices, my dear?'

'Oh, yes.' She gathered herself, wishing she hadn't sighed so loudly and given the wrong impression. She'd missed the discussion entirely. 'They will be lovely. Thank you again, Aunt B.'

They rose and Aunt Benedicta made arrangements for fittings and delivery. 'We're off to the milliner's now. Hats and then gloves and shoes, girls.' She smiled cheerily as if she meant to reassure Cora. 'All will be well,' her aunt whispered as they passed the Duchess's coterie. 'The Duke isn't the only *eligible parti* in Town, you'll see. There are second sons, vicars with good livings, barristers, doctors, gentlemen with large estates and the income to match.' Aunt Benedicta gave Cora a sly twinkling glance as they stepped out into the street. 'Your uncle has friends. We might even find you a baronet if your heart is set on a title.' Perhaps they would. Cora merely nodded. She understood her duty and she would do it.

Declan Locke, Duke of Harlow, knew his duty and he would see it done. He would not let the Harlow cradle go empty any longer than necessary. The year of mourning for his father was past. Protocol had been satisfied, now it was time to get serious about the future. Beyond himself, there was no obvious heir except a distant cousin he'd never met who lived in Upper Canada.

Unfortunately, the future meant facing the much-anticipated Harlow Ball. It hadn't even started yet and he was already done with it. Over it. Declan poured himself a drink from the collection of decanters on the sideboard while his mother talked. And talked. And talked. About the ball. His ball. The place where he'd pick his wife.

The ball had been the obsession of London for weeks now, even before the Season began. The gossip pages had been leaking little details each week—the colour of the roses, the style of the decorations—all to tease the masses. He didn't know who was anticipating the event more, his mother or the guests. Both parties were worked into a fevered pitch about it and there was still a week to go. With any luck, everyone would burn themselves to cinders in their excitement.

'Shall we go over the list again?' His mother reached for a sheaf of papers on her writing desk. It wasn't really a question. They were going to go over the list despite his preferences. Declan took a swallow from his drink and looked out the window at the street below. It was crowded and busy and he'd give anything to be away from the noise, back at the family seat, riding his horses and fishing in his rivers. Had his father felt this way? Torn between duty and desire? The title meant his life was never truly his own, and yet his father had taught him that duty must always come first. He would honour that because he wanted to honour his father.

'There's Lady Mary Kimber, daughter of the Earl of Carys. She's an excellent young lady. We're lucky she's still available. There was a chance she'd go to the Creighton Dukedom last spring. Fortunately, Creighton married his portrait painter instead.' She waved a hand. 'What a scandal that was, as if Devlin Bythesea wasn't enough of a scandal on his own, son of a third son and an Indian woman.'

'Bythesea's mother is the daughter of a raja,' Declan pointed out. 'I like Creighton. I've met him at Travellers. He's got a good head on his shoulders. He and the Duke of Cowden are business partners in the Prometheus Club.' That was a club he'd like to join now that mourning was behind him and he was fully settled into the title. He had submitted an application for membership when he'd arrived in Town.

His mother's eyes narrowed and she huffed. 'The Creighton Dukedom is a cautionary tale as to what can happen when a man doesn't fill his cradle with sons. We cannot risk waiting another year.' She cleared her throat and returned to her list. 'There's also Lady Elizabeth Cleeves, the Duke of Colby's girl. She's been out for two Seasons, has good polish on her. She knows her duty and she'll be keen to marry this year.'

Declan turned from the window, his temper bristling. He loved his mother and he knew she had his best interests at heart, but it did not make this discussion any more palatable. 'You read that paper like it's a racing sheet. These are real people, Mother. They are not fillies entering the lists at Newmarket.' And he *knew* what that made him: a prime stud, nothing more. Something to be mated with the best bloodlines in order to produce yet another finely blooded thoroughbred.

It was a rather humbling realisation. He wanted to be so much more: a good father to his children as his own father had been to him, a father who played with them, who spent time with them. He wanted to be a loving husband, to be in partnership with his wife. He wanted to leave behind a legacy at Harlow Hall that positively impacted the quality of living for all those who depended on him. To perhaps build a school in the village, or improve farming so that the land was reliable, providing sustainable living far into the future.

He could do those things—but in the end no one would care about them if he didn't put sons in the cradle. Strip it all away, and that was what was left. First and foremost, he was to stand to stud, and like the stallion covering the mare, it hardly mattered how he *felt* about the mare in question, only that she be worthy of his seed and produce an heir that was a credit to the bloodline.

'How would you prefer I read the list, Declan? Like a fairy tale? Would you like me to sugarcoat it? Do you want me to pretend you can simply pick any girl you want to be your wife? Because that's not how it works.' His mother set the list down and fixed him with a hard, grey stare. 'Let me remind you how I met your father.'

Declan took a long swallow. 'I've heard this tale before. His parents selected five young women to attend a house party at Harlow Hall. You were one of them. Father spent the party with each of the five and at the end he held a ball and announced his engagement.'

His mother smiled. 'Exactly so. The five of us were selected because we had the requisite pedigree, backgrounds, fortunes, and connections. And yet, there was a flare of the romantic to it. Two weeks to win a duke's heart, to be plucked from the other contenders. And I won. When I waltzed with your father the night of the ball after our engagement was announced, I felt as if I was floating on air. I was that happy. Not because I'd fallen in love. I was not that naïve. There is no such thing as love at first sight, Declan. But I *was* happy because your father and I understood one another. I knew my duty, he knew his and we had done it. Together. Just as we navigated many things together in our marriage. And it was a good marriage. I do not regret it. I also know we were lucky. There is room for error when one only gives their son five women to choose from.'

She waved a hand. 'You are being given far more than five girls to select from. You have more choice than your father did. Be thankful for that. I promised myself when I had children, and the time came for them to marry, I would lay the best of London at their feet and let *them* choose. You may pick anyone you like from the guests.'

This was his mother's idea of being progressive, magnanimous even. 'Thank you, Mother.' It was meant sardonically as he drained his glass. He was thirty-one. He ran the estates, oversaw the Dukedom, paid the bills, sat in the House of Lords and voted his seat, making policy that governed the whole of the land. And yet despite all of that responsibility, he felt as if he were still tied to his mother's apron strings.

'You're just nervous,' his mother consoled. 'This time next week, it could all be over.'

He knew what she meant by that and it did not soothe him. If he selected a bride at the ball and announced the engagement that night, it would be finished. The papers would love it. London would talk of nothing else all Season but how he'd swept his bride off her feet and married her forthwith.

He gave a dry chuckle. 'But Mother, if I did that, what would become of the house party you've so carefully planned to follow the ball? I'd hate to see those efforts go to naught.' The ball was his mother's opening gambit, but the real bridal hunt was to be at Harlow Hall, an homage of sorts to his father's own courtship. To Declan, the house party was both an annoyance and a type of reprieve. It offered him two more weeks to postpone the inevitable. Of course, he could always hope for a miracle, that somewhere on his mother's guest list was a girl he could love, a girl who was more interested in him than she was the duchy.

Chapter Two

'Oh, miraculous day! The dresses are here!' Elise burst into the bedchamber with an envious exuberance that had Cora looking up from her letter writing—another letter home to Kitty and Melly. Elise grabbed her hand and pulled her from the writing desk, her excitement irrepressible as a parade of deep, white dress boxes tied with Madame Dumont's signature pink satin ribbon marched into the bedroom.

'Oh, my, there are so *many* boxes.' Cora hugged her sister, Elise's enthusiasm was contagious in the best of ways. She wished she could be a bit more like her sister and give herself entirely over to the London experience, but part of her was still tethered, still worried about how everyone was doing in Dorset without her. Kitty wrote almost daily asking for instructions: What should she have Veronica read for her studies? What should she take to the Robertses' for the baby's croup? The questions seemed endless.

'Did we really order so much?' It hadn't seemed like it at the time. Cora laughed in disbelief as the boxes kept coming. What a thrill it was to see them piling up on the bed until the covers were hardly visible. Perhaps it was vain and selfish to delight in such largesse, but it had been so long since she'd had anything new, let alone fashionable. The closest she had come was making over some of her mother's dresses for Elise and herself last Easter, but her mother's dresses had been far from new. Surely, she was allowed a few moments of simple joy over new clothes, as long as she didn't let it go to her head.

'Where shall we start?' Elise clasped her hands together, her face a mixed expression of abject joy and disbelief that mirrored Cora's own. A silent message passed between them, sister to sister, a shared understanding of just how miraculous it was—after years of hardship and loss—to be standing in this airy chamber, surrounded by boxes of beautiful clothes, with nothing to worry about but who to visit, what to wear and which balls to attend. For Elise, it was clear that the sun had come out at last. But Cora wondered how long the sun would last, and when would it rain again? For it surely would. Nothing lasted for ever, especially if it was good.

The combination of that joy and disbelief turned her sister's face ethereal. It was no wonder early suitors were already comparing Elise to an angel. The sight of her sister's happiness filled Cora with another type of happiness, one that had less to do with dresses, and more to do with the affection she felt for her family. At last, she cautiously dared to believe things might come aright for them after all. Elise would marry well, she was sure of it. Elise had been an instant success at the small entertainments they'd attended so far.

Perhaps she, too, would find someone. How could she not, with all of these dresses to help? Just because she hadn't found anyone who appealed yet didn't mean she wouldn't find someone soon, maybe even tonight at the Granton soiree. It was still early days—the sight of the dress boxes piled three high on the bed did much to buoy Cora's spirits, which had been lagging of late.

'It will take all afternoon to unpack this,' Elise exclaimed, but it was clear from her tone that she didn't mind.

'Perhaps we should wait for Aunt Benedicta,' Cora suggested, deferring their own excitement out of polite consideration for their generous aunt. In truth, deep down, she was just as eager to see the finished gowns as Elise. There'd been a round of fittings, which gave them some idea of what the gowns would look like, but there was nothing like seeing the finished product.

'Perhaps we should. It would only be kind after all she and Uncle have done for us. I know she was looking forward to seeing them.' Elise sighed reluctantly.

Mrs Newton, their aunt's redoubtable housekeeper, bustled forward, shooing the footmen out now that their delivery task was done. 'You are too sweet! But Lady Graylin gave me explicit instructions that if the dresses arrived while she was out, you weren't to wait for her.' She flapped her hands towards the boxes with a knowing smile. 'Have your fun, girls.'

Cora laughed as Elise dug in immediately, hastily untying the first ribbon, tossing it aside and plunging her hands into the depths of the tissue paper layers to come up with a daffodil yellow promenade gown. 'This is divine!' She held it against her and whirled about the room with a shout of glee. 'I can hardly wait to wear it walking in the park.'

Cora turned her attention to her boxes, choosing to savour the moment with a more deliberate unboxing. She carefully untied the length of satin ribbon and rolled it into a neat coil, before removing the lid and gently pushing back the tissue. She would fold the tissue later so it could be used again. 'Oh...' she sighed longingly, removing the delicate, gauzy white ball gown with flowing lines. Perhaps white wouldn't be so bad after all. She made her way to the long pier glass and held the dress to her. Elise came up behind her, still clutching the yellow gown. 'It's a little like Christmas morning, isn't it?' Elise said with uncharacteristic solemnity.

'Yes, it is. Christmas in May.' Cora exchanged a glance with her sister in the mirror and said what they were both thinking, both feeling. 'I wish Mama could see us. She would have loved dress shopping.' Mama had missed so much, *would* miss so much. She wouldn't be there to see them married, to see her grandchildren born. She wouldn't be there to hold the family together, and they so desperately needed holding together. Despite her best efforts, Cora felt she was failing—it was too much. How had Mama done it all those years and made it look so easy? So effortless?

'She wanted us to have a Season, Cora.' Elise gave a soft smile and gentle laugh. 'Although I doubt she expected it would be this grand.' Elise sobered. 'She would want us to enjoy it, every minute of it, and I mean to do just that. She'd want you to as well.'

Elise shot a meaningful look at the writing desk.

'Even now, when we are surrounded by every luxury, you bury yourself in worry. We are days from Wimborne Minster, we cannot control what happens there. But we can manage what happens here. We can make good matches and affect long-term change for the family and it's no sin, Cora, to enjoy doing it, to put yourself first.' Elise left the mirror and began opening another box. 'Perhaps we can help the family most by helping ourselves. Perhaps sacrifice isn't always the answer.'

Or perhaps that was what people told themselves to justify doing what they wanted, but Cora kept that thought to herself, let it be overridden by her mother's last words to her.

'Promise me, Cora, you will seek your own happiness. You give so much to others, I worry you don't keep enough for yourself.'

Cora wiped at an errant tear while Elise wasn't looking. Maybe there *was* merit in what her sister said. Maybe she ought to loosen the reins on hope just a little more. After all, things had been good so far. Elise was doing well and so would she, given time.

'You're as slow as a tortoise,' Elise called from the bed, where she was holding up a pink gown for at-homes. 'We'll never get through the boxes at this rate.'

Cora smiled. It was exactly the prod she needed to throw off the megrims and indulge for an afternoon.

They proceeded through the boxes at their own paces, Elise plunging in and Cora taking her time. The coils of satin ribbon piled up on the bedside table in pink pyramids as she unboxed dress after dress, cognizant of the privilege it was to be the recipient of such beautiful clothes. Beneath the joy she was cognizant, too, of the responsibility that went with these gifts. These gowns were her tools to advance her family and herself. They were meant to help her change things.

So far, despite Aunt Benedicta's efforts to see them temporarily gowned in a few quality, ready-made dresses and shown off about Town at smaller venues until their bespoke gowns were done, Cora had been a little disappointed with either her progress or, if not *her* progress, then the selection of men who had flocked to her muslin banner. There was nothing technically wrong with them. They'd been well-mannered, well-tailored and well-spoken, but none of them had put a spark to her blood or to her mind any more than the men of Dorset had. Her practical self warned that perhaps she simply wanted too much, had set the bar too high. She would need to readjust her standards to avoid being disappointed.

Cora reached for a box, mentally calculating the dresses she'd already unpacked—the green and blue day dresses, and the white ball gowns. What could be left? Perhaps the remaining boxes were Elise's and had ended up in her stacks? She untied the ribbon, lifted the lid and gasped. Swathed in tissue lay a gown done in the cerulean silk she'd admired at Madame Dumont's. Tears of gratitude smarted in her eyes. Had Aunt Benedicta guessed how much it had meant to her and ordered the gown anyway? Guilt over the additional expense pricked at her. She would be sure to thank her aunt for the unexpected extra kindness.

The moment Cora drew the gown from the box she knew that wasn't the case. This gown was above and beyond what her aunt and uncle could afford. This gown wasn't practical. It was…magical. 'Elise, come see this.'

'Oh, my word, where did that come from?' Elise breathed in awe, a fingertip daring to stroke the silk. 'It's lovely. You would be breathtaking in it with your dark hair.'

'I don't know. It's not ours.' Cora sighed wistfully. Best not to get too attached, though. She began carefully putting it back in the box but Elise had other ideas.

'No, you don't! We are *not* putting the dress back until you try it on. Right now. With *all* the trimmings. I'll get your new corset and undergarments.' She was already rummaging through the bureau drawers, collecting the needed things. 'Do it for my curiosity, if nothing else,' Elise called over her shoulder. 'I want to see you in that.'

It was hard to resist when Elise was arguing for the exact thing Cora wanted. 'I suppose it couldn't hurt,' Cora relented, letting her heart win the argument against realism, but reality still managed to get the last word. 'Don't get your hopes up. It's not likely to fit since it's not mine.'

Cora let Elise help her out of her clothes and into her new things, let Elise slip the wondrous gown over her head, the soft slide of silk slipping over her body quietly defeating reality's argument with an argument of its own.

This dress is meant for you, it whispered before she even looked in the mirror.

The silk felt light as the gown settled over her and Elise's fingers worked the fastenings. Had anything ever felt so delightful to wear? A little furl of fear uncurled in her belly. What if it looked awful on her, this gown meant to be beautiful? What if it didn't look as good as it felt? What a tragedy that would be. Cora craned her neck for a glance in the mirror only to be scolded.

'Not yet. You're not ready. Put on your gloves.' Elise passed her a pair of new, pristine, white satin elbow-length gloves and she slid them on. 'Now, you may look.'

Elise led her to the pier glass and for a moment all Cora could do was stare. Was that truly her staring back? She'd never spent much time thinking about her looks before. Her days were too long, too demanding, and vanity was a sin. Mama had always said she was beautiful, but Mama and Papa thought all of their girls were lovely. Whatever looks she might have, this gown definitely enhanced them.

The off-the-shoulder cut of the neckline showed off her bosom in a way that made her want to tug it up a bit. The snug fit of the bodice called attention to the slimness of her waist before falling away into the most delicious skirt she'd ever worn—wider and fuller than the current fashion, it gave the gown its own unique flavour. There would be no other gown like it. She gave an experimental twirl and sighed with delight. The gown felt like air and moved like water.

'For a dress not made *for* you, it definitely fits as if it was,' Elise breathed in awe. 'You're beautiful, Cora.'

'It's a bit low,' Cora tugged at the bodice and Elise slapped her hands away.

'It was meant to be worn that way, leave it. It's perfect,' Elise scolded. 'You're perfect. Don't look for ways to criticise, to minimise. Just accept.'

'It's not mine,' Cora protested, but she had to agree with her sister. The dress did put her in fine looks. The proof stared back at her from the looking glass, and it was harder still to argue with the yearning in her heart. 'We have to send it back.' A dress like this would be missed. This gown was meant for someone, but not her.

Mischief glinted in Elise's eye as her glance strayed to the bed. 'Do you think there are ball gowns in the other boxes? I'm sure we've opened all that we've ordered. I think we should look.'

There was. And more. They opened the remaining boxes together, revealing an exquisite gown in sea foam, one in a vibrant aquamarine with teal hints and another gorgeous evening gown meant for suppers and soirees in a sophisticated bronze. There was also a riding habit and a carriage ensemble in blue. 'Whoever ordered these dresses likes her blues and greens.' Elise gave a sly smile. 'What good fortune those are also your best colours.'

'They're not ours,' Cora said sharply against the growing temptation. Oh, to have clothes like these… 'Someone will be expecting them.' Cora firmly replaced the lids on the boxes. Perhaps she'd be less tempted if they were out of sight. Perhaps she could pretend she'd never seen them. Whoever had ordered them had been of her own build and age, and someone who could wear something other than white.

Elise gave a shrug, ever hopeful. 'Maybe they will miss them, but not yet.'

'It's no good.' Cora sat down carefully on a chair, the lovely fullness of the skirt spreading about her. 'Where would I wear a gown like this? Not to the Granton soiree. It's a beautiful dress but we must be reasonable. It doesn't suit our purpose.' Such a gown would look out of place and that would not help her cause. The last thing she needed to be was a misfit. Perhaps white ball gowns weren't such a bad idea after all.

Elise was beside her immediately, the other gowns forgotten. 'You *will* meet someone, Cora. You're pretty and witty and well-spoken and kind. You just haven't met the right one yet. It's only been two weeks and we've made so much progress already. We've been to teas, card parties and a few musicals. Now that we have our full wardrobe, there will be bigger events, balls and routs, and the theatre. You'll see. Even so, Sir Richard seems keen on you and Mr Tidewell has all but begged to partner you at whist at every card party so far.'

'Because I win!' Cora laughed and squeezed her sister's hand in appreciation. Elise always knew how to encourage her. 'But I must disappoint you. I have it in strictest confidence from Letitia Corning that Mr Tidewell will be calling on her father shortly to confirm their previous "understanding".'

'Oh, I'm sorry,' Elise consoled. 'Mr Tidewell has lovely dark hair and a good smile. I thought him quite handsome.' He'd clearly become less handsome in Elise's opinion now that he was no longer eligible.

'I'm not sorry.' Cora wouldn't let her sister believe she regretted Letitia Corning's news. 'He loves the city, as he should, given that's where his business interests are, but he hasn't a place in the country. And beyond whist, we have no common interests.' If she could choose, she'd prefer a husband who enjoyed riding and fishing and outdoor pursuits, who preferred raising a family in the country. She supposed she could tolerate him being a bit of a bore in exchange for the country. She had to be practical, realistic about her options, although the thought was definitely deflating. She did not think she'd meet the perfect man at the Granton soiree. Tonight all the perfect men would be dancing the night away, out of reach, at the Harlow Ball.

But enough of that. She would not sit here on this glorious spring day, in a room full of new clothes, and sulk over what could not be when there was so much to celebrate, and so much that needed putting away.

Cora gestured to the room. 'Look at what a mess we've made! We'd best get busy folding up tissue paper and rolling your ribbons. I was thinking we should send some of the pink ribbon home to Kitty and Melly. They can trim their spring hats and dresses with it.' She stood, carefully brushing out the blue silk skirts. 'Perhaps you should help me get out of this dress.'

Elise shook her head with a laugh. 'Not yet. It can't hurt to enjoy it a little while longer.'

They were in the middle of rolling ribbons when the door to the bedroom burst open. Aunt Benedicta entered in high colour, gloves and hat still on. 'I heard the dresses arrived, I want to see every one of them! Plus, I have the best surprise…' Her voice trailed off, her eyes going wide at the sight of the blue gown. 'But perhaps the surprise is all yours. Where did that lovely creation come from?'

Cora took a twirl, showing off the skirt. 'It got mixed in with our dress order. Isn't it divine?' Hopelessly so. In a few minutes she'd pack it away and get out one of her new white gowns for the Granton soiree. And she *would* be grateful for the dress and the opportunity. 'What's your surprise, Aunt B?'

Their aunt's eyes sparkled. 'How would you like to go to the Duke of Harlow's ball tonight?'

They may have actually squealed in their delight at simply hearing those words. Then, she and Elise were talking at once, their questions overlapping.

'How did you manage it?'

'We were not invited.'

Aunt Benedicta's smile turned playfully smug. 'Consider me your fairy godmother. I remembered an old friend of mine from my school days.' She gave a merry laugh. 'Tut-tut, girls, don't look at me like that. School days weren't that long ago for me. Anyway, my *friend* Lady Isley is in Town for the first time since her daughters married. She's been invited and has asked if I might like to come and bring my nieces.' She ended her recitation with a wide smile.

'*She* asked? Really?' Cora hoped her aunt hadn't begged for an invite. She would feel horrible if her aunt had put herself out. She shouldn't have been so obvious in her interest about the event. Their aunt and uncle had done so much for them already.

'She did,' Aunt Benedicta insisted. 'I may have mentioned I had two girls to bring out this Season, but she did the rest, I assure you. Her carriage will pick us up at nine. We'll miss the receiving line, but it can't be helped. She has a short prior engagement.'

'But we're promised to the Grantons,' Cora reminded

her, simply because this was too good to be true. She fought the urge to pinch herself. Surely, there was a catch. When things sounded too good to be true, they usually were. Or they came with an unaffordable price.

'Your uncle will go to the Grantons so we won't desert them entirely, and we'll invite them to share the theatre box later in the Season to make up for this evening,' her aunt assured them. 'All has been arranged for your magical night.' She sobered and reached out a hand for each of them, squeezing tight. 'But do remember, girls, it's just one night. One night out of time. Something to tell your own daughters about some day.' There was a wistfulness in her tone, perhaps for the daughters she'd never had, perhaps for salad days that had passed. 'You can tell them you danced at a duke's ball. That's a pretty good tale for two vicar's daughters from Dorset and their apparently wizened old aunt.' She smiled.

The three exchanged long, bittersweet looks, a wealth of meaning passing between them. They should not expect these gentlemen tonight to do more than dance with them. There would be no morning calls, no further interest pursued. Tomorrow it would be back to work, charming the Sir Richards of the world at card parties and lesser balls in white dresses made a block or two off Bond Street.

'Since it is just one night out of time, as you say, Aunt B,' Elise began, 'I think Cora should wear the dress. Just once. No one will know it's not hers and they won't see her again.'

Elise's suggestion was audacious in the extreme. Cora tried to mount a protest but Aunt B was quicker, a sly smiling teasing at her lips. 'I completely agree, Elise. Cora should wear the dress.'

And so she did.

Chapter Three

The way Declan saw it, he had done his duty. He'd endured the receiving line, standing beside his mother, bowing over hands, exchanging a polite word with fathers, flattering the mothers and smiling, always smiling, at the daughters in order to put them at ease. No easy task given that, on the whole, the daughters were quite a nervous lot. He felt for them. Perhaps they were no more interested in being paraded about than he was.

He saw to it that everyone could go home content with the 'gift' of his attentions. They could recount for friends the conversation they had had with the Duke. No one could say they'd been overlooked. He'd been careful to give his attention as much to the first girl as the last, the first being Lady Mary Kimber, and the last being Miss Clara Brighton, both of whom were high on his mother's list of candidates. There were many in between, all of whom had their credentials whispered in his ear by his mother as a running litany between guests.

Oh, he'd definitely put his time in tonight, and the evening was just beginning. There was still the first dance to lead out and the ball itself to get through. His dance card had been masterfully managed by his mother.

All but the first dance. She'd left that for him to arrange. He had to tread carefully there. He knew how she'd use his choice. She would wave it about as a sign of his preference and she would waste no opportunity in pushing that girl forward. Unless...

Unless the girl was highly unfavourable—which would be unlikely since everyone on the guest list had already been vetted by his mother. In that regard the playing field was relatively equal, all the girls starting in the same place—acceptable. All of them were from good families, good bloodlines, decent wealth. Not much separated the girls from one another in his mind, and that was decidedly *not* an advantage. They were copies of one another at worst, slight variations on a theme at best. Or, there was the other option.

He could find a girl that actually interested him, who stood out and stood apart from the white and pastel clad crowd with gazes as blank as their minds. It was the option he preferred, but so far there'd been no one who fit the latter. It seemed highly unfair. Declan thought there ought to be a sense of quid pro quo. He'd done his duty. Fate ought to do its and provide him with someone who was at least interesting, different, someone with whom he might stand a chance of finding a spark.

'I've given the orchestra a five-minute warning. You'll be expected on the dance floor shortly.' His mother ushered him through the crowd, nodding here and there to friends, using her eyes and nods to expertly cut a path through the guests without needing to stop every few steps to make conversation. Never let it be said that Her Grace the Duchess of Harlow couldn't navigate a ballroom. With a glance and a smile she kept the wolves at bay. If he wasn't the fatted calf on display he'd have admired her efforts more.

'Are you listening to me?' Her tone turned sharp, catching him out for wandering thoughts. 'I said Lady Elizabeth Cleeves was unable to attend tonight. Her mother wrote to say there was a last-minute problem with her gown and some other wardrobe issues.'

'Perhaps she didn't want to meet me.' Declan chuckled. He wondered if *he* could get away with such an excuse as wayward clothing.

His mother didn't share his humour. 'She absolutely wants to meet you. Her mother was *très desolée*. We are all interested in the match. Lady Elizabeth Cleeves would make an outstanding duchess, her father...'

Yes, yes, yes... Declan's mind impatiently dismissed his mother's recitation of the Duke of Colby's impressive bloodlines. As for the 'all of us are interested in the match', he wasn't sure he agreed. How did one reason that a woman who couldn't go to a ball without a new dress made a good duchess? Why couldn't she just wear another gown? Surely, she had more than one?

He wasn't sure he wanted a duchess who would give up so easily in the face of such a slight calamity. The future Duchess of Harlow must have bottom. A bit of cynicism sprang to mind. If Lady Elizabeth was using this as a strategy to claim a personal call from him, she'd be sorely disappointed. He was not going to give the impression of running to her side, or remarking on her absence in any way that might be construed as undue interest in her. The ton's matchmakers might play games, but he did not.

The orchestra played a preliminary tune and Declan felt his stomach tighten. The moment would soon be upon him and he still had no idea who to choose. There was motion around him, a small surge. He looked about. 'What's going on?'

'I've asked all the eligible girls to line up at the top of the ballroom,' his mother informed him.

Declan grimaced. 'Really, Mother?' He did not like that at all. He was to walk the line and lead one of them out. 'This feels more and more like a cattle auction all the time.' He studied them as they assembled, pale and pretty, innocent and empty. He knew instinctively he did not want them, any of them.

'Lady Mary Kimber is the second from the end,' his mother coaxed. 'Perhaps in the absence of Lady Elizabeth Cleeves…' She flashed him a scolding look. 'Smile, my dear, or you'll have them swooning from fright. You don't want them to fear you.' His mother offered her parting wisdom and stepped back from his side, leaving him alone. He'd reached the beginning of the line and it was once more time to do his duty, as disheartening and distasteful as he found it.

He straightened his shoulders, aware that all eyes of the ballroom were upon him and the girls. He walked the line, slowly, with a smile. Each girl curtseyed as he passed, doing her desperate best to make a last impression before the selection. Some were more desperate than others—those who didn't have a place already on his dance card.

He absolutely hated being in this position for his sake and for theirs. He knew what kind of pressure his mother was putting on him, but he was a duke and a man full-grown. He would manage. These were girls barely out of the school room. He hoped they would not be severely berated for not being chosen. He reached the end of the line, having given the girls the courtesy of his attention. He could put it off no longer. Perhaps he would lead out Lady Mary Kimber after all and be done with it.

He turned to walk back down the line when a murmur susurrated through the ballroom, starting in the back and working its way forward, growing as it came like ripples on a pond. Declan's eyes followed the sound, the murmur parting the crowd until its source was revealed. Two latecomers—one a pretty blonde vision in white, who held no unique allure for him at first sight. He had a ballroom full of girls like her.

The other, however, surely *she* was the source of the murmur, with her dark hair brushed to a glossy walnut sheen, and eyes that sparked with a shrewd intelligence, evident even at a distance. Her slender form was shown to advantage in a cerulean blue that put the sky to shame and outshone the pastel palette currently on display.

All else became a backdrop, as if it were a stage set specifically for her. The sight of her was like a lightning bolt to his heart. Some might say fate had taken pity on him at last, but pity was not at all what he felt. What he felt was not relief or mere satisfaction, but a bolt of desire so raw and so hot that it filled his blood with both recklessness and surety.

Without hesitation, he turned from the line of debutantes and made his way towards her, his strides decisive, their briskness cleaving a path amid the guests. His gaze found hers and held it, making his intention clear—he meant to claim her. She stood her ground, not intimidated by the boldness of his gaze. She answered his pursuit with a smile of honest surprise and a gaze full of a genuine appreciation that fired his blood. There was a moment where she didn't know who he was, did not guess, where she saw him only as a man that pleased her and it stole his breath. When had a woman last looked at him thus without seeing his title first?

He reached her side, bowed over her hand and realisation settled in her gaze. Who else could he be but the Duke? She took the shallowest of gasps before sinking into a deep, elegant curtsy. He raised her, holding her gloved hand in his, his gaze steady on her. 'My lady, may I have the honour of the first dance?' On cue behind him, the orchestra played the opening strains of a waltz.

'How can I refuse when the music has already begun?' She smiled, a tease flirting on the upturn of her lips. Whoever she was, she was lovely, had a bit of wit and the ability to send his blood racing, his heart pounding. Perhaps fate had a sense of quid pro quo after all. Or perhaps it was just toying with him, teasing him with this woman in blue who seemed like a dream come true. He put his hand to her waist and drew her into the dance, before the dream could vanish.

She must be dreaming. Cora's pulse skipped at the feel of his hand closing around hers, his touch at her waist, the warmth of him rocketing through her as her mind grappled with the reality—she was dancing with the handsomest man in the room and she didn't need to look about her to know it. She was dancing with the Duke. He'd crossed a room for her, blazed a path through the crush for her, claimed her with the heat of his gaze before he'd even reached her, and, oh, what a gaze it was.

He had the bluest eyes Cora had ever seen, blue like an ocean in summer, deep and steady. That gaze became her anchor in this sea of strangers, and she could not look away as they moved into the steps of the waltz, all eyes of the ballroom on them. But she had no time for them, her gaze was riveted solely on him and his on her. Exhilaration hummed in her veins. This was heaven come down to earth and she was alive with it!

He took them through a turn, swift and sure, the full skirt of her gown belling out deliciously with the speed of it. A burst of rare, pure joy swept through her like a wave dragging her from the shores of reality. Had she ever danced like this? Ever felt like this? As if the world ceased to matter and there was only this moment to live in, to claim? To relish? She laughed, elation spilling out of her. His blue eyes crinkled at the corners, twinkled at their core. He'd caught the magic, too, and they were lost together in it, in a world that existed only for the two of them. In this world, they were not strangers.

He favoured her with a smile so bright she nearly stumbled, mesmerised by the dazzle of it, but his firm grip quickly righted her, his hand tightening at her waist, a silent message in his eyes saying, *It's all right. I've got you. I won't let you fall.*

What a wondrous, exhilarating thought that was, to

have someone who wouldn't let her fall, someone who would be there to catch her. To not have to shoulder burdens alone.

She would dance with him all night if she could. She didn't want the waltz to end, the moment to end, the feeling of being alive, of being free and unfettered. How was it possible to feel so much from a dance? Perhaps it wasn't the dance. Perhaps it was the man? She wasn't ready to let either go, to let the dream end. The rest of the night would pale by comparison. And yet she could not halt it. The music slowed as the waltz wound down like a music box.

His hand lingered at her waist, her fingers still in his grip as if he, too, were reluctant to let the moment go, to let *her* go, even though the whole ballroom was looking on. 'Might I have the pleasure of your name?' he asked in a low, private tone meant for her alone.

'Cora Graylin,' she breathed. A name seemed such a trivial thing after the communion of the dance floor. It was no wonder the waltz was considered the most intimate of dances.

'Cora Graylin, thank you for the dance.' He made her a small bow as guests applauded. For the first time since he'd called her onto the floor, she felt self-conscious of the attention. 'Would you walk in the garden with me? Or would you prefer I return you to your companions? I see dance partners are beginning to swarm.'

Cora slid a look towards the place where her aunt stood with Lady Isley, the two women now surrounded by men waiting to lead her out upon her return. Apparently, dancing with a duke made one instantly popular. It was a fickle sort of popularity though, one that wouldn't last the night. Vicars' daughters had to be realistic about such opportunity. Cora wrinkled her nose in distaste at the thought of dancing with anyone else. The choice was easy. She would have chosen the garden with this man who set her veins afire even if the King himself had been waiting for her.

'The garden, please.' She took his offered arm. 'Thank you for the rescue.'

His spare hand closed over hers where it rested on the sleeve of his jacket and leaned close so that the words were for her ears only. 'It's the least I can do since you rescued me first.'

Chapter Four

The first whispers of cool spring evening air bathed the heat of Declan's body, but did nothing to lessen the desire this woman evoked in him, a desire that was running hot even now after the initial excitement of the dance had passed. She'd not disappointed. How brave she'd been, how courageous—to take his hand and dance in front of the entire ballroom without warning or preparation.

Declan manoeuvred them down the paths towards the fountain at the centre of the garden. 'Perhaps we are rescuing each other. I must confess, my motives aren't entirely selfless. I wasn't ready to return to my duties, not when there's such lovely company to be had with you.'

She gave a light laugh that had him smiling all over again. 'I don't blame you. How do you do it? Waltz so divinely with everyone watching?'

'You seemed to have no problem. You did admirably.' He winked and leaned close, breathing in the soft jasmine and vanilla scent of her. 'Shall I tell you my secret? I forget about them. I focus on what is right in front of me, what is in the moment.'

'Yes, I know what you mean. All I had to do was look in your eyes and everything else disappeared.' The honesty in her words evoked an appealing boldness. Here was a woman who spoke her mind. How many others would dare to speak so openly with him?

'And I yours,' he replied, holding her gaze and willing the world to disappear once more. Whatever magic she wrought upon him, he wanted more of it. He'd not approached this evening thinking to feel this way.

She tipped her head up to the sky, giving him an unadulterated glimpse of the elegant length of her slim neck. She surveyed the sky. 'Ah, there *are* stars up there. I was beginning to doubt it, you know. London skies are not the clearest. In the country we have hordes of stars. They seem nearer, too. It's like you can reach up with your hand and pluck them from the sky.' She sighed wistfully and he thought he detected a moment of homesickness. His angel was a country girl.

'Is that where you're from? The country?' Now he was the one doing the plucking, grabbing at pieces of information about her as if *they* were stars in the sky. His mind was hungry for it—who was she? Where was she from? The country would explain why he hadn't met her before. 'Is this your first time in London?'

'Yes. My first Season, my first visit to Town. My first formal ball.' She was not coy. There was something natural and unaffected about talking with her.

'How do you find Town? I admit it's been a long time since I've seen London through fresh eyes.' Through beautiful, green eyes full of intelligence and consideration. When she looked at him, he felt seen. He was likely being fanciful now—how could a stranger really see him?

She gave his question some thought before replying. 'London is a riddle. Every day I wake up, excited to be here, to see something new. There are a thousand adventures to be had, to be sure. But it's also intimidating, even frightening. Amid the grandeur there's poverty and crime. It's a city of extremes. I wouldn't have missed the chance to come, but at the same time I miss the freedoms of home.'

She gave a guilty smile. 'At home, I walk where I please, go where I want. I needn't rely on an escort. I don't worry about pickpockets. And I think that home misses me.' She paused, her dark brows furrowing as she formulated a thought. 'It's interesting. Here, I have the ability to be free of responsibility, but that freedom comes at the cost of connection. I am not connected to anything here, no one would miss me. But at home, everyone misses me. My family writes almost daily. I am needed there in a way I am not needed here. Yet, that connection requires I give up a certain part of my freedom in order to belong, to be beholden to them.'

They'd reached the fountain and Declan stared at her for a long while, mesmerised by the truth she'd captured so exquisitely, a truth he felt to his bones and battled with every day. He gave a wry smile. 'That dilemma is eloquently put, Miss Graylin. It is one I find myself quite familiar with, the eternal struggle between duty and personal desire. A duke is endowed with endless personal privilege but also endless responsibility to others. There is often very little time or space in which to be oneself.'

She gave him a considering smile. 'Not even at a ball.' How insightful of her to understand.

'*Especially* not at a ball, at least not this one.' Declan grimaced. He'd have to return inside soon. Ladies were going without their dances, without their chances to dazzle him into matrimony. He tossed a pebble into the fountain. 'I'm supposed to pick a bride this Season. This ball is the opening salvo in that process.'

'Do you not want to wed?' She sat at the edge of the fountain and trailed her hand in the water. He joined her, his leg brushing the fullness of her skirts.

'I do, but not just anyone. My mother seems to think I can and should pick a bride out of the Season's debutantes, any one of them will do. It was how my father chose his bride and that turned out fine, my mother likes to remind me. But I'd like something more than a pattern card bride.' He cleared his throat. He needed to rein himself in, show some ducal discretion or he'd be disclosing all his secrets to this woman with the green eyes and the blue dress. 'But I didn't bring you out here to bemoan my fate.' He smiled. 'I wanted to know more about you. What do you love best about the country?'

She played a little with her skirt, suddenly less bold in the face of a personal question. Or was it the attention being turned on her she didn't like? 'I ride and fish on occasion, although I don't like baiting the hook. We're near Wimborne Minster where the River Allen joins the Stour. The Stour has good trout. We've made many a summer meal out of it.'

He smiled at the image her words conjured. 'That sounds like my version of heaven—a cookfire roasting trout on a spit next to a river. Be careful, or I might think you're extending an invitation.' He was teasing, but something shuttered in her gaze. His jest had made her retreat.

He cast around for a suitable topic, one that would lead the conversation back to safer ground. 'We are sitting on Italian travertine. The fountain was purchased from a villa outside of Rome and transported here in three pieces. It's called *la Fontana dei Desidera*, the Fountain of Wishes.' Good Lord, he was babbling now.

'The Fountain of Wishes. Does it work?' She smiled, her eyes lighting once more.

'I like to think it does. Shall we try?' He reached into his coat pocket and took out two coins. He pressed one into her palm. 'Close your eyes, throw it in and make your wish.' He demonstrated, making his own wish. 'Now, your turn.'

She smiled and closed her eyes, thinking of a wish. His blood heated at the sight of her in contemplation, so intent and sincere. For a moment recklessness tempted him to steal a kiss, but he refrained. He would not ambush her while she thought. She tossed the coin and the moment passed. She opened her eyes. 'No one will think it odd in the morning that there's money in the fountain?'

'Not at all. Guests throw coins in all the time when they come to tea or dinner. Mother even makes it an after-dinner activity for some of her parties. At the end of the Season, we dredge the fountain and donate the coins to a charity.' He nodded towards their two coins glistening at the bottom of the fountain. 'Ours are the first two of the Season. Perhaps that makes them extra lucky.'

'The Duke has a fanciful side, I see.' She gave another of her soft smiles but Declan was swift to interject.

'Declan, please, I insist.' She had not called him Duke or Your Grace all evening, and he didn't want her to start now. It seemed wrong after such a beautiful dance and lovely walk.

She hesitated just for a moment, knowing full well his request was too forward. Would she refuse him? He found himself holding his breath until she gave a small nod of her head as if she understood why he'd asked. 'All right, then. *Declan*, what did you wish for?'

'What did *you* wish for?' he teased and then nodded knowingly when she was silent. He chided her with a laugh.

'One cannot tell wishes or they won't come true,' she said, smiling softly.

It was so easy to laugh with her, to be himself. Caught up in the revelation, he leaned towards her, wanting to connect with her, wanting to touch her…

'There you are, Her Grace has been asking for you.' Alex Fenton strode towards them, his voice raised to give fair warning of his approach. Declan drew back, reestablishing distance between himself and Cora.

'Don't tell me Mother has put you on errand duty.' He greeted Alex with good humour that he didn't quite feel, but Alex was his best friend and it wasn't his fault Mother had made him the messenger.

Sensing her cue, Cora rose beside him. 'I should be getting back as well. I did not intend to monopolise your time.'

'You have not monopolised it,' Declan corrected. 'I invited you out here if I remember rightly.' He turned to Alex. 'Lord Alex Fenton, may I present Miss Cora Graylin? Miss Cora Graylin, this is my dearest friend, Lord Alex Fenton. He's put up with me for more years than you can imagine.'

Alex bowed. 'May I see you in, Miss Graylin? There's a set forming and it would be my pleasure to stand up with you.'

'I would be honoured, Lord Fenton.' She smiled at Alex graciously. The intelligence Declan had credited Cora with was not misplaced. She comprehended quite well the undertones of this exchange. She was not to return to the ballroom with him. He was to return alone, all the better for him to get back to the business of his dance card without ruffling any more feathers. But at the sight of her hand on Alex's sleeve, Declan felt a prick of loss. He didn't like thinking of her dancing with Alex. Alex was good looking, charming and kind. Alex could afford to spend his attentions on her, whereas Declan's own attentions needed to be divided.

'Wait, just a moment.' Declan halted their departure. 'Miss Graylin, my mother and I are hosting a house party at our estate in Richmond in two days' time. I would like to extend you an invitation.' This was madness. These were words he'd not thought through, brought on by the same recklessness that had him cutting through the ballroom to claim her.

He'd shocked her. He could see it in her eyes, and for the first time he saw uncertainty there, too. Why did she hesitate? Surely he'd not misread the situation or her interest?

'I would need to bring my aunt and my sister.'

'Bring whoever you like.' He felt marginally better,

knowing when he'd see her again, even as she disappeared into the ballroom with Alex.

That hope got him through the three remaining dances until the midnight supper. He entertained the wild notion of eating with her, but when he looked for her, Cora Graylin was nowhere to be found. Like Cinderella, she'd slipped through the cracks at midnight.

Chapter Five

Any moment now, Cora *knew* the other glass slipper
would fall. This kind of happiness didn't last. She'd turn
into a pumpkin and the dream would unravel. When
it did, she wouldn't just float back down to earth, she
would flat out crash like Icarus into the sea. But it was
approaching noon the day after the ball and she was *still*
buoyed with the euphoria of last night. The dress, the
dance, the Duke—*Declan*, with his piercing blue gaze
and warm touch that sent shock waves through her as
they'd danced. She gave a little skip to her step as she
entered the sunny breakfast room where her aunt and
uncle and Elise were assembled for a delayed morning
meal after sleeping late.

'There she is, our lady in blue!' Elise cheered, beaming. 'You're a celebrity, Cora. All the Society pages have
written about you. Listen to this one, "Duke of H is
swept away by an unknown guest in blue at his own
ball. Blue will no doubt be the colour of the Season given
the results of the Harlow Ball where the Duke, who has
made no secret of his intention to marry this Season,
shunned the usual line-up of well-bred debutantes to
lead out the opening waltz with a new beauty, and then

promptly disappeared into the garden with her. Are wedding bells, or should we say blue bells, in the offing?"'

Elise gave a dreamy sigh. 'Was it as wonderful as it seemed, Cora? You looked so happy waltzing, and the dress was divine. It was like a fairy tale—no, it was better than a fairy tale. He saw you from across the room, Cora. Oh, the look in his eyes, it was delicious. Every girl in the ballroom wanted to be you.'

Cora took a seat at the table. 'It was wonderful, Elise. I liked him. We had a good conversation in the garden.' The words didn't seem adequate to describe their walk. How did she explain what they'd talked about? Freedom and responsibility. How did she explain that they'd shared more than words? She'd felt a kinship with him, as if she knew him far better than a simple conversation allowed. She wasn't in a hurry to find the right words, to share the experience, not even with her sister, whom she usually told everything. But this—her moments with Declan—were personal. She wanted to keep them to herself, to tuck them away like a precious treasure.

Aunt B gave her a long look and a short smile. 'We have supper at the Stanwicks' tonight and we'll all go on to the Templeton rout afterwards.' It was a gentle reminder that last night was supposed to be a night out of time, and now it was back to the work of finding a suitor in earnest, one who could be brought up to scratch for a vicar's daughter. 'Then, tomorrow, there's the Danfields', which should be quite nice. Lady Danfield has just redecorated the ballroom.'

The day after tomorrow, Declan expected her in Richmond. Cora looked up from her eggs. 'Might I suggest an alternative to the Danfields'? We've been invited to Riverside for the Harlow house party.' She glanced at her aunt. 'I thought we might attend,' she said casually, as if she hadn't accepted the invitation already.

'Oh,' Elise gave a squeal, turning wide eyes in Aunt B's direction. 'Mr Wade will be in attendance as his sister, Philippa, is going.'

'Wade? Viscount Grave's son?' Uncle George entered the conversation for the first time, looking up from his newspapers. 'Good family. Quiet family, spend most of their time at their country seat.' Cora noted the look that passed between he and Aunt B. She could interpret most of it.

Aunt B set aside her napkin, her gaze settling on Cora. The same shrewdness that had argued her father into letting them come to London was once more weighing the costs and benefits of this next move. 'Come walk with me, dear. I want to show you the daisies while they're fresh.'

Aunt B waited until the French doors of the house were shut behind them and they were strolling amid her prized flowers, arm-in-arm. 'You've flipped the fairy tale,' she said simply. 'You were to have one night dancing among the *haute ton* in a pretty dress, but now it's gone much farther than that.'

It had gone much farther the moment the Duke had asked her dance. Although she argued with herself that she might have had the dance, the walk, the talk, and *still* let him go without much repercussion beyond a notice in the newspapers, which would fade once someone else claimed the spotlight. It had all been salvageable right up until he'd issued the invitation to the house party and she'd said yes. It might be salvageable yet.

'You think we should decline.' Just breathing the words brought a little pain to her usually practical heart. She thought she'd trained it better. But it had never been tested like this. It was easy to be practical when there was nothing to tempt her. To decline would mean to never see him again.

Her aunt gave her a sharp look and a shake of her head. 'It is too late for that, thanks to the papers. If you think you can just disappear, think again. Right now, you're the girl who danced with the Duke. You don't want to become the girl who *ran* from the Duke. What happens to him if you vanish?' It would make her mysteriously conspicuous and it would make him look… less. People would wonder what could be wrong with him if a girl hid from his attentions. This, she realised, was the kind of scrutiny he had referred to last night.

Her aunt stopped at the daisies and pulled a few weeds that had been overlooked by the gardeners. 'Let me ask you very seriously—what do you want from the Duke? What do you want from the house party? Think carefully, because the longer your association goes on, the less available to other suitors you will become. People will assume the Duke is courting you.' She paused. 'What I am asking you is, do you mean to bag the Duke? And do you think you can do it? It's a zero sum game. If you go after the Duke, there won't be any other suitors.'

'I don't think he'd like to be thought of as prey at the hunt or described thus.' The conversation made Cora uneasy. She'd not thought in those terms. She'd thought only of extending the fairy tale one more day. All she'd wanted, all she'd wished for when she'd thrown her coin in the wishing fountain, was more time with him.

'I'm sure he's used to it. Goes with the territory.'

'I just thought the house party would be an opportunity for Elise to meet some eligible men or to reconnect with anyone she met at the ball. This Mr Wade sounds promising.'

'At the price of meeting the Duke again,' Aunt B reminded. She patted Cora's hand. 'Do you see these daisies, so fresh and white, their yellow centres bright. They're lovely when they're newly bloomed, but a rose will always outpace them. Come and sit.' She nodded towards a stone bench amid a bower of blooms. 'What do you think happens with the Duke?'

Magic. Moonlit waltzes in lantern-lit gardens. Morning rides over the parkland. Long walks, dazzling smiles, feeling his hand at her waist once more, the thoughtful intent of his gaze, feeling her blood heat at a look, at a touch, joy coursing through her. She wanted to feel alive again. What was wrong with her? This was not like her at all. She'd trained herself to practicality, to embrace her reality. This fancifulness was Elise's style, not hers. There was nothing practical about what she wanted or what she could have from the Duke.

Aunt B took her hand. 'Cora, I don't want to be unkind, but I do want to be honest. Right now, the Duchess is wondering who you are. You upended her plans for that ball, and the plans of other matchmaking mamas who have designs on the Duke for their own daughters. Her Grace will be wondering who you are, where you are from. Likely the Duke is wondering the same. What happens when he learns you're a vicar's daughter from Dorset, the niece of a modest baronet with no dowry to speak of? No real connections?'

Cora was tempted to say she didn't think Declan would mind, that he liked the country, that he thought fishing the Stour sounded grand. But she didn't want to argue with her aunt, and she wasn't obtuse regarding the larger message her aunt was sending. Dukes didn't marry vicar's daughters. There was no future, there never had been. Up until last night, there hadn't needed to be. But then they'd danced, they'd talked, and everything had changed. Had it really changed though? There was still no future.

They sat in silence for a while, listening to the birds chirp, each lost in their own dilemmas. It had been foolish to say yes to the invitation. She'd been caught up in the moment, the romance of the ball. Seeing him again only prolonged the inevitable, and it came with the risk of discovery. She didn't belong in the Duke's circles. They would decline. She could feel it in her bones. It was the right thing to do.

Aunt B drew a breath. 'All right, here's what we'll do. We'll go to the party. It's only a week and it's unlikely anyone will unearth much about you beyond your relationship to us in that time. You will simply be a baronet's niece. By the time anyone learns more, the excitement over you will have died down. Elise will have a chance to use the party to get to know Mr Wade better and you, my dear, will have a few more days in the sun.' Or not.

Cora understood the risk. Perhaps the Duke wouldn't

like her as much in the daylight without the need to be rescued. Perhaps he wouldn't have time for her. Perhaps the attraction she felt was the attraction of a moment only. And perhaps it didn't matter. Her aunt was right. Nothing good could come of it even if there was something genuine between them. And yet, an undeniable thrill ran through her at the thought of seeing Declan again.

Aunt B rose and smoothed her skirts. 'Start packing. Take the other dresses. You'll need them.'

Cora shook her head. 'No, we agreed, just the blue dress, just one night. Those gowns belong to someone else.'

'I made enquiries with the dressmaker. The delivery service is shared among four other modistes. So many dresses go out every day that, at the height of the Season, it's almost impossible to keep track if a mix-up happens.' Aunt B sighed. 'Madame Dumont has been called out of Town to care for a relative. The assistant left in charge is too overwhelmed just keeping up on the orders to sort through this mess, assuming it's even her mess to sort through. The dresses might have come from one of the other shops that share the delivery service.'

'But the cerulean! I saw that bolt of fabric the day we were there,' Cora argued.

'Dumont's isn't the only place with that colour.' Aunt B gave a kind smile. 'Perhaps this is a stroke of good fortune. I saw how you looked at those silks that day. Can't you just accept that fate has done you a favour? Goodness knows, after the last few years you've had, you deserve it, my dear.'

'The world doesn't work that way, Aunt B,' Cora protested. It hadn't worked that way for her mother, the kindest, most loving woman Cora had ever known. For all of her goodness, her life had simply got worse and worse. The scales had never balanced in her favour.

'Well, if it makes you feel better, your uncle did offer to pay for the gowns, but Madame Dumont's refused to take the money, since they weren't sure the gowns were theirs to start with. We have tried our best to make it right, my dear.' Aunt B rose and smoothed her skirts. 'I'll write to Her Grace today and tell her we accept the invitation.'

'You've invited *her*?' His mother set down the newspaper and fixed him with a stare that travelled the length of the breakfast table with barely disguised angst. Declan did not think she'd looked at him in such a way since he was ten, when he'd taken apart her Swiss music box in an attempt to figure out how it worked. Her tone had not changed in the last twenty years. But he had. He would no longer be managed with a look and a scold.

Declan took a long, calm sip of coffee, savoured it and swallowed before answering, although he was sure his mother had heard him perfectly well the first time. 'I invited Miss Cora Graylin to the house party. I trust that won't be a problem. She'll be attending with her aunt and her sister.' He imbued that last statement with a bit of ducal authority, meeting her gaze with a steely one of his own as the footman refilled his coffee.

'This is beyond audacious. It does in fact border on

insulting.' His mother's tone had moved beyond horrified disbelief to aghast anger.

'Insulting to whom, Mother?' He reached for a sweet bun.

'To the other girls, to the other families. To our *friends*. It is not bad enough you chose a complete stranger to lead out the first waltz with, and then further snubbed the other girls by taking said stranger out to the garden, whereby you absented yourself for three dances? Those three girls were counting on you.' Someone was always counting on him.

'I thought the purpose of the ball was for me to meet someone I *liked*? I rather liked Miss Graylin. I invited her to the house party because I would like to get to know her better.' He chewed the sweet bun. 'I thought such news would please you. Your efforts have borne fruit.' His mother ought to be crowing about the success of last night.

'Think about how this makes us look.' She ought to be gloating that she was right. She was doing neither, and her anger was genuine, even if Declan thought it was misplaced. It made him wonder if something more was amiss than upsetting her balanced numbers for the house party.

Declan furrowed his brow. 'I cannot please everyone and there is bound to be disappointment, since I will inevitably favour someone over the rest. I simply can't marry them all.' And thank goodness for that, since only Cora had interested him. 'All the girls last night started as equals—some had birth, some had wealth, some had station, some had all three. Your list ensured that. No one need feel lesser for it.'

'Except one,' his mother snapped. 'Miss Graylin was *not* on the list. I know nothing about her, and yet you chose her over Lady Mary Kimber, an *earl's* daughter, over Clara Brighton, an heiress and a granddaughter of a viscount. Need I go on? These girls were *known* to us. We knew exactly what we were courting with each of them.'

'You mean me. That *I* knew exactly what I was court-ing,' Declan corrected. 'There is no "we" in this, Mother. I will be the one married to them, living with them, sleeping beside them, making children with them.' And he'd not been nearly as enchanted with Lady Mary Kim-ber or the absent Lady Elizabeth Cleeves or the wealthy Miss Clara Brighton as his mother had been. But Cora Graylin had been freshness itself, with her honesty and boldness.

'Don't be vulgar,' his mother scolded. 'You're miss-ing the point. *You* know *nothing* about Miss Graylin or her family and you've invited her into our home. You've shown her preference over girls that have more to offer.'

His mother was wrong. He *did* know Cora Graylin. He knew it was her first time in London, that she un-derstood the dichotomy of the city, that she saw its hy-pocrisies as did he. He knew that she danced as if she were on clouds, that she'd not been afraid to hold his gaze, unlike other dance partners who spent the time looking off into the space over his shoulder. But Cora had not been able to look away, nor he from her. She'd made him feel like a man, not a title, with her straight-forward conversation. Oh, how he wished she'd stayed. He had a hundred questions for her.

'Not knowing her sounds like all the more reason to

invite her. We can make her acquaintance at the house party. You can vet her all you like there.' Declan gave a sharp smile that conveyed finality. The discussion was over. He was not worried about Cora Graylin passing his mother's inspection. A dress like hers did not come cheap. No doubt, she'd turn out to be the daughter of a viscount or the relative of an earl. That would please his mother but he found the prospect slightly deflating. He rather liked the mystery of her. He wasn't in a hurry to solve it. She'd not been on his mother's list. The revelation had only added to her intrigue.

'Your father used to have that same smile when he was finished with a topic,' his mother huffed. 'I suppose we cannot uninvite her, not when every Society page has commented on the two of you last night. But I don't like it. She *is* a stranger, a veritable bolt from the blue, literally, given the colour of her gown.'

'I *liked* the colour of her gown. It was different. *She* was different,' Declan said in Cora's defence, and in his own. He didn't like having his opinions challenged as if he didn't have sense to make a good decision. He and his mother had that in common. It was a difficult trait to share, both of them stubborn by nature.

His mother gave a look beset with resignation and retreated the field with a final salvo. 'Different can be dangerous. Invite her and you will see.' In other words, his mother was giving Cora Graylin enough rope with which to hang herself. But for now, he'd take the victory.

Declan rose from the table. 'Excuse me, I need to pack for the house party.' The house party had suddenly become a much more interesting proposition. Perhaps it was the prospect of proving his mother wrong, or perhaps it was simply the prospect of seeing Miss Cora Graylin again. He offered a cool smile. 'Perhaps it will be you, Mother, who shall see.'

Chapter Six

Cora had never seen a house like Riverside, with its smooth cream stone and Palladian architecture standing boldly at the end of the drive, reigning like a queen over the vast expanse of verdant, manicured parkland. The sight of it left her in awe and set her pulse pounding, this time with nerves. Not for the first time since she'd left the Harlow garden she wondered what she had committed herself to. Had she let a moment of rashness go too far? Should she have taken Aunt B's advice? She'd had her night, her fairy tale. Perhaps she'd gone too far? Such recklessness was uncharted territory for her. She had no map for this. She'd not only changed the fairy tale, she'd outrun it—now there was no turning back. Her own nerves aside, it would be worth it for Elise, though.

Cora glanced at Elise, who was looking pretty and fresh in a yellow carriage ensemble. This was a grand opportunity for her sister. The guest list to the house party was honed to perfection in order to put the best girls forward for His Grace. But he was not the only eligible parti here. There'd be other fine young men in the form of the brothers and cousins who'd been pressed into service to escort the girls. Elise could continue acquaintances she'd made at the ball.

The weather was fine and Aunt B had allowed them to travel in the barouche with the top down for the journey to Richmond. Now, their barouche joined the queue of other vehicles in the circular drive. Busy valets and maids disgorged from carriages and began unloading trunks. Elegant ladies were handed from their vehicles by gentlemen and escorted to the top of the steps, where the Duchess of Harlow waited to greet each guest.

Even as their carriage inched closer to the unloading area, Elise leaned forward and gave a wave, a smile lighting her face, as a pleasant brown-haired gentleman approached. 'Mr Wade, how lovely it is to see you again,' she exclaimed with genuine sincerity, offering her hand.

Mr Wade bowed over Elise's hand, favouring her with an answering smile. 'How fortunate it is to find you in all this hubbub. There is a tea on the veranda this afternoon. I shall look for you there as soon as you are settled.' He took his leave then, but Elise's smile remained and her gaze followed him into the house. Ah, so this was the young man Uncle George had spoken of at breakfast— the one with the quiet, respectable viscount for a father. Cora would have met him at the ball if she'd stayed after dancing with Lord Fenton.

'He's perfectly acceptable,' Aunt B said with quiet reassurance. 'They're a sedate but enduring family. No doubt such circumspection appeals to Her Grace.' Aunt B gave a nod towards the Duchess at the top of the steps. 'The Dukedom of Harlow has remained scandal free for centuries. She'd like to keep it that way.' Hence the line-up of biddable, respectable, scandal-free debutantes who wouldn't dream of being the ones to break the streak of scandal-free living. It was a reminder of sorts that *she* would be a scandal simply by dint of who she was—a low-born girl who'd managed a dance with the Duke. She'd already succeeded in snaring the attentions of the gossip columns.

It was their turn to unload and a footman helped them alight. Cora looked again for Declan and did not find him. Would Declan still be glad to see her? What would it be like to see him again without the magic of the ball? Cora glanced around, searching for Declan. Surely, he would be somewhere in this mêlée? When she could not find him, she reminded herself he'd have hosting duties. Perhaps he was out back on a veranda, entertaining guests who'd already arrived? Or giving a tour of the stables, or a hundred other things. She was not his only guest. It was a rather lowering reminder that she had to share him with the other guests, with the other young ladies. Perhaps he'd only invited her to be polite, to return the favour of dancing with him, of having been put on the spot at the ball without warning.

'Don't worry,' Elise whispered behind her. 'If the Duke were out here, no one would get through the door, they'd all stand about gawping at him and trying to get his attention.'

Elise was probably right. The observation made Cora feel marginally better as she made her way up the steps to meet the Duchess.

Aunt B took over at the top of the steps. 'Your Grace,

please allow me to introduce my nieces, Miss Graylin and her sister, Miss Elise.'

Cora did not think she imagined the Duchess's gaze narrowing in speculation as it rested on her, a cool smile at her lips. It occurred to her that the Duchess was not merely a hostess at the top of the steps, welcoming people in, but rather a gatekeeper determined to keep the wrong sort out. 'Lady Graylin, how lovely to see you. Our encounters are rare indeed. And Miss Graylin, it is good to see you at last. I hope you enjoy your time at Riverside.' The Duchess dared not be anything but polite, but those polite words carried their own damning connotation. Encounters were 'rare' because the Duchess did not run in the Baronet's circle, and the phrase 'at last' implied her displeasure that the Graylins had eluded her prior receiving line.

'We shall enjoy it very much,' Aunt B replied with equally polite coolness.

'And I shall enjoy it immensely,' Declan said in a warm tenor, contrasting with the coolness between the women, as he strode towards them. Cora's heart tripped an excited beat at the sight of him. Day suited him as well as the night had. He looked confident and at ease in buff trousers and a bottle-green jacket. His blue eyes landed on her and, for a moment, she forgot to make introductions, forgot almost to breathe, as she let the sight of him happen to her all over again.

'Your Grace, this is my aunt, Lady Graylin, and my sister, Miss Elise.'

'Charmed. Thank you for coming. I know it was sudden. I hope it didn't upend any plans?' He was all solicitous concern as he greeted her family. It was a very different reception than the one they'd received from the Duchess. 'You have rooms overlooking the garden. I hope you will find them pleasant.' He turned to Cora and offered his arm. 'There's refreshment on the veranda, if you'd like to join me? I can introduce you to some of the other guests.'

'Perhaps the ladies would like to change?' The Duchess's disapproval was clear on her face.

Blue eyes clashed with blue. 'The ladies look perfectly fine to me.' Declan saved Cora from refusing the Duchess. 'Unless you'd like to change?' He put the question to Cora.

'I'd be glad to accompany you and meet your guests.' Cora smiled and slipped her hand through Declan's arm, aware of all eyes in the foyer on them and the little ripple that ran through the hall.

'Well, well, well, that's her. The girl in the blue dress.'
'Who is she?'
'Where is she from?'
'Why haven't we seen her before?'

'Ignore them,' Declan murmured beside her. 'I am glad you're here. I was watching for you.'

At his words, her heart gave a dangerous, incautious thump. Never mind that she could feel the Duchess's eyes boring into her back as they left, or that she might have made an enemy or two. It was enough to be here, with Declan, to know that he had been waiting for her. Let others whisper. Who cared what anyone says? Her heart gave another radical leap. Oh, dear heavens, such audacious, impractical thoughts stirred whenever she was with him—a sure sign that she was definitely in over her head. It was time to sink or swim.

He'd not just been watching for her the way someone might watch for a delivery to arrive, but he'd been *waiting* for her with a mixture of excitement and anticipation, as if he could not fully give himself over to the house party until she was here. There was anxiousness, too. Declan worried that what had appealed in the moonlight would pale by daylight, that he'd acted precipitously at the ball out of desperation and seen something in her that simply wasn't there. He'd been on the watch much as the prodigal's father had been on watch for his child, so that he could run to his son's aid if needed. Declan had feared she might need his aid if she had to get past his mother, who seemed determined not to make this easy.

His fears had been unfounded on both accounts. Miss Graylin had not cowered before the Duchess nor did she disappoint on second glance. She look composed and confident in a blue travelling ensemble, cut to emphasise the slimness of her waist and the femininity of her curves, her dark hair tucked beneath a pert hat tilted prettily on her head, a pristine blouse of fine white linen peeping beneath the jacket. Miss Cora Graylin knew how to dress to impress. Then, she'd smiled at him and he was reminded once again that here was a woman who was more than the sum of her wardrobe, that it had not been her ball gown alone that had appealed to him.

Declan led her out to the back veranda with its shady view of the yard and its crowd of guests taking a casual tea. 'I want you to meet a few of my friends.' Actually, he wanted more than that. He wanted to escape the veranda with her. He wanted to take her through the maze to the wishing fountain that matched the one at the townhouse, where they could sit and trail their hands through the basin of cool water and talk uninterrupted. Such an adventure would have to wait. If he did that, the guests would talk of nothing else, and his mother would be livid. He was Duke enough, diplomatic enough, to know he had to balance his desires against the desires of his guests.

The little group near the steps widened to make room for them as he approached. 'Everyone, I'd like you meet Miss Cora Graylin.' He paused for a moment, thinking he ought to add something, but what would that be? From Wimborne Minster? The daughter of? But he couldn't offer anything more because he didn't know more. It reinforced the mystery of her and perhaps his mother's own concerns. Who was this woman in the exquisite blue travelling costume? He covered his hesitation with a smile. 'Miss Graylin, you already know Lord Fenton.'

Fenton took Cora's hand, his usually neutral features transforming with a smile. 'It is my pleasure to see you again, Miss Graylin.'

'As it is mine,' Cora replied sincerely, favouring Alex with a smile. 'Truly, I am thrilled to recognise a friendly face.'

'We are all friends here, Miss Graylin,' an eager young man said as he stepped forward, 'especially when the friend is as lovely as you.' He was flirting gallantly. 'I regret we weren't introduced at the ball, I was out of Town. I am Jack DeBose and this is my sister, Miss Ellen DeBose. She will be your friend as well, Miss Graylin.'

That was a bit forward, Declan thought, even for the normally enthusiastic Jack. A bit suspicious, perhaps. What was Jack playing at? Genuine interest or a larger game?

Ellen was a pretty girl who'd been out for a Season, her greatest claim to fame being that she'd turned down three offers last spring because she was hoping for better. Declan suspected that 'something better' could very well be him. Jack's father was a viscount and their holdings were minimal. He and Jack were friends because of their love of riding. They'd met at Tattersalls a few years ago. Did Jack think to influence Ellen's chances by doing him the favour of having her befriend Cora? Ellen's connection to him through her brother's friendship was the one advantage Ellen had over the other girls. Or perhaps it was nothing. Perhaps it was just Jack being Jack.

It was the curse of being a duke. One never quite knew where they stood with their friends—except for Alex. Alex was genuine, but friends like Jack DeBose always wanted something. He slanted a look at Cora charming the group. He preferred to think Cora was more like Alex—genuine and sincere, that she might be the only female present who didn't care he was the Duke, who was simply herself, unmotivated by an agenda or intimidated by the agendas of others. It was an assumption based on the intuition of a moment—that singular instance when their eyes had first met in the ballroom, when it had not registered with her who he was beyond the initial frisson of attraction that had fizzed between them, a woman responding to a man.

'Your Grace.' A throat cleared in an attempt to discreetly get his attention. 'Might I make an introduction?' As the gentleman beside him drew him away, Declan flashed a look in Alex's direction that said, *Take care of her*, noting that as he did so, Alex immediately took up the newly vacated place at Cora's side. He discreetly watched long enough to see Cora smile. He relaxed. She seemed to enjoy Alex's company, nodding her head and smiling in apparent agreement.

Thank goodness for Alex, as Declan had difficulty getting back. The introduction had led to another and then his mother had appeared at his side, gently insisting he greet a few of the later arrivals, among them Lady Mary Kimber, who was an ardent botanist, requiring a private tour of the rose garden at his mother's urging, and to his great disappointment.

'I'd be glad to show you, Lady Mary,' he offered politely, exchanging a stern look with his mother, making it clear he would not tolerate being manipulated. But neither would he exhibit bad manners and make Lady Mary bear the brunt of his squabble with his mother.

He knew this would be only the first of many skirmishes this week. He'd need a few flanking manoeuvres of his own, or else he'd be so busy showing ladies the rose garden, the stables, anywhere his mother could think of, that he wouldn't have a moment alone with Cora. It was a thought that sat poorly with him, for more than one reason, as he escorted Lady Mary down the steps, leaving Cora in Alex's company. Lucky Alex. And unlucky him.

He would not be likely to see Cora again before supper

and, even then, she would not be seated anywhere near him. He cast a final glance at Cora and Alex on the veranda. They had moved apart from the group. At least he was leaving her in capable hands. Alex would be a good friend to her. Declan needn't worry he'd abandoned her among strangers. Among her many qualities, it appeared Cora Graylin was good at putting others at ease the way she'd put him at ease that first night. An unlooked-for thought rose hot and unbidden in his mind—such a quality for making friends would be useful in a duchess.

'You've made enemies,' Aunt Benedicta said pointedly, taking up her post on a chair in the girls' chamber, from where she could oversee everything that went on in the airy, powdered pink and white room.

Cora turned from the vanity where her aunt's maid was putting up her hair. 'I've made *friends*, Aunt B,' she corrected with some incredulity. 'Everyone has been so nice. Jack DeBose, Lord Farnhurst, Lord Townsend and, of course, Mr Fenton.' Cora laughed. 'But he has to be, as we've met before.'

Aunt Benedicta arched a sharp brow. 'I daresay cornering the market on the most popular young men here, in addition to the Duke, did *not* endear you to the other young ladies,' she cautioned.

'All except Mr Wade,' Elise pointed out gaily from the bed, waiting her turn for dressing. Aunt B's maid was doing for all three of them, Aunt B insisting they dare not trust a maid outside the family who was sure to report downstairs anything that happened in their chambers.

Aunt B relented for a moment, softening. 'Yes, dear.

Mr Wade seems quite taken with you. Wear the white dinner gown with the pink sash tonight.'

'Ellen DeBose seems kind,' Cora continued to make her case.

'Ellen DeBose thinks to get to the Duke through you. All her mother could talk about were her three offers last year. None of which were good enough for the family.' Aunt Benedicta surprised Cora with her shrewdness, just as she had the day she'd argued the right to bring the girls to London with her.

Cora smiled. 'Aunt B, you look like a nice, normal human being with a gentle soul, but in truth you are a matchmaker's version of an amazon.' She thought Aunt B might laugh at the comparison, but instead her aunt's eyes flashed with serious intent.

'Cora, darling, London's marriage mart is not for the faint of heart. There are no fairy tales here, no happy accidents. The Duchess wants her son wed, the mothers of the ton want him wed. The other men don't have a chance until he's off the market and the debutantes are setting their sights elsewhere. I promise you, Society will see that man brought to the altar before the summer is out. He might as well circle a date in his diary. The only question is *who* will be standing beside him, and even that answer is finite. It will be one of the young women here this week. The mothers know it, the fathers know it. The girls know it. No one here is your friend unless it advances their case with the Duke.'

Perhaps that was another reason why Aunt B had consented to the house party. The Duke would be forced to move on from her, forced to pick one of the eligible girls. Amid such a crowd, she would fade into the background.

Aunt Benedicta's speech brought the innate energy of the room to a standstill. 'I am sorry, Aunt. I did not mean to appear cavalier. I understand what is at stake for all of us.' Cora sobered. No wonder Declan had looked at her as if she were his lifeline. Her heart went out to him, listening to Aunt B describe his circumstances. He was being swept along an inexorable current to an inevitable end. And so was she. He was not the only one expected to make a life-changing decision in the next twelve weeks. But her current seemed gentler at present.

The maid brought forward two dresses for Cora's approval. 'The white or the bronze, Miss?' Cora slid a look her aunt's direction. The white was one of hers, but the bronze had come from the other order that had landed with theirs by mistake. It was silk, lush and sophisticated, designed to stand out. She fingered the bronze silk, thinking of how it would look against the dark sweep of her hair, how it would bring out the depths of her eyes. But that was vanity speaking. She hesitated, although it was silly to prevaricate now. She'd packed the dresses purposely to wear, knowing full well she'd need them to keep up appearances. *To keep up the ruse.*

This was the sticking point she'd been debating over the past two days. *Was* she perpetuating a ruse? *Was* she pretending to be someone she was not when she wore them? Was she misleading Declan? Or even herself? Perhaps she was merely boosting her confidence when she wore them. It was a fine line, and she wasn't sure which side of it she was on.

'I feel like someone else when I put the gowns on.' When she'd worn the blue dress she'd felt like she could take on the world, that she could claim her happiness. The Cora Graylin who worried over making ends meet, who felt blessed to simply just get by, was replaced by someone who believed all things were possible and that she was allowed them. 'She sent a pleading look to her aunt, hoping for wisdom.

Aunt Benedicta cocked her head in a studying stare. 'Then, I'd say those dresses are doing what they're supposed to do—enhance. Clothes transform us, they make us into our best selves.' She nodded towards the gowns. 'Wear the bronze, embrace your boldness. Let the gown be your armour. You may need it tonight. The Duke's attentions did you no favours.'

Chapter Seven

Aunt Benedicta was correct. The dinner table was a battlefield, laid out with a general's precision. It was a carefully veiled competition, orchestrated to be covert, everything overtly justified from Cora's placement at the table, which was as far down from the Duke as one could get but still be in accordance with what her aunt's title allowed. She and her sister were split up, ostensibly so that her sister could spend the meal with Mr Wade on one side, but perhaps the more cynical among them would see it as a chance to divide and conquer, leaving her without support. She was surrounded by no one she knew.

Ellen DeBose and her brother were much further up the table, as was Lord Fenton, leaving her surrounded instead with fathers. On her left was Clara Brighton's father, a man without a title, and on her right was the local squire, who'd been invited to round out numbers at the last minute. She didn't need to be a genius to know what had made that necessary. Her invitation had upset the order of things. Now, she'd been relegated to a no man's land at the vast table, not near the Duke *or* the Duchess but in the lower middle where guests went to be forgotten. Or ignored.

Still, it was a pleasant meal and instructive. Cora was not one be daunted by circumstance or to let any opportunity go to waste. At a distance, it was both easier to study Declan and avoid his mother's censure while she did. Lady Mary Kimber was at his right hand, and a young woman Cora didn't know at his left. His dark hair was brushed back and the candlelight emphasised the strong bones of his face. But there were no smiles on that face, his expressions limited to nods of politeness, his gaze straying just once to her end of the table to catch her eye.

When supper ended, everyone rose as one, foregoing the custom of leaving the men to their brandy, in order to enjoy a musical evening together—an entertainment, Cora noted, she was not asked to join. The girls crowded into the seats placed nearest the piano, leaving her to take a seat in the back with her aunt. Elise sat with Mr Wade, talking quietly. Cora's heart warmed at the sight of the two of them, early hope surging that perhaps something would come of this Season in London for Elise.

Lord Fenton slid into the empty chair beside her. 'Will you perform tonight, Miss Graylin?' he asked congenially, settling the split tails of his coat.

'No,' Cora laughed. 'This evening I shall enjoy the talents of others. I'll save my skills for the field. I've been assured there are outdoor pursuits scheduled later in the week.'

'You're an athlete then?' he enquired.

'You are too generous, Lord Fenton. I am merely an outdoorswoman.' It was easy to talk with him. There was no spark as there was when she spoke with Declan, but there was an ease where she felt she might be herself, where her boldness would not be held against her.

His hazel eyes twinkled. 'Perhaps *you* are too modest, Miss Graylin.' He leaned close as the first performers, a pair of sisters, situated themselves, one to sing and one to accompany on the harp. 'Perhaps we might partner one another for the archery competition?'

Cora gave him a considering stare. 'Before I commit to that, may I ask, are you any good, Lord Fenton? Because I am and I mean to win.' She might not be able to pluck a harp, but she could hit a bullseye at one hundred feet, further if the bow and the weather were on her side.

Lord Fenton gave a low chuckle. 'I knew you had spirit.' He winked. 'I won't disappoint.'

The evening did, however. The musicale was interminable, perhaps because the talent was tepid. Too many girls trying too hard, Cora thought. She was doubly glad she'd not attempted to join their ranks in a bid to capture Declan's attention. If the mothers had arranged this in an effort to push their daughters forward, and to push her to the rear, the efforts had backfired. The girls all looked the same in their white gowns and sounded the same with their mediocre renditions of Bach and English country ballads, their faces pale as they dared to glance in Declan's direction as he sat beside his mother on the settee. He was pressed into service a few times to turn pages at the pianoforte. Mothers' fans came out as the evening drifted along, and fathers began to shift, growing increasingly restless on the chairs.

'I don't think I've ever been so relieved to see a tea

cart in my life,' Lord Fenton whispered drily as Miss Clara Brighton sang the off-key notes of the evening's finale and the tea trolley rolled in. 'I'll get us some tea.'

Cora drifted over to study the Constable landscape while the other girls congregated to receive compliments on their performances. Aunt B hadn't been wrong. The evening had been constructed to be many things, one of which was an attempt to remind her of her place. The Duchess had several allies in that regard. No one had been insulting to her face, but their exclusion of her had sent its own message. Well, now at least she'd taken their measure. She'd been glad of the confidence imbued by the bronze dress.

'I see you've found our Constable.' Declan was beside her, holding a teacup. 'I told Fenton I would deliver your tea. I hope you don't mind?' There was a question in his eyes as if he worried she might prefer Alex Fenton's company to his. 'Fenton can be entertaining.'

'He has been generous with his time. I am grateful.' She took the tea and set it aside on a small table.

'I must apologise about that. It was not my intention.' He leaned close and her pulse ratcheted at the nearness, the intimacy. 'If it were up to me I'd send them all home.'

She shook her head. 'No apology is necessary. You are the Duke. You have responsibilities. I cannot dominate your attentions. In fact, my aunt reminds me that to do so does not make me likeable. I think many of these girls have already put a target on my back.' She offered the words laughingly, but the private look he exchanged with her said he understood the silent message—*Whatever we are playing at, be careful with me.*

'It is my fault if my behaviour has caused you to be singled out. I will take your counsel and pursue a more discreet course of action.' She felt his hand curl about hers, something pressing into her palm for the briefest of moments, the motion hidden by the folds of her skirt. He nodded towards the painting. 'Do you recognise it?'

'That's the River Stour. Constable came to Wimborne Minster to paint a series of rural scenes. My family had a chance to meet him at a reception while he was there. *The Hay Wain* is his most popular from that collection. This one also came from it. One can see the similarities.' Cora sighed. 'I think I would know Constable's clouds anywhere.'

Declan smiled the first smile she'd seen him offer all evening. 'Very impressive. You shall have to tell me more about Mr Constable.' Because Constable was safe, a public topic no one could fault them for discussing. But Cora didn't want to be safe. The bronze gown was made for boldness, and her time with him would be brief.

'I'd rather talk about you. Is a house party better or worse than a ball?' Cora shifted the conversation with a laugh. She might have spent the afternoon with Lord Alex Fenton, but Declan had never been far from her gaze. She'd tracked him as he moved from group to group, from pushy mother to pushy mother, always calm, always polite, always doing his duty.

'House party,' he answered with a chuckle. 'It goes on for days and there's no escape. But I've survived worse. It is tedious, nothing more.' Declan dismissed it but it was tedium that would characterise his life, Cora thought, and her heart went out to him. It was quite similar to how she lived her own days in Dorset, moving from task to task without complaint, because they simply must be done and there was no one else to do them. But beneath that calm exterior, sometimes she secretly rebelled against the demands made on her, not that anything ever came of it.

She gazed longingly at the painting. 'There are days when I go down to the river and dream about sailing away. Do you sometimes resent it? All the responsibility?' she mused quietly.

'Yes.' His word was a whisper at her ear, a plea, maybe even a prayer. In the hidden folds of her skirts, she reached for his hand, the urge to hold on—to hold *him*, to be held *by* him—rocketing through her, hot and unlooked for. His fingers closed around hers. For a moment in this room of strangers, there was just the two of them, two souls looking for escape.

Alex returned. It was time to send Declan away. She gave Declan a final smile. 'You should tell Lady Mary how much you enjoyed her rendition of Bach's minuet in G,' she advised quietly. 'Thank you for the tea.'

The evening broke up soon after, but it wasn't until she was safely upstairs in her room that she unfolded the scrap of paper he'd pressed into her hand.

Meet me in the maze tomorrow morning at seven.

So that was what discretion looked like…what life beyond the fairy tale looked like. A clandestine meeting. Meeting in secret was certainly one way to defuse those who resented his time spent with her.

Cora folded the scrap of paper. She would have liked

to say the prospect of a private meeting away from watchful, resentful eyes pleased her. On the surface it did. Uninterrupted time with Declan was a luxurious commodity, and it was what had drawn her here—one more day, one more chance to experience the magic of being with him. It was the undertones that troubled her.

The truth was, anything they did in public together would be food for speculation, and her aunt had warned her there was speculation aplenty to be had. *Where did she come from? Who was she? How much money did she have?* People were intrusive when there was a duke was on the line and a debutante to bring down. The Duchess was already asking those questions and Aunt B was right—within the week everyone would know the truth of her. They weren't hiding it, but neither were they trumpeting it, letting social nature take its course, at which point she'd become *de trop* to the Season soon enough as far as the *haute ton* were concerned.

Until then, however, there were rules to follow, which prompted the question—did he see the risk in this request to meet? It would be devastating if they were caught alone. For a moment, Cora considered not keeping the appointment in order to protect him. Perhaps it was the least she could do for him after all he'd done for her and for Elise, even if he didn't realise it.

She debated the merits of not showing up right until the clock in the hall struck seven in the morning. She was already late. But in the end, it was the magic that won out. She could not have for ever with him, but she could have one more day, one more conversation, and for those she was apparently willing to risk everything.

Chapter Eight

Declan took out his pocket watch as he paced a circle about the fountain at the centre of the maze. The sun was up. The sky was cloudless and blue. The songbirds were in glorious voice. It was a gorgeous spring morning in the country and it was ten minutes past the appointed meeting time. She was either late or… He didn't want to think of the 'or'.

Rapid footsteps crunched on the gravel path. She'd come! He let out a sigh of relief and inhaled the freshness of her, a smile curving at his mouth at the sight of her. She was morning come to life in her sprigged green muslin, the sun glinting off the walnut depths of her hair. 'I thought you weren't coming.'

'I almost didn't,' she confessed, keeping her tones low and casting a nervous look about the square courtyard at the centre of the maze. 'Being alone like this is dangerous. If we were discovered…'

He laughed and reached for her hand. 'We won't be. We're in the middle of a maze at the crack of dawn by house party standards. Most of the ladies won't even have a tray brought up to their rooms for another hour, and if the men are up they're out riding far from the gardens.' He led her to a bench set near the fountain. 'I assure you, we're quite safe here. You're safe here,' he amended. 'You are always safe with me, Cora. I want you to believe that. Was it selfish of me to invite you out here?' Declan stretched his long legs out beside her skirts. 'I was tired of sharing you.'

Tired of watching her with Alex, tired of not being part of the magic she could weave with her smile, her gaze, with the lightest of touches on the arm that said, *You have all my attention, I am entirely present in this conversation, nothing is more important right now.*

Last night at the Constable painting had nearly slain him when she'd talked about responsibility and wanting to escape. How was it that she could pick out the very thoughts in his mind and express them as her own?

Her eyes sparkled and held his. 'Then I am selfish, too. I was tired of sharing you, although that is the nature of house parties and the nature of my life. I should be used to it. I have four sisters, I am always sharing something.' It was easily said and Declan took the opportunity to pry open the treasure chest of her a little further, to know a little more about this woman who'd come to captivate his thoughts in such a short time.

'Any brothers?' he asked, sopping up the little facts of her life like bread to gravy. Her brightness faded as she shook her head, and he instantly regretted bringing the subject up.

'None that lived. But my father says a man doesn't need sons when he has five pretty daughters.' She loved her sisters—he could hear it in her voice.

'I know there's Elise, but who else? Tell me about

them.' They were sitting close together on the bench, the fountain burbling, birds warbling, and there was no place Declan would rather be. This was a simple, straightforward conversation. He needn't be on his guard, he needed only to listen, to be. It had been that way at the ball. Her very nature put him at ease, allowed him to set down the burdens and politics of his title.

'I have three younger sisters at home. Katherine—we call her Kitty—is fifteen and Melly, or Melisandre, is thirteen and a half.' She gave a delightful, earthy laugh and he knew his face had given him away. 'If you're doing the math, the answer is yes, Melly was something of a surprise coming so soon on the heels of Kitty's birth. Then there's the baby, Veronica. She's seven.'

'An unusual name,' Declan commented, doing another sort of math. The baby boy must have been born between Melly and Veronica.

She nodded, soft reflection in her green eyes. 'My father is a biblical scholar. She's named for the old church legend about the woman who wiped away the tears of Jesus on the road to Golgotha. The family had been through great sadness before she was born. Her birth was a happy occasion, proof of life renewing itself.'

Ah, evidence then that his assumption was correct. It was an interesting insight into her large family. Perhaps that would put his mother's worries to ease. Her father was a gentleman who'd been born the younger son of a baronet, who was now brother to the current Baronet— a man who could afford to be a biblical scholar while raising five daughters, and sending two of them to London with his eldest turned out in gowns as fine as the one she'd worn to the ball. Last night's bronze silk had been testament to that.

'What of you, Declan? Do you have any siblings?'

He liked her quiet, casual use of his name. With her, he might be an ordinary man for a while. 'Sisters, two of them. Both older. Both married with children.'

That seemed to please her. She favoured him with one of her warm smiles. 'So, you're an uncle. Do you see them often?'

He knew before he spoke that his answer would disappoint her. 'No, actually, I don't.' He found he was ashamed to admit it to this woman who so obviously loved her family. 'They live in the country and my sisters' husbands' estates are not necessarily close to mine.'

'That's too bad.' Her sorrow was genuine. 'If I had nieces and nephews, I'd want to see them all the time. I hope that when my sisters and I marry we'll live close to one another. I want our children to grow up with their cousins.' There was an enchanting wistfulness in her tone that touched him.

'You'd be content to stay in Wimborne Minster all your life?' What a novel thought that was. He spent his life on one giant progress. Spring and early summer in London. Late summer and autumn making a tour of the ducal estates, timing his visit up north to coincide with grouse season. He would often return to Town briefly before the holidays, and then a month or two at his estate in Sussex for the winter, before starting the cycle all over again.

'I'd be content to be wherever my family is,' she said softly. At the sincerity in her tone, the feeling returned that, despite the shortness of their association, he could trust her, that she saw him as the man first, the Duke second.

'You're close to your family. I think I might envy you that.' Whereas he hardly saw his. One of his sisters lived on the Welsh border, the other in Cornwall. He had three or four letters a year from them filled with news about events that he felt quite removed from. He saw his mother of course in the spring. They shared the town-house during the Season. This would be the last year for that, he realised. Once he married, she would move to her own place. He would see decidedly less of her, which wasn't entirely a bad thing, but it would cut the last of the strong ties to his childhood family. There was a certain sadness that came with the acknowledgement.

'You have what I've always longed for—a real family, a family focused on each other instead of the succession.' He gave her a thoughtful smile, an image creeping to mind of what her life in Wimborne Minster might be like. Big family dinners, a noisy family riding to the hunt, taking hedges in the countryside, picnics beside the river on sunny days, roasting fish on a spit beside the river. Every day a bucolic idyll fit for a Constable painting.

'Family is the most important thing in the world to me. They are always there for you. It doesn't matter if we've quarrelled, we end each day knowing the constancy of their love.' She gave a wry smile. 'And quite often the constancy of their forgiveness. Five girls cannot live together without stepping on some toes.'

Declan laughed. 'It sounds chaotic and wonderful.'

He was filled with a longing to see her home, to see her amid her Dorset life. More than that, to be part of it with her, to leave the demands of London behind.

'Most of the time it is. I miss my other sisters dreadfully. I am grateful to have Elise here. I don't think I could manage London without her.' She paused and studied her hands. 'But I worry that I may not have her for much longer.'

'Because she will marry?' He'd noticed Mr Wade's attentions, and not only his. Several other gentlemen had been interested in Elise Graylin's pretty charms. 'But you will marry as well.'

She sighed. 'Yes, I suppose so. It's the whole purpose of being in London, after all. Everyone has twelve weeks to find a match. I don't like to dwell on that, though. It's too mercenary, too desperate, all of us swanning around in finery trying to impress each other, when deep down we're all as desperate as the next person.'

'A very apt assessment. Not a very popular one, though. I wouldn't advise saying that out loud to anyone else.' They laughed together and Declan cocked his head, considering her situation for the first time. 'Must *you* marry in twelve weeks? If no one suits, you can come back next year and try again once you've taken London's measure.' Surely, she had time. She had no obligation to fill a ducal cradle.

Her gaze moved from him, going to the fountain instead, and he had the sense she was searching for the right words, perhaps wanting those words to protect something or someone. 'I don't want to hold Elise back. Some feel that the eldest daughter should marry before the younger one. I would not want Elise to wait on my account and risk losing a happy match. Besides, there's Kitty to think of. She'll be sixteen next month and she'll be wanting her own Season all too soon.' It was the proper thing to say, the socially accepted reason, but Declan didn't think it was the entire truth. There was a moment's hurt in knowing she was keeping something from him.

'Still, marriage should not be rushed,' he probed gently around the thing she was determined to keep secret.

'Except in your case,' she said bluntly and he laughed. He laughed a lot when he was with her. The only thing he did more in her company was smile. He liked that.

'Except in my case,' he agreed. 'But I have extenuating circumstances—an empty nursery, no brothers and an heir presumptive whom I haven't seen in seven years—a distant cousin I hardly know who lives in Upper Canada.' He paused, directing her gaze back to him. 'What are your circumstances, Cora?' he asked quietly. 'Is there someone in Wimborne?' His chest tightened at the thought although it seemed unlikely. Why come to London if she had a suitor at home?

She shook her head and he felt himself ease. 'No one that I want, that is. There is a man who's offered—a widower who wants a caretaker for his children and his home more than he wants a wife. I have refused him.' But, Declan sensed, the man was proving persistent.

'And should London fail to turn up a better offer, his may be back on the table?' A little rill of anger pulsed through him at the thought of this beautiful, vibrant woman, who was filled with love, being forced into a loveless union.

She flashed him a brief look, dark and wry. 'If not me, then one of my sisters. Five girls is a lot for my father to launch.'

Declan grimaced. 'Still, it is his job. It is every father's job to see their children, male or female, launched into adulthood.' His father had believed that, had worked with his mother when it had come time for his sisters to marry. His father had seen to marriage settlements, to protections so that their husbands didn't run through those generous settlements, so that his sisters and their children would always have financial protection. He would do the same for children of his own when the time came.

'You must understand.' Cora pressed his hand in earnest. 'My father suffered greatly when my mother passed two years ago. It's simply too much for him.' She was protecting him, shielding the man from blame. Because she loved him, even at the expense of her own happiness, her own future. His picture of her life in Dorset just became a little bit darker. His own protective urges surged.

'My own father passed not so long ago. We spent the last year in mourning, transitioning. We miss him, *I* miss him.' The confession surprised him. He hardly ever spoke of his father with anyone. 'But here I am, moving forward because people are counting on me.' There was a scold in his words for this father he'd never met, who was willing to give his daughter to a dour man devoid of the love she deserved.

'Don't be angry with him, Declan. He is doing the

best he can,' Cora soothed. 'Still, in truth, it's nice to have someone stand up for me.'

'Does no one stand up for you in Wimborne?' Declan laced his fingers through hers and held their hands up, studying her hand in his, feeling that sense of being intertwined in his bones and marvelling at it. This woman with her love of family, a desire for a close-knit family of her own, spoke to his own heart, his own dreams, in a way he'd not thought possible.

'No, but I am thankfully capable of standing up for myself.' She gave him a warm smile. And for others, he'd warrant. She'd stood up for her father, she was cognizant of her sisters' needs. She put others ahead of self. Not unlike him.

We are alike, you and I, compromising ourselves and our wants for those around us, for those who need us.

The longer he was with her, the more he knew her and the more he knew himself. He was already wondering when he might steal more time with her.

'Fenton tells me he's partnering you for the archery competition. Perhaps you would do me the honour of being my partner for the horseback scavenger hunt tomorrow?' That seemed like an eternity from now. 'My mother can't abide killing foxes any time of the year, so she has devised her own more seasonally appropriate version of the hunt.' Somewhere in the maze came the clip-snip of gardening shears, a reminder that the morning was advancing. The house would be rousing—their time was up.

'I would like that.' Cora rose with a teasing smile. 'Be warned, though, I like to win.'

'As do I,' he assured her with a wink, and then sobered, taking her hand one last time. 'Thank you for coming to meet me. If you can find your way back, I'll let you return first.'

Declan watched Cora's green skirts disappear into the maze, missing her already. They'd laughed and talked—really talked—about hopes and dreams, about family and loss. They'd found common ground in those hopes. He could not imagine sharing like that with Lady Mary Kimber, who would partner him later today for archery. With Lady Mary, his whole life would be one, long, continuous masque, always playing the part of the gentleman—calm, controlled, without cares.

To let down his guard would likely shock her sensibilities. Certainly, Lady Mary Kimber would never think to shock *his* sensibilities. She would never speak her mind openly out of concern of contradicting him. He'd felt sure that if he'd said a yellow rose was white she would have agreed wholeheartedly, despite the obvious truth staring her in the face. But Cora Graylin was something different. His first impressions had not been wrong.

She was a breath of fresh air, and that breeze was disrupting his world, blowing preconceived notions amok the way wind through the windows rustles loose papers left on tables. When he was with her, he was himself, out of 'the game' of matchmaking. He could set aside responsibility, he could speak his mind. And she could speak hers. She treated him in a way no one else ever had.

Declan kicked at the gravel on the path as he started back towards the house. He did see the irony surrounding the situation. How had this happened? He'd thought it unlikely to find a mate, let alone something that resembled love, in twelve weeks. Yet he'd not needed nearly that long to feel as if Cora embodied the other half of him, the better half of him that wasn't swallowed up by compromise and conditions. The question now was what was he going to do about it? A few days ago, he would not have believed it possible, but it now seemed entirely possible that Cupid's arrow had aimed true.

Chapter Nine

Everyone had chosen sides, Declan noted, now that the team archery competition was down to the last four pairings. He watched several 'gentlemen's' wagers being exchanged discreetly out of earshot of his mother, who would be appalled to discover her genteel entertainment had become a source of gambling.

'Could you help me fasten this?' Beside him, Lady Mary held up a forearm that was draped in a leather brace, dyed a deep rose to match her gloves, strings dangling. Lady Mary had turned out to be a highly competent, highly competitive archer. Thanks to her, they were one of two teams left.

They'd face Alex and Cora in the 'archery finals', a match-up that had guests angling for front row seats on the lawn for reasons that went beyond affinity for the sport. People were eager to see two leading contenders for the Duke's hand square off, as if the target at the end of the alley was his heart instead of merely a hay bale.

Declan tied the strings of Lady Mary's brace with dispassionate dexterity, wondering if this request was a ploy for his attentions. If so, Lady Mary wasn't nearly as adept at flirting as she was at archery. 'Are you enjoying yourself?' he asked as he tied off the last string and stepped back. 'You're shooting well, today.'

'So you *were* paying attention. I was beginning to think I could put an arrow on the moon and you wouldn't notice.' She gave him a shrewd smile. 'As for enjoying myself, I might be enjoying it all a bit more if I wasn't certain I was about to be jilted.'

Ouch. The truth hurt. He'd not been as discreet as he'd hoped. 'I must apologise if I seemed distracted,' he began. 'It is nothing personal.' Would she contradict him? Call him on the obvious lie? Of course not. She was too well bred for that.

She gave him a sad smile. 'I will beat her, you know, your lady in blue, the one you can't take your eyes off except to shoot. It will be my consolation prize for being passed over by two dukes in two Seasons.' She plucked an arrow from the *petit poche* at her side, polished an arrow tip with a tassel hanging from her belt, feigning an air of indifference as if such matrimonial games didn't matter a whit to her.

Declan immediately felt guilty. He didn't want another hurt by his own behaviour. Lady Mary Kimber was fast becoming an innocent casualty in his mother's matchmaking.

'Jilted may be too strong of a word.'

Lady Mary slid the arrow back into the *poche*, her tone harsh. 'You're right. Jilted would imply some sort of understanding, that either of the two dukes my parents coerced had made more than passing conversation with me.'

Declan did feel sorry for her, then. Creighton had never been serious about her and Declan knew he never would be either. Whoever he married, it wouldn't be her. Lady Mary Kimber was a pretty enough girl with a surprising amount of bottom and all the right qualifications… for someone else. But with him, there was no spark, no passion, no common ground except that they were both being pushed towards one another by parents who wanted a match. That was not enough to build a lifetime on.

Lady Mary slipped her arm through his with a wry smile. 'Let's go get my consolation prize.' She slid him a considering look with a hard set to her hazel gaze. 'Don't even think about going easy on her and Lord Fenton. I won't let you take this victory from me, too.'

Declan nodded. 'You're not the only one with a competitive soul. I owe Fenton payback for shooting at Manton's. I lost by a whisker in a very controversial decision.'

Lady Mary smiled. 'Good, I am counting on it. I must take my wins where I can get them.' Their *tête-à-tête* as they strolled towards the targets garnered attention from the older guests. Declan was too much a veteran of matchmaking wars to miss them, particularly the satisfied look his mother exchanged with Lady Mary's mother. Well, there'd be time to disabuse his mother of that hope later. Right now, he had an archery competition to win. It was the least he could do for Lady Mary as a parting gift.

Declan did do his best. He shot well, better than Alex, much to Alex's good-humoured chagrin. 'That last arrow just edged me out infinitesimally,' Alex groused as they departed the field and took up their stances on the sidelines. Lady Mary and Cora marched on to the shooting range, one in white and rose, the other in white and blue.

'That's what I said at Manton's about my last shot.' Declan clapped his friend on the back.

'My shot was closer than yours that day,' Alex retorted.

'And mine is closer today.' Declan grinned smugly. 'Now it's up to the ladies. At least you gave Cora a fighting chance.'

'Cora? You mean Miss Graylin,' Alex corrected with a raised brow at the familiarity. 'Yes, I suppose I did. She's a fine archer. They must have archery societies where she comes from. Where was that again?' His probe was not subtle.

'Dorset. Wimborne Minster, where Constable painted last summer.' Declan let those three pieces of information roll off his tongue with confidence, as if to say, *'Ha, she is not so much of a mystery now. People cannot keep saying we know nothing of her.'* He'd spent a large part of today mulling over everything he'd gathered about her, replaying their morning conversation, the conversation last night, their dance...the encounters were mounting, and with them his desire.

Alex slid a look in his direction. 'A country girl? There's a lot of sheep in Dorset. I suppose that appeals?'

'More than you know,' Declan said in low tones. The question wasn't if Cora's life appealed to him, but if his life would appeal to Cora. Could he make her happy? She would want to spend time in Dorset, close to her sisters. She would not want to be on constant parade, going from estate to estate, never settling long enough anywhere to put down roots.

When people talked of an earl or a duke as figureheads of their rural community, they meant it quite literally. Just figureheads. Not really invested in the hands-on day-to-day running of that community. Just someone to write a few cheques and alternately give orders or a stamp of approval. It was the vicars and the squires who really ran things, who got things done. It was one more way in which Cora was different. He doubted any of the girls here had ever thought if they *wanted* to be a duchess or if they would even like it.

Declan watched the two women line up at their targets—one blonde, one sable-haired, both turned out in white archery dresses, bodices devoid of bows and frippery so that their bows risked catching on nothing. Both with intent expressions on their faces as they sighted their targets. Lady Mary spared a cool glance at Cora before nocking her first arrow.

'What a look,' Alex commented. 'The lady means business. How does it feel to be fought over by two lovely women?' He elbowed Declan playfully. 'Every man's fantasy, eh? Would you like to wager your girl against mine? I'll put up five quid that Cora beats Lady Mary to make it interesting, although I think the odds are in your favour.' He shrugged. 'Easy money for you. Unless you'd like to wager against your lady?'

Declan shook his head. 'You know very well I can't wager on either of them without everyone reading volumes into it. Everyone will see it as a declaration. I think declaring so soon would put a damper on the rest of the party. As much as my mother wants me to make a choice, she wants her drama, too.'

They paused, watching Lady Mary's first arrow lodge

in the ring closet to the bullseye. They joined in the smattering of applause. For the finals, the ladies were shooting at the same target and alternating turns. Declan felt his body tense as Cora raised her bow. Her arrow lodged in the bullseye, sending a murmur through the crowd. She'd taken round one.

'You're smitten with her. You held your breath while she shot,' Alex commented quietly as Lady Mary prepared for her second shot. 'I don't think I've ever seen you like this.' It was a fair point. Declan didn't think he'd ever seen himself like this either, at least not for a long time.

'Not smitten. Intrigued,' Declan insisted, not wanting to give too much away even to Alex. 'To that, I will admit. I am intrigued. She wants what I want.' Which wasn't necessarily what he could have. For a duke there was often a difference between the two. 'We share certain similarities that go beyond the superficial.'

'How convenient and appealing.' Alex's dryness caused Declan to give him a sharp look.

'What are you insinuating?'

Alex put a placating hand on his arm. 'Nothing evil, my friend, only caution. If you've only known her a few days and, even though you won't say it out loud, you think she's perfect, exactly what you've been looking for—don't you think it's strange that she's come out of nowhere? No one knows anything about her, and yet she knows all about you, speaks to you on a level that has you looking starry-eyed? Doesn't she strike you as perhaps too good to be true? For a duke at least.'

Alex just meant to help, but Declan didn't appreciate

it. 'She's not like that. When she looks at me, she sees me, not the title. It's hard to explain. I just want a chance to get to know her better.'

'What happens when intrigue becomes smitten?' Alex needled him a bit. 'Are dukes allowed to marry for love?'

'It's not that it isn't allowed, it's just rare,' Declan replied gruffly, letting his imagination run away with him for a moment as Cora's second shot went a little wide, matching Lady Mary's first shot. He'd be the first duke in the history of his line to marry for love. The Duke who married the archer from Dorset. Love would be a scandal all its own. The first to marry for love, the first to cause a scandal. These were perhaps not the 'firsts' his mother had in mind when she thought about his contributions to the Harlow legacy. It was not a position he'd ever thought to find himself in.

A short intermission was called to push back the target a few feet further. 'I should go offer encouragement to my partner.' Alex flashed him a smile and strode towards Cora with a proprietary air, calling out with jovial good cheer, 'My dear Miss Graylin, don't fail us now. I live to best Harlow in shooting competitions.' The remark earned him a laugh from the spectators.

For good form's sake, Declan went to join Lady Mary, offering up words of encouragement, but he couldn't quite defeat the stab of envy that poked at him as he surreptitiously watched Alex laughing with Cora, giving her instruction she didn't need and she wouldn't heed. Cora was her own person, with her own rules, a woman who understood herself and what she wanted. When he was with her he understood himself better, too. That was a rarity not often afforded to dukes, who were not really men but placeholders.

She could not afford to miss this shot. Cora studied the target. It wasn't the distance she was worried about, it was the wind. The breeze had picked up since the shooting had started. Breeze provided resistance, making it harder for the arrow to go the distance with force. It also made it more difficult for it to stay on course. Even a gentle breeze might cause the arrow to veer just a fraction from the bullseye, and only a bullseye would do. Lady Mary Kimber shot nothing but. The one shot that had gone astray earlier was an anomaly.

Cora had been watching her all day. In part because Lady Mary was paired with Declan, but also because she was good. Cora had thought it inevitable the competition would come to this since the moment it had started. It seemed unlikely the Duchess would have paired her son with an inept archer, and Lady Mary Kimber was the best the Duchess knew, in terms of archery and in terms of a marriage match—an earl's daughter with a fortune. Perfect for a duke with a fortune.

Like married like. That's how real-world stories ended. Cora was not naïve enough to think winning the archery tournament changed that, nor morning meetings in mazes. She glanced at her sister and her aunt on the sidelines, Mr Wade attentively at her sister's side. Winning would certainly enhance their status at the party. People always flocked to a winner, but that would also bring questions, and perhaps some animosity.

Not everyone would be pleased if she won. If she were canny, she might miss the shot on purpose so that the 'right' girl could win. It would avoid making any further enemies. It would make her human, no longer the girl in the blue dress who'd appeared out of nowhere and stolen the dance with the Duke.

That dance had been the beginning of unlooked-for entanglements, each one leading to another. Sometimes, a part of her wished she'd not tried the dress on. It had allowed her to be the princess in her own fairy tale, someone she was not, someone to whom good things happened, someone who could have dreams come true. That dress had complicated things. And now, it would make it all the harder to let go when those dreams didn't come true. And yet, her heart cried that she wouldn't have missed these moments for the world, no matter the pain that came afterwards.

She glanced at Lady Mary and made her decision. She would shoot to win. Cora Graylin of Dorset was an excellent archer who held back for no one. Today, she wore one of her own gowns. She was entirely herself, so she would darn well shoot like it. Lord Fenton strode up, full of bonhomie. 'Don't fail us now,' he joked, holding a finger up to the breeze. 'You'll need to account for the breeze.'

'I've already noted it.' She laughed. He'd been an excellent partner, not only in his skills but in company. He'd been easy to talk with between flights. If she'd had a brother, he would have been like Lord Fenton—Alex, as he insisted, although she'd not relented on that account. She was aware of Declan with Lady Mary just a few feet away, wondering what kind of advice he was giving her. She ought not be jealous. She had no unique claim to him nor could she make one. She knew how this story ended. At the end of the week, she would return to her own circles and he would continue in his. Their association would be done.

Cora watched as Lady Mary took her shot with determined calm and steadiness, staring down the alley for a long deliberate moment before letting loose, the arrow hitting the bullseye, her slight exhale the only sign of relief. Evidence as to how much the shot had meant to her, how much she was counting on it to perhaps put her forward with the Duke.

'If you tie with her, there will be a shoot-off, you'll get a second chance,' Lord Fenton whispered from his position at her shoulder. 'Just put the arrow beside hers.'

She shook her head, her own mind already made up. No second chances. This was for her. To prove to herself that she was still Cora Graylin, that *haute ton* house parties and dances with dukes hadn't changed her and would not change her. It was a reminder she desperately needed. At the end of this, she was still going to be Cora Graylin, archer, rider, daughter of a vicar too poor to sponsor his own daughters in Town.

'What are you going to do?' Fenton sounded slightly agitated at having his strategy ignored.

She plucked an arrow and fitted it to the bow, sparing him a brief glance. 'I'm going to telescope it.'

'You mean Robin Hood it? That is an unnecessary risk,' he began. 'There is no need.'

'There is every need,' she snapped sharply. 'Step back

please, Lord Fenton.' The time for thinking was past. It was time to do, to let her body go through the motions it knew effortlessly. In a fluid movement that was the antithesis of Lady Mary's long, deliberate gaze before shooting, Cora raised her bow and drew a breath, feeling the brush of the arrow's feathers against her cheek, her fingers loosing the arrow without thought, sending it straight into the feathers of Lady Mary Kimber's bullseye and an enthusiastic round of applause from the guests.

'I think you've immortalised the Duchess's archery competition for all time,' Lord Fenton murmured, but she hardly heard the words as her attention was fixed on Declan making his way towards her, wearing one of the smiles she'd come to feel were reserved just for her.

'Well done, Miss Graylin. That was splendid shooting. I had it on good authority you meant to win and you certainly did that.' The sparkle in his gaze sent a private message, that he was thinking about their conversation in the maze. A footman came up with the prizes, and beyond the impromptu winner's circle afternoon tea was being laid out al fresco, but Cora was aware only of Declan's blue-eyed gaze, fixed on her, full of awe and appreciation.

He presented Lord Fenton with a silver flask etched with the competition and the date, and for her a pin done in the shape of a golden arrow, the date engraved on the back. His hands were warm and steady as he pinned it to her bodice. That, she thought, was perhaps the real prize the women had been after—the privilege of having the Duke's hands on them, having the Duke so close that one could smell the clean, citrusy scent of him, to know such an intimate detail about the man who bore the weighty title. The pin was merely a ruse to claim the Duke's touch. But it would be formal and perfunctory. Not at all like the way he'd laced their fingers together in the maze, or the way he'd reached for her hand, assuring her they would not be seen.

The crowd dispersed for tea and Declan offered his arm. 'Walk with me? I think folks expect it given that you're the victor of the moment.'

'No wonder Lady Mary Kimber wanted to win so badly. The real prize isn't the pin at all. It's a chance to have time with you, to have you all to oneself.' They were careful to stroll the perimeter of the tea party, private but still in full view of the guests. They could be seen but not heard. No one could find fault.

Declan gave a half-smile. 'She just likes to win. Lady Mary Kimber doesn't care about time with me.'

'On the contrary,' Cora argued. 'I am sure she does, even if she masks it well. It doesn't serve her to be too easy.' She paused as another strolling couple passed with a nod to them. 'I've heard you were going to dance with her that night at the ball before I arrived. I've stolen her moment of victory twice now. She's going to hate me.'

'I don't think she's someone who hates,' Declan disagreed.

'Then you don't know women very well. Remember, I have a household full of sisters. I will tell you, females have a long memory and a penchant for vengeance.' Cora flashed him a smile. 'My sister, Melly, once "borrowed" Kitty's good Sunday sash without permission and got a stain on it. Kitty retaliated by putting a toad in Melly's bed, knowing full well how much Melly hates the creatures. She's downright frightened of them. The result was that Melly slept in my bed for weeks before she had the courage to go back to her room. She snores, she and Elise both. The point is, we all suffered Kitty's wrath. Don't think for a moment that Lady Mary Kimber is immune to these defeats.'

Declan laughed, manoeuvring them towards the huge trunk of an oak on the edge of the lawn. Two, three steps more and they were hidden from the party by the enormous trunk with its thick roots. They might be back in the maze again. Alone, private. 'A cautionary tale, to be sure. Remind me not to anger your sisters.' He said it as if he'd actually meet them. What a novel thought that was, and an impossible one. That would never happen. She didn't want him to see the vicarage with its leaky roof and weedy garden, sheets hanging out to dry.

'You can laugh now, but take the tale seriously,' Cora counselled. 'Every girl here covets time with you. You're the real prize, not pins and silver flasks.'

He chuckled. 'Somehow I don't think you mean that as a compliment.'

Cora slanted him a soft look, leaning against the tree trunk. 'I don't. In truth, I feel badly for you.' How would he take that blunt assessment? One never pitied dukes. It was probably a rule written down somewhere.

'I don't pity me, not right now at least.' Declan propped one arm against the tree trunk, the nearness of his body to hers sending a warm fizz through her veins. 'I get to be here with you. That's my prize. This morning seems ages ago already.' His blue eyes rested on hers, the air around them beginning to crackle with intent. They were not out here for simply another conversation. His thumb caressed her lips in a soft gesture, his voice low and seductive. 'I'd claim another prize as well, if you'd allow.'

'Would that be wise?' Her breath caught despite her words. Her practical self knew the answer. It wouldn't be wise. To kiss Declan would change everything. It would force them both to venture questions that had currently escaped being asked, and truths that had managed to avoid being told—that nothing could come of this. In fairy tales, kisses solved problems, turned frogs into princes and broke curses. But a kiss now would only do the reverse.

'I'm not interested in wise at the moment, Cora.' He reached a hand to stroke her hair. 'You've turned my world upside down in the best of ways. When I am with you, I am more myself than I've ever been. I tell you things I don't share with others.'

'Declan, you shouldn't say such things, you hardly know me...' she began but the protest was feeble. It was hard to argue with the truth, and she hadn't the heart for it. She wanted only to live in this moment, practicalities and realities be damned.

He pressed a finger to her lips. 'When I look in your eyes, I see my heart reflected back to me. You feel it, too, Cora, tell me you do.'

They were standing close now, bodies touching, her heart racing with the truth. Resistance would not win this fight. Every bone, every thought and pulse, begged for him, answered to him. 'Yes,' she whispered as his mouth bent to claim hers, 'I feel it, too.' She would have this moment, this kiss, her body seemed to say—let the aftermath fall where it will.

Chapter Ten

Even as she gave herself up to the kiss, it was as if a craving opened inside her for more. The kiss did not satisfy as much it awakened—hunger, want, passion. She was aware this was not merely one kiss, a brief, contained meeting of mouths, but mouths and bodies coming together, entwining about one another. Her arms were about his neck, pressing him close. Her body pressed into him, mouths fully engaged, tongues tasting, tangling in pursuit of fulfilment.

There was wildfire in her veins, intense and obliterating, a match lit to a fuse. Once the kiss started, she didn't want it to stop, didn't want to leave the sanctuary of his arms, the shelter of his body.

At last he broke from her with a ragged breath. She lolled her head against the tree, looking up into the sky through the boughs of the oak, gathering her own breath as if they'd both come up for air. 'Are kisses supposed to feel like that?' All she could do was *feel*…the weakness of her knees, the racing of her heart, the heat in her veins. She'd never felt anything so intensely that it obliterated the ability to think.

He drew a steadying breath, his eyes mirroring those

feelings of awe, of surprise, of unlooked-for heat. 'No, not usually. At least not for me.'

She smiled at his confession and tentatively offered her own. 'Not for me either.' John Arnot had kissed her once. It had been demanding and insistent. It had roused none of the reaction Declan's kiss raised in her. It certainly hadn't made her want more.

'I didn't expect...' She trailed off, unsure how to complete the sentence. *What* hadn't she expected? 'Perhaps I should have, though. It's always been different with you, nothing with you has ever been by the book.' She fussed with his cravat, straightening it, feeling an uncustomary mix of shyness and boldness over her confession. Had she said too much?

'What do you mean by that, Miss Graylin?' he teased, leaning in to steal a quick peck.

She tilted her head and took his hand. 'Well, we're a fairy tale in reverse aren't we?' She lifted his hand and twined her fingers through his, studying the elegant, lean length of his hand. 'We began where most fairy tales end—a dance with the Prince. And now, we've tumbled off the edge of the page into uncharted territory.'

'Am I the Prince in this scenario?' He laughed. Now that the kiss was behind them, euphoria enveloped them in the aftermath.

'Yes.' She laughed as he stole another kiss.

'If I recall the fairy tales correctly, the princess was usually in hiding, subjugated to servitude. Snow White was a scullery maid and so was Cinderella.' He laughed against her neck, nipping at her ear. 'Are you trying to tell me *you're* a scullery maid?'

No. Just a vicar's daughter.

The thought went unspoken. Cora worried her lip, the feeling of being a fraud settling over her again. What would Declan think if he knew there was no substance to her? That what he thought he saw was all smoke and mirrors? She was the niece of a baronet, but beneath that there was nothing a duke would find merit in. She hadn't the lineage of a Lady Mary Kimber. That was where their fairy tale unravelled. Briar Rose went from being a peasant to being a princess. Cinderella was the daughter of a nobleman. Snow White was the daughter of the King. But she was none of those things. Her trajectory would be the opposite. She would not be elevated but demoted.

She could have a kiss among the oaks, a week of house party fun, but that was it. Then she'd return to London and it would have to be over. To prolong it risked the full truth coming out, which would embarrass them both. The same urge that prompted her to protect her sisters surged in her now to extend that protection to him. How odd to think a duke needed protecting, but perhaps he needed it more than anyone realised. Everyone watched him. He was always under the quizzing glass. She didn't want to be the one who caused him to stumble.

'We'd best get back. People will be missing us. I'm sure the requisite time allotted for a "victory lap" with the Duke has been exceeded. The other girls will want their turns.' She gave a half-hearted laugh, meaning to make light of it, but a cruel-spirited thought occurred as they began a slow stroll back towards the party. She could not expect to keep Declan's kisses for herself.

There would be a moment when he'd steal away, by necessity, with perhaps Lady Mary, to test the passion between them. If he did, what would he find? Would all the girls go weak in the knees? Would all the girls kiss him back with the same verve she had? She found she did not like the idea of that possibility at all.

Something stilled in Declan's eyes, his gaze going hard, his tone stern. 'No, Cora. The answer to what you're thinking is no.' She'd offended him mightily. Even his touch had gone to steel, his arm stiffening beneath her hand as they walked. He stopped walking and turned to face her, eyes smouldering with the blue fire of insult. 'I do *not* indiscriminately pin women to oak trunks and kiss them until we're *both* senseless with desire.'

She did not want to argue the issue. There was no point to it. Her heart wanted their kiss to mean something, wanted to believe every word he'd spoken in the forest—words that had come dangerously close to a declaration of love. His heart had been in his blue eyes, both of them swept away by the moment perhaps. But reality suggested otherwise. Whatever he might feel for her at present, he would not choose her in the end. He couldn't. He would see that soon. And that meant he had to kiss others, no matter what he thought in this moment.

They rejoined the party. He escorted her to where her aunt and sister stood with Mr Wade before taking his leave. Cora watched him go, her heart in her throat.

Everything was topsy-turvy. This was what she'd feared would happen with a kiss. It was no longer enough to simply look forward to one more conversation, one more day. That kiss had been an admission of feelings, a declaration of its own. The things they'd said to one another, the things they'd done and felt, all flirted with the impossible. The stakes had just got infinitely higher for them both. They weren't just courting each other. They were courting scandal. This was precisely why people shouldn't fall in love. She turned to Aunt B and pled a headache, which was becoming all too real, and fled to her room.

Cora had just loosened her laces when Elise blew in from the corridor full of worry. 'Are you all right? Aunt B said you had a headache.'

'I'm fine, I just wanted some time to think.' Cora stretched out on the bed, smiling to reassure her sister. But apparently seclusion wasn't to be her lot.

Aunt B came through the connecting door between their rooms, sinking into what was becoming her customary chair. 'The party is going well. Her Grace must be pleased. Many matches are getting off the ground. If things keep up at this rate, the Season of 1824 will be known for the amount of weddings it produced.'

Cora managed a laugh. 'I do believe you're a romantic at heart, Aunt B, despite your shrewdness.'

Aunt B gave a contented smile. 'A practical romantic, but I suppose that still counts. Love is something, but it's not everything.'

Elise sat on the bed, legs crossed, as she took the pin out of her straw hat. 'Mama and Papa were a love match,' she said confidently.

Aunt B's smile turned soft. 'Yes, they were. I remember their wedding. Your uncle and I had already been married for a few years. We came out from London for it. It was a beautiful May day, the sun was out. Your mother wore a wreath of daisies and her hair loose. It hung down her back, all the way to her waist, one long, glossy walnut skein. Like your hair, dear Cora.' She gave a gentle laugh full of memories. 'Your father was beaming as he stood at the altar waiting for her. When he looked at her, he looked like a man who had the world by the tail. He had everything he wanted. He had a lovely wife, he'd just received his living. The world was laid at his feet and he knew it.'

Cora stared at her hands, blinking hard against the tears. Father wasn't that man any more. He hadn't felt that way for years. Even before Mother had taken ill, the light of living had dimmed for him, worn down by too many mouths to feed and too little funds. Reality had outpaced what love could provide.

'Mama showed me her dress once.' Elise grinned, bouncing a little on the bed with her natural energy. 'It was made out of linen with a lawn overskirt, and she'd embroidered the daisies at the hem by hand. What about you and Uncle? Were you a love match or a practical match?'

'Elise,' Cora admonished quietly, 'you're prying.' But she was curious, too. One of the unlooked-for benefits of this trip to London was the chance to get to know her aunt better. Aunt B and Uncle George had been rare visitors to the vicarage over the years. Of course, she could understand why. They were busy and the place hardly appealed. It was too crowded, too unkempt to properly host anyone, and it was rude to make family stay at an inn.

Aunt B waved a hand, dismissing Cora's concern. 'I don't mind, child. It's good instruction to hear family stories. One should know what they're getting into. I don't hold with girls being unprepared for marriage. Not just the marriage bed, but the whole of it. There's a lot more to it than bedding and heirs.' Cora felt her cheeks heat, the memory of Declan's kiss still warm on her lips.

'Uncle and I were a little of both,' Aunt B went on. 'I met him during the Season. I thought he was handsome if quiet. But I knew little about him other than that he would eventually inherit your grandfather's title. He would have a title, land, an income that was comfortable. He was not riddled with debt like so many others are, and he seemed kind. He was interested in making himself agreeable to me. I met his family's requirements. My father was the younger son of a viscount and I had good marriage settlements. I came with a small property in Oxfordshire and good manners, and your uncle thought I was pretty.'

She gave a becoming blush that made Elise laugh. 'It was enough to start with and all else followed in time. One can hardly expect more when there's only twelve weeks to make a match.'

Elise sighed dreamily. 'That's a wonderful story, Aunt B. A quiet fairy tale, I'd call it.' Cora felt Elise turn her gaze towards her. 'What about you, Cora? How are things with your Duke? Is it a quiet fairy tale or a whirlwind romance?'

'Are those the only two choices?' Cora tried for deflection. She didn't want to make what happened between her and Declan a panel discussion. 'Besides, it's a private matter.'

Aunt B was all sharp alertness, sitting up straight. 'It's hardly a private matter. Nothing that happened at the ball or at the house party is private. Everyone is watching everyone. It's one giant chess game,' she scolded. 'Today, you're the front runner. You won the archery contest. You took a stroll with the Duke.'

'Yes, but Lady Mary Kimber had his attentions during the competition as his partner. She had more of his minutes than I did,' Cora prevaricated.

Her aunt gave a sly look. 'All of her minutes were spent in plain view whereas a few of yours were not. And I didn't see the Duke standing behind her, helping her adjust her bow or any other such nonsense people contrive in order to touch if they were truly interested in each other.' Like attaching a pin to a bodice. Like sneaking kisses behind an ancient oak. 'The stakes are high for Lady Mary Kimber. Creighton overlooked her last year when she was the most obvious choice for his duchess. This party ought to be her chance to gain an advantage over the absent Lady Elizabeth Cleeves and instead she's lost ground to an outsider—you.'

'She has nothing to worry about from me. I can't be a front runner. There can only be this week. When we go back to Town, I'll need to focus on finding a more appropriate suitor.'

'Do you think the Duke will allow that?' Aunt B quizzed. 'I don't think he believes this week is just for fun. He is in deadly earnest of a wife and his sights are fixed on you.'

Cora shook her head. She couldn't allow herself to believe that. It would only set her up for disappointment when he discovered the whole truth. 'I am a moment's intrigue to him. I am different, that is all.'

Elise gave a snort from the bed. 'I don't think it was "intrigue" I saw in his eyes today.'

That alarmed her. She'd seen it, too, she'd heard his words. 'It has to be. It can't be more. If he finds out who I really am…' Cora pressed her fingers to her temples. She flashed a plea for help in Aunt B's direction. 'This was only supposed to be a chance to extend the magic of the ball a little longer, a chance for Elise to meet suitors she couldn't encounter elsewhere. And she has. Mr Wade—'

'Stop! That's enough.' Elise leapt from the bed. 'Don't do this, Cora. Don't make this about me. You always make it about me or about the girls. When we were unwrapping dresses, your first thought was about sending the pink ribbon to Melly and Kitty. When you saw that blue dress, your first reaction was to find its owner. Can't you just let something good be about you? Do you always have to give away your happiness? Can't the Duke fall in love with *you*? There is no one more deserving of a fairy tale than you, dear sister.' Elise seized her hands. 'Can't we be here for you?'

Elise's outburst stunned her for a moment. She didn't know how to respond. But Elise had words enough for them both. 'Ever since Mama died, you've taken everything on yourself—the house, the budget, managing Father, managing the parish when he forgets to. You've sacrificed so much. You don't paint any more, I know how much you loved that. I thought after Constable's visit you might start again, but you put it off saying there's no time or money for supplies, that Kitty and Melly needed new shoes instead. But this time is ours,' Elise pleaded. 'This is your time.'

'To find a husband who can help me set the younger girls up, to make sure Father wants for nothing,' Cora supplied. She might not know how to answer Elise's outburst, but she knew her duty.

Elise shook her head. 'And to find love. You heard Aunt B. Be a practical romantic. You can have both with the Duke. He likes you.'

'Elise, it simply can't be. Dukes don't marry vicars' daughters. He doesn't know me and didn't Aunt B *also* say that love is not enough?' It certainly wouldn't be when or if Declan learned of her rather lowly antecedents. Love would not ensure a lack of scandal if Declan officially pursued her, or, heaven forbid, proposed. How many times did she have to say it? Cora felt like she was howling in the wind.

Aunt B rose in a rustle of skirts, giving them a strong look. 'It seems that you girls have a lot to talk about. I'll excuse myself and let you do that in private, where you can talk freely. I'll just be next door if you need me.'

Elise flopped back on the bed, a hand flung over her eyes. 'You're so exasperating sometimes, Cora. I can't imagine ever being as good as you.'

It was said without meanness and Cora sank down beside her with a sigh. 'You know how bad things are at home. We're hanging on by the proverbial thread. We must marry well and immediately. I am already being selfish enough by coming to the house party and indulging the fantasy. The only redemption is that you have met and impressed Mr Wade.'

Elise turned her head and giggled. 'And he has impressed me, Cora. I like him. We have fun together. He makes me laugh and we enjoy the same things—long walks, outdoor pursuits, and some of the same writers. He wants to start a school on his estate. I'd like that kind of work. He lives quietly. He's not enamoured of Town. That's fine with me. It's been good to see London but I don't need to come every year.'

'It's only been a few days, a few dances. Is that really enough time to know someone?' She would hate to lose Elise. Yet, she knew what her sister meant. Didn't she also feel the same way with Declan? That she knew him far beyond a waltz and a walk? That Declan was right—it seemed that their hearts spoke to each other.

'Mr Wade and I have made good use of our time, not that you've noticed,' Elise said with a sly grin. 'You heard Aunt B. She didn't have long with Uncle George before she knew they'd suit. It is possible to be a practical romantic, Cora.'

'Better a practical romantic than a hopeless one, I suppose.' Cora sighed and let out a long breath.

Elise squeezed her hand. 'It's not hopeless—you and the Duke. If you can't have him in the long run, perhaps you can at least have him for the short term? Love is precious and rare and fragile. It can be lost in a moment, shattered with the slightest effort. The world does not always handle love with the delicacy it deserves. We must enjoy it while we can, before the world intrudes, before we have to choose.'

That was easy for Elise to say. She wouldn't have to choose. Mr Wade was offering her both. But what Declan thought he could offer her was based on a false premise. Her case was different. She had a clear duty to Declan and to her family and those duties did not coincide.

'Cora?' Elise murmured with afternoon drowsiness. 'Is the Duke a good kisser?'

'How should I know?' Cora's eyes flew open.

'Because he kissed you in the woods today. When you came back from your walk your lips were puffy and your hair was a little dishevelled. I don't think anyone else noticed.' Elise turned on her side and punched her pillow into a comfortable form. 'If all I could have was a week with a man I cared for, and who cared for me, I would take it. I wouldn't look for reasons to ignore what was in front of me. At least then, I'd have something to remember while I did my duty.'

Elise fell asleep shortly after delivering her verdict. Cora laid awake long after, wishing she didn't find her sister's words quite so compelling. It put her mind up to all sorts of mischief. Perhaps the only way to seize happiness was for the short term, with the knowledge that it would end.

Chapter Eleven

His mother wanted a moment before supper. Declan poured a splash of brandy into a glass—not too much though, given that the brandy was his hourglass. When the brandy was gone, the conversation would be over. Mother could say her piece but he would not tolerate a full-blown harangue. He took a seat at one of the two Chesterfields facing each other near the cold fire, his mother on the other.

'I wanted a chance to connect with you, to hear your impressions of the girls so that I know how best to assist,' she began as he took a sip. In her own way, he knew she wanted to help. He was sympathetic to the reality that this was the work of her lifetime. Seeing to the succession of the Dukedom was as much her responsibility as it was his. Only, for her, there was the added realisation that she was picking her successor, whereas he was choosing a partner. His wife would replace her, take her title, while she would assume a new one as the Dowager Duchess. But empathy was not a reason to entirely surrender to her choice, her wants.

He gave the brandy a thoughtful swirl. 'The girls are all well-chosen, Mother. You've outdone yourself, truly.'

He appreciated it was no small feat to have gathered twenty-five of England's finest girls from the best families under one roof.

The compliment pleased her. Her face softened. 'What do you think of Miss Brighton? I've seated her next to you for supper. You've not had as much time with her as some of the others.'

Declan nodded, appreciative of the effort she was going to on his behalf, if not the outcome. 'That will indeed allow me some conversation with her.' It wouldn't matter. He did not think he'd like Clara Brighton any better if he had fifty conversations with her. She was a pretty girl with a rich father and a tendency to sing slightly off-key.

'How do you find Lady Mary Kimber? You've had considerable time with her—supper last night, the musical, and the archery today. It was a shame you and she didn't win.'

Declan took another swallow. 'I found her much as I find the other girls. They're all very much the same. It's as if my choice is to pick the least objectionable among them, the one who is least boring, as opposed to the one who is *most* interesting.' One who captivated his senses and his thoughts, one who challenged him when she disagreed. One who kissed like wildfire in the woods, whose body had answered his against the trunk of the oak tree, as if all of their encounters had been leading to that moment. Cora was simply herself, honest in word and deed. The longer he knew her the more convinced he was of that.

'There is always Lady Elizabeth Cleeves back in

Town. It's a shame she was not able to attend.' His mother sighed. 'She's a diamond to be sure. I had hoped perhaps in her absence, these other girls might not be overshadowed, that they might shine. Certainly, Lady Mary Kimber has done some of that,' she pressed. 'Her father is eager, Son. It would be a good match if Lady Elizabeth isn't to your liking.'

'To my liking?' Declan said grimly. 'This is not about mixing a perfect cup of tea.' He took another swallow. He had two swallows left and the conversation had gone exactly where he'd expected it to go—winnowing down the list of candidates, funnelling him towards a choice, while making it seem that he had a hand in the matter. It was time to speak up. 'There is one here who does have my liking and my interest and that is Miss Cora Graylin.'

His mother's face went stern, her jaw set with a stubbornness he knew well. 'She is an outlier. We hardly know her.'

'That's a poor argument all the way around. I hardly know *any* of these girls. They are at least a decade my junior. When I was their age, they were barely ten years old, still playing with dolls while I was touring Europe with my tutors.' Having a very controlled taste of the world's great art and vices, becoming a man. His eighteen-year-old self would have had as little interest in those pinafore frocked girls as his thirty-year-old self did now. Time had not changed that.

'They are on the cusp of womanhood now. Lady Mary Kimber is twenty, if you want someone not quite so freshly out of the school room. She has polish on her, as does Lady Elizabeth Cleeves.'

He gave a snort at that. 'Lady Elizabeth Cleeves will not change in thirty years. She'll still be as petty as she is now. A truly grown woman doesn't throw a tantrum over a dress order gone awry. That does not speak of great maturity on her part. I enjoyed my time with Miss Cora Graylin today.' He steered the conversation back to where he wanted it. His mother had been quick to hold up her candidates and he was done discussing them. 'She speaks her mind.'

'She is too bold,' his mother countered. 'She does not know her place. She is not *haute ton* and has overreached herself. Perhaps we can excuse the ball. That was Lady Isley's error, but she should have known better than to have come here and put herself among the diamonds.'

'I think it was brave. It speaks well of her courage.' Declan fixed his mother with a stare. 'I need a wife who will stand up to me, who will tell me when I am wrong. You were that for father. You never hesitated to speak your mind,' he reminded her. 'Much good came of that, too. Thanks to you, there is a small lending library in the village so that all have access to books.' He offered his mother a smile to soften his scold. 'You have set the bar for my bride very high. Why should I settle for less in a wife than what my father had?'

'If she were all that, perhaps I would reconsider,' his mother said slowly. 'But it's only been a few days. She is lovely and vivacious and gorgeously attired at every turn. I can see why she has turned your head. She's turned the head of nearly every man here, and those who haven't had their heads turned by her have been charmed by her sister.' She was pandering to him before making her case. 'But we have known these other families for generations. One need not know the girl if one knows the family.'

'What is there to know?' Declan leaned back in his chair, feeling some progress had been made. He crossed a leg over one knee. 'She is the granddaughter of a baronet, the niece to the current baronet. Her father is a biblical scholar, a man of learning and intellect.'

'She is gentry, nothing more,' his mother scoffed. 'Surely, you can do better than that. I've given you daughters of earls and viscounts and dukes. What do we know of Miss Graylin's father? Is he an intellect of some renown? Has he published a book? Presented papers at Oxford?' Declan could see his mother's mind starting to work. She was at least considering, wondering how she might package this to Society if her son proved intractable. If Cora's father was famous even in his own circles, she could tout him as having celebrity. Heaven forbid her son marry an ordinary gentleman's daughter.

'I do not know,' Declan ceded. 'But I ask myself this— what does it matter who he is? What good is having a duke's privilege and station if I cannot use that privilege on occasion to my personal benefit?' Declan asked.

'Because you would not have that power for long if you used it so arbitrarily. Such decisions would undermine your authority. How long do you think anyone would respect a duke who married a milkmaid? Being a duke means duty and compromise above all else. Your father taught you that.'

He stifled the petty urge to point out Cora was not a milkmaid. Why was the compromise always at his expense? Why were his needs and wants always sacrificed? Declan said nothing. Sometimes the best argument one could offer was silence. He finished his drink and set aside the tumbler.

'I shall make enquiries, then, so that we're certain of what we're getting into.' His mother rose. 'Of course, you don't have to decide this week. Perhaps I was a bit hasty in thinking that would be possible. We may want to host a variety of smaller entertainments once we're back in Town. I hadn't counted on Lady Elizabeth Cleeves being absent, among other things.' Those 'things' being a gentleman's daughter catching her son's eye.

'Thank you, Mother.' Declan could be gracious. He had had two victories. His mother had not said no to Cora, only caution. And the bridal search had been extended. There was hope on both fronts. 'I'll join you directly in the drawing room.'

The enormity of what had just happened was not lost on him. He'd been granted another reprieve, an extension on his matrimonial commitment. They would go back to Town and continue to consider candidates. All because he'd chosen a girl who was less than appropriate in his mother's eyes. *Chosen.* What a powerful word that was. *Chosen.* Had he chosen Cora tonight?

Declan helped himself to another small splash of brandy. He knew why his mother had conceded. She wanted time to send letters, to research Cora more thoroughly. Perhaps she was hoping that something would emerge in Cora's background to put him off. It would be interesting to see what she would do when nothing disgraceful emerged. He was certain nothing would. How disgraceful could a young woman be, living her whole life in Wimborne Minster? And Cora was too straight-forward to have secrets.

He studied his brandy. By putting Cora forward with his mother, he'd taken a step closer to choosing a bride. The thought should have alarmed him, and a few weeks ago it would have. But tonight, the only anxiety he felt was centred on whether or not Cora would accept.

Of course she'll accept, his conscience prodded. *She needs to wed or face the consequences in Dorset.*

But he didn't necessarily want her that way—as simply a choice under duress. He wanted her to choose him no matter how many options she had. The question arose once more—would she want to be a duchess? Would she be willing to make the necessary compromises? It would be a lot to ask when the time came. And yet, as fanciful as the notion was, love might be enough. Their kisses and their conversations suggested as much.

Declan set aside his brandy glass, the second serving untouched. His thoughts regarding Cora Graylin were complicated and the brandy wasn't helping. He'd been swept off his feet, even though he was supposed to be the one doing the sweeping.

She was being swept off her feet, despite her efforts to the contrary. It was not supposed to have happened like this—finding herself mid-house-party, kissing the Duke behind an oak tree, her heart engaged to the full-est. For someone who staunchly felt love was an over-estimated emotion, this was not a comfortable spot to be in. And that kiss...oh, that kiss had undone her.

Cora had not anticipated the lingering effects a kiss could have, like the desire to follow Declan around a room with her eyes, or to let her gaze drift down the length of the dining table and her thoughts with it. *What was that delicious mouth of his saying?* She choked on her wine at the salacious thought.

'Are you all right, Miss Graylin?' Lord Fenton solicited on her right.

'Quite fine, thank you.' She offered a polite smile with the lie. She was decidedly *not* fine. Hours later, that one kiss had turned her thoughts decadent. She'd become wanton. But it hadn't been just one kiss. It had been a series of kisses, each hotter than the last, a veritable siege of her senses. Even then, those kisses had not acted alone. They were the culmination of conversations full of discovery, moments and touches that had built a history between them.

Her gaze drifted again, and this time Declan caught her eyes with his—another brief moment added to the history between them, his blue stare lingering on her lips, as if he wanted nothing more than to slip from the room, away from prying eyes, and plunder her mouth with his kisses, pressing her body against his. She wanted that, too—to forget reality for a moment, the responsibilities she owed others. To lie down with him skin to skin, to feel the bare strength of him beneath her fingertips, to touch, to feel, to taste…

The fantasy shocked her with the depth of its recklessness. She was bold, but never rash like this. Her family could not afford it, and here she was contemplating the ultimate recklessness a girl in her situation could contemplate. Well, it was only reckless *if* anyone knew. It was very much like the tree that fell in the forest. If she kissed the Duke and no one knew, did it really happen?

At the foot of the table, Her Grace rose, signalling the removal of the ladies, and Cora stood, reluctantly. She would not get close to Declan the rest of the evening. There would be cards after the men finished their port. The Duchess had already arranged partners. She'd be partnering Jack DeBose. She felt Lord Fenton's hand brush hers.

'There are other men here, Miss Graylin, who would delight in your company,' he said softly. It was both an encouragement and a gentle scold. He'd caught her staring. He was warning her against transparency, and perhaps even impossibility.

She offered him a small smile. 'Yes, thank you, Lord Fenton. You've been a gracious dinner partner.'

'I won't be so gracious at cards. Good luck tonight. We'll see if you play as well as you shoot.' He gave a winning grin, something both warm and warning in his tawny eyes. She did not want to encourage more than friendship from him, although it might be too late for that. He would likely be one of those men he alluded to if given the chance.

Perhaps she ought to consider that, Cora thought as she followed the other ladies out to the drawing room. Perhaps she should set aside reckless fantasies, forget the passion she experienced with Declan and use the opportunity to find a gentleman with a title or strong connections to one. After all, who knew better than she that passion and love wasn't enough? Practicalities would win the day and see her family safe.

In the drawing room, Cora took up a position at the window, hoping no one would join her. She could do far worse than Lord Fenton.

Except that he was Declan's close friend.

That brought its own perpetual awkwardness with it. There'd be a lifetime of encounters, of wonderings, of what-ifs, that would eventually wreck a friendship and perhaps even their marriage. All parties involved deserved better than that.

Ellen DeBose approached with a smile, looking pretty in a pale peach gown. 'You get to play with Jack tonight. You're sure to win. He's good at cards.' She looped an arm through Cora's, oblivious to Cora's desire to be left alone. 'Come stroll with me. We'll take a turn about the room. It won't hurt your cause to be seen being friendly.'

'What cause is that?' Cora enquired as they walked. She couldn't decide if she liked Ellen or not, despite her earlier hopes that Ellen would be a friend. Ellen was a pretty, sharp girl, but one who always seemed as if she had an agenda.

'You've made no secret of setting your cap for the Duke.'

'Every girl here has done the same, or at least their parents have. It's the point of the house party, after all,' Cora corrected. She found Ellen's assessment rather unfair. Declan had set his cap for her. He'd been the one to initiate all of their interactions, and yet she was the one to blame for stealing his attentions. How like Society to blame the woman when a man broke the rules of engagement.

'But *they* haven't managed to capture his attention.' Ellen's eyes dropped to the skirts of the aquamarine gown Cora wore. 'It's amazing what good tailoring can do.' Ellen leaned confidentially close. 'I've given you the name of my dressmaker but I think I must have the name of *yours*. If you catch the Duke, she'll be in high demand next Season.' She laughed, oblivious to the insult she'd dealt the Duke by assuming Declan was only interested in looks. 'Are you looking forward to the hunt tomorrow?' she asked coyly. 'You'll have the Duke all to yourself yet again.'

'I enjoy riding and being out of doors,' Cora redirected, casting a glance towards the drawing room door, hoping the gentlemen would come through.

'And I'm sure being outdoors is even better with a duke,' Ellen whispered naughtily, 'although I'm certain the Duchess disagrees. It's clear she thinks someone like Jack is more your level.'

Cora merely gave a neutral smile. She understood Ellen's message—birds who flew too high had their wings clipped. It was not all that different than the lecture she gave herself. To dally with a duke came with consequences, whether she'd chosen them or not.

Chapter Twelve

There was nothing like a good gallop to sort out angst in Cora's opinion, and she had more than her fair share of it. She'd spent the night tossing and turning over Declan's kiss and Ellen DeBose's remarks. In that regard the mounted treasure hunt in the morning was well placed. It was her partner that might prove to be problematic. Would she be able to sort through any of her thoughts with the object of her angst so near to hand? And yet there was no one else whom she'd rather share the blue-skied late spring day.

Declan was waiting for her at the mounting block when she joined the guests milling in the stable yard. He was comfortably turned out in breeches, boots and hacking jacket, looking every inch the country gentleman and entirely at ease with it. 'I chose her for you myself.' Declan showed off the mare, a compact coal-black hunter named Magic who sported a white sock on her back left leg.

Cora petted the mare's nose and stroked its shoulder, wishing she had Declan's *savoir faire*. Did he think of the kiss when he looked at her? Was he just better at hiding his reaction? Assuming he was still thinking about it. She certainly was. Whenever she looked at him, all she could think about was that kiss. Her eyes seemed to naturally drift to his mouth. It had been a problem last night at dinner, and that problem had not been solved this morning. If anything, her awareness of him was heightened further this morning by his nearness. He stood beside her, chatting easily as she inspected the mare and tried not to look at his glorious mouth, tried not to think of the steely strength of those arms.

'Will she do?' Declan asked, offering her a hand on the mounting block steps.

'More than do. She seems delightful.' Cora settled into the side-saddle and picked up the reins. The mare tossed her head, perhaps as eager as she to be gone from the noisy stable yard. Cora patted the mare in agreement. The sooner they were off, the sooner she could regain her equilibrium. She'd gallop the angst out of her thoughts.

The Duchess called for attention and gave instructions for the treasure hunt. Lists were distributed as Declan sidled close to her on the back of a big chestnut, the prospect of a day out of doors lighting his eyes. 'We'll go west when Mother gives the signal,' he murmured. 'Stay close to me. These horses want to run and I know exactly where we can do that.'

The Duchess dropped the flag and the guests took off in a mêlée of excitement and horses, laughing and jockeying for position. As soon as Cora and Declan cleared the stable yard, they kicked the horses into an easy canter, breaking to the front of the pack. Cora easily picked up Magic's smooth rhythm, keeping pace with Declan's chestnut.

'This way!' Declan gestured to a path off to the right as the other riders began to surge and split off in varying directions to begin their hunt. She followed him, taking a hedge as the path opened up into a meadow. 'We can gallop here and then find a quiet spot to look at the list,' Declan shouted over his shoulder. 'Are you ready?'

'Always!' A good gallop was what she needed to clear her head. She gathered the reins, gave the mare a kick and they were off, racing across the meadow, the warm spring air in her face. Cora could hear Declan yell something about fairness, and then the pounding of his big chestnut's hooves warned he was closing the gap. 'Come on, girl, we won't let those boys catch us,' she called to the mare. The mare surged. Perhaps she felt it, too, or perhaps it was just the mad joy of living on a warm spring day. Elation coursed through her, obliterating all thought but the thought of the race.

At the last, Declan pulled even. 'A tie!' he declared, catching his breath and slowing his horse. 'That felt good.' He laughed. 'I've been missing that.' He was a revelation with his windblown hair, his dancing eyes, his wide grin and easy laughter. It was as if she was seeing him, the *real* him for the first time. Here he was in his element, free of all constraints. He clapped the shoulder of his horse with genuine enthusiasm, and his joy was positively intoxicating, the sight of him fizzing through her veins like champagne. 'How do you like her?' He nodded towards the mare.

'She's a darling, there's no quit in her,' Cora complimented. She let out a long, contented breath and couldn't help but smile. 'I've missed this, too. I didn't realise how much until this morning. London keeps one so busy that it's easy to forget.'

'What sort of horse do you have at home?' Declan asked as the horses walked side by side towards a leafy canopied bridle path.

She smiled. 'A roan mare named Delilah. She's seventeen now, but she's been mine for ever,' she explained, telling him the story of how Delilah had come to the vicarage. 'An elderly parishioner without any close family had passed away unexpectedly and his livestock needed homes. Delilah was for riding, so there were few folks who had the need or ability to care for a luxury animal that didn't pull a plough. We took her in. My mother insisted her girls learn to ride like ladies. We all learned on her, but somehow she became mine.' Cora smiled again, starting to relax. Her angst had indeed passed with the gallop. It was easier to be with him out here, just the two of them. 'What about your horse? Have you had him long?'

'This is Samson, ironically enough. He's ten.' Declan laughed. 'Perhaps the two of them should meet. It seems a little bit like fate, except that a lot of horses are named Samson.'

'Perhaps they shouldn't meet—' Cora shot him a teasing look '—given how that turned out for the real Samson.'

Declan gave a conceding shrug. 'Perhaps so. At any rate, I'm glad you like Magic. I thought you would. I suppose we should get down to business. Do you have the list?'

Cora pulled the list from the skirt pocket of the blue

riding habit, focusing on the task. 'There's only seven items.' The hunt was entitled 'Signs of Spring', and all the items on the list were meant to be found outdoors. 'A bouquet of wildflowers containing at least three different varieties, a bird's feather, a caterpillar, lichen on a twig, a pinecone and a wreath of oak leaves.' She shot him a look. 'And the ornamental eggs, of course.' The Duchess had announced this morning before teams mounted up that twelve decorated egg-like casks had been hidden around the estate for teams to discover, each one containing a piece of jewellery featuring a birthstone, one for each month of the year.

Cora pondered the list, wondering where to start. 'The oak leaf wreath will have to be made. That might take some time.' She tapped a finger against her lips absently. 'No one will rush through this. It will take most of the day.'

Declan chuckled. 'I think that's the point. Midway through a house party is usually time for people to get to know those who interest them.' He gave a wry smile.

'I'm surprised your mother allowed me to partner with you if that was her intention.'

'Oh, it wasn't,' Declan replied with light-hearted honesty. 'She wanted me to partner Ellen DeBose, but I told her I'd already asked you and I wouldn't back out.' He stopped his horse in a leafy grove, and surveyed the trees. 'There are oak leaves here. I'll climb up and gather some and we can turn them into a wreath.'

He dismounted with enviable ease and came to help her down before stripping out of his coat. He draped the coat over a low branch and shimmied up the tree with more of that admirable athleticism. He'd not lied. He was definitely comfortable out of doors, and comfortable with himself, his body.

Sans coat, that body was on glorious display for her — muscles flexing beneath the thin linen of his shirt as he climbed. She was aware of a new heat stoking low in her belly as she watched him, the awakening of an awareness that went beyond appreciating handsomeness. This went deeper. It was desire and want. It was primal and possessive. He was hers. She wanted to claim him and be claimed by him. To touch and be touched in ways that went beyond a kiss in the forest. She ought to find such thoughts wicked, but she did not. She found them natural, intuitive, and that, too, was shocking, new territory.

Declan dropped to the ground feet first. 'I've got the leaves but I don't know the first thing about making a wreath.'

Cora laughed. 'Don't worry, I do. Give them to me.'

They settled in a hollowed-out area between the roots at the base of the trunk while the horses grazed nearby. Birds twittered overhead and the sun managed to peek through the leafy canopy. 'I wonder if it wasn't your mother's intent to select a task that required cooperation,' Cora mused, laying out the leaves. 'Perhaps she anticipated that most of the ladies wouldn't be quite up to tree climbing, and that their partners wouldn't know how to make a leaf wreath.'

Declan cocked his head. 'Show me the list. It would be just like my mother to teach a lesson like that.' She handed him the list and watched his eyes scan the items, a little smile forming at his lips. 'I think you're right,

Cora. This scavenger hunt might be better named ingredients for a successful marriage.'

Cora leaned towards him, reading the items. 'I see some of them. The task of the leaf wreath emphasises cooperation, and the birthstone eggs are an obvious nod to family and children.' She furrowed her brow trying to puzzle out the rest.

'The oak itself is significant,' Declan mused. 'Oaks stand for strength, and endurance. Also for fertility, so there's quite a few ingredients there.'

'The three types of wildflowers support the importance of variety being the spice of life. One must be careful not to take one's spouse for granted,' Cora offered, solving another item on the list.

'Pinecones often stand for enlightenment of thought and also for eternal life. Marriage is for ever, and a strong marriage is valued in the eyes of the Church, so this is a nod to the religious ingredient, I suppose,' Declan added.

In her enthusiasm over solving the puzzle of the list, Cora leaned close, her body brushing Declan's arm. 'That leaves the bird's feather, the lichen on the twig and the caterpillar.' She slid him a teasing glance. 'I wonder if we get extra points for decoding this.'

'The bird's feather could have two meanings. It could be an additional reminder that marriage is for ever, one cannot fly away at the first sign of trouble as birds often do, or it could be a reminder that marriages moult like birds. They change and are reborn with new plumage throughout the seasons.'

Cora wrinkled her nose. 'Moulting is not a very romantic prospect, but I do like the idea of new plumage in new seasons.' It hit rather close to home when she thought of the new dresses she'd acquired and the reasons for them. 'The lichen has me stumped, though.'

'You need to spend more time in the woods,' Declan laughed. 'It's about stability. Lichen grows on trees because the trees provide a stable source of life-sustaining ingredients. The tree is home, a place where the lichen is safe and can flourish. But the lichen gives to the tree as well. Lichen helps enrich soil. Their relationship is of mutual benefit, each giving to the other. I daresay the application to marriage is obvious from there.'

'I daresay it is.' Cora beamed, enjoying this exchange. This was yet one more side of Declan revealed to her. Most gentlemen she knew were outdoorsmen because they fished and hunted. They took without understanding nature. But Declan was an outdoorsman and a naturalist. 'You are a wonder.' She gave him the full attention of her gaze. 'How do you know so much?'

'My father took me out when I was a boy, taught me about our land, how it worked, how we needed to work with it if we were going to sustain it. Not just crops and harvests, but the wildlife that roam here, the trees and plants that grow here. Everything plays a role in keeping our estates healthy and thriving. He taught me it was my privilege to be the caretaker of our estates, and that great responsibility came with it.' He cleared his throat, his body shifting, and she was suddenly aware that her breasts had pressed against his arm as she'd leaned in to read the list.

'Excuse me, I'm a little…stiff…sitting on the ground.'

He clambered to his feet and turned away, making a show of stretching, but not before she'd caught sight of the hard length of him pushing insistently against his breeches.

Cora fought back a blush and searched for something neutral to say. She held up the wreath. 'I've finished it. What shall we seek out next? We'd better get busy or we'll finish last.' They didn't dare finish last. If they finished too far behind the others, people would wonder what they'd spent the day doing. That was hardly what she wanted. She had a reputation to protect. The last thing she needed was for anyone to think she'd trapped the Duke—only she didn't think of him like that. He might be the Duke to everyone else, but he was Declan to her.

He followed her to the mare and helped her mount, his hands firm at her waist. 'Let's go after the wildflowers next. I know a place where we can find all the varieties at once.' He swung up on his chestnut beside her and favoured her with a smile, apparently recovered now. 'We have the advantage today. These are my lands and I know every inch of them. My father would take me out in the summers. We'd go on horseback and explore acre by acre. Sometimes we'd even camp out overnight and stargaze.'

She liked those images. His boyhood didn't sound all that different from her own childhood growing up. It was too easy to imagine him trotting along on his pony, an ordinary boy beside his ordinary father, enjoying ordinary pleasures. But those were imaginings as dangerous as his kisses. Both made him accessible, as if this was a real courtship that could be carried to a very real end. When, in reality, this was just part of the fairy tale she'd catapulted herself into with her blue dress. Dresses changed lives, and for a short time it had changed hers, put her into the orbit of this extraordinary man.

They gathered wildflowers, Cora naming each variety as they went, sharing stories of her and her sisters picking wildflowers along the River Stour. 'We'd make necklaces and crowns and pretend we were princesses. My mother would come with us, and she'd be the queen. She could make the best circlets of flowers and we'd wear them on our heads. She would pack a picnic and we would sit on old quilts and we'd take turns braiding each other's hair while she told stories.' Cora gave a wistful sigh.

'Your mother sounds very different than mine.' Declan laughed. 'I can't imagine my mother ever making daisy chains and sitting on the ground.' They stopped beneath the shade of a tree at the edge of the wildflower meadow and sat.

Declan offered her his coat to sit on, but she waved the offer away. 'I'm not so delicate as all that.' She tucked her skirts around her. 'I'm quite comfortable with sitting on the grass.' It was pleasant and quiet beneath the tree, quiet enough to hear the bees buzzing in the meadow, quiet enough to tease her with drowsiness. Her head leaned against him and his arm found its way about her shoulders with a casual ease, as if they shared such comfort countless times before.

'Your mother may have been a stickler for formality, but I think your parents cared for one another,' she said softly, thinking about the list. 'I think she based that list on what made her marriage work. Perhaps that list is what she wants for you, her son.'

Dear lord, this woman knew how to grab his heart and hold on to it—with her words, her insights. 'Yes, they cared for each other very much.' He matched his tone to her softness. They were exchanging secrets now, even though there was no one to hear but the birds. 'They started out hardly knowing one another beyond a dance and a house party. But by the end they'd created a grand love, something deep and abiding between them.'

'Ah, our last mystery on the list solved.' Cora sighed against his shoulder. He liked the weight of her there. It felt right. 'The caterpillar. The idea that something can grow from nothing. That from something simple, something beautiful can form.'

'I fear that is a double-edged sword the way my mother wields it. She seems to think that I can grow a marriage with any girl here. That in time, everything will take care of itself if the girl is well born enough.' Declan leaned against the tree trunk, Cora snuggling against him.

'But as I recall, you are more fanciful than that,' Cora commented. 'You believe in wishing fountains.'

'And that love, real love, has power.' It felt right to confess such a thing, here in the spring afternoon with Cora in his arms, this woman he'd not known a week ago, but who had become so very important to him— whose body spoke to his, whose thoughts seemed to so clearly echo his own. She understood him.

'Not enough power, not to do all we expect of it,' she

said drowsily. 'We expect it to conquer all, but it can't, it simply isn't strong enough.'

'Why do you think that?' he asked, but there was no answer. 'Cora?' he called her name softly but she was sound asleep. Well, he'd let her and her contrary opinion be for now. There were worse ways to pass an afternoon than holding the woman you thought you might love. Even if it meant hurrying to finish the scavenger hunt.

They were down to their last item, the twig with lichen, when Cora tripped over something at the base of a tree. 'There's something down there.' She fell to her knees and rooted around in the pile of forest detritus. It was most unladylike and Declan loved it. How many other of the ladies here would be willing to dirty themselves in search of treasure? He knelt down beside her and they dug together, unearthing the rest of what had tripped her. 'It's one of the eggs! I'd not thought to find one,' Cora cried with glee, holding it up. It was a beautifully wrought casket made of pretty paste jewels that could endure being buried or stuck in a tree.

'Go on,' Declan urged, entranced by the smile on her face. 'You open it.'

She flicked the clasp and opened the top half of the egg. On a bed of deep blue velvet lay an opal pendant on a thin, elegant gold chain, decidedly not *faux*. 'The Duchess was not pranking us when she said the casks might be fake but there were real jewels hidden inside.' She held up the pendant, dangling it from her fingers. 'It's beautiful.' She moved the pendant this way and that, smiling as the light danced over the leaves. 'Did you know the opal is one of the twelve stones in Aaron's breastplate of judgement in Exodus?' It was her turn to dazzle him with information.

'No, I had no idea.' Declan laughed. 'I suppose knowing such things is one of the benefits of being the daughter of a biblical scholar. Shall I put it on you?' Declan reached for it but she shook her head and put it back in the casket.

'No, I'll save it for one of my evening gowns. Between the blouse and my riding jacket, I haven't got the neckline to do it justice.' She hesitated. 'Unless you'd like to keep it? Perhaps you should keep it.'

Declan took the egg-shaped casket from her. 'I'll carry it for you until we get back, but it's yours. I want you to have it.' He let his gaze reach for her, holding her dark eyes with his, letting her see the intent in them, the want that he'd kept leashed today. After yesterday's kisses, he'd not wanted to overwhelm her, had not wanted her to think he expected kisses now every time they were alone, although it had taken all of his willpower to refrain. There'd been that moment under the oak tree when her breasts had brushed against him, testing his willpower to its utmost extent. It had nearly broken. 'Every time you wear the necklace, I want you to think of our day together.'

She blushed, clearly touched by his words, but she didn't look away. 'I won't need a reminder to recall today. It was wonderful. Thank you for your time, your stories, the chance to get to know you, the real you.'

Yes, indeed she had. He couldn't recall the last time he'd shown so much of himself to another, and yet he'd not hesitated to share with her. He'd hungered to do it, in fact. He'd been filled with a desire not only to know but also to be known.

'It is I who should be thanking you.' He took her hand and raised it to his lips. 'I haven't had a day as enjoyable as this for ages. I am myself with you, Cora, you cannot know how much that means to me. Do not underestimate what you've given me today.' Everything they'd done and said was imprinted on his mind. Like her, he would be remembering these hours for a long time. When he was with her, he was transformed—and there were still three days to go. What other magic might she wield?

Chapter Thirteen

The Duchess wielded her fan like a weapon in the drawing room before supper that night, making it clear to Declan she wanted a word with him, without making it look that way to anyone else. But Declan was very good at reading his mother, and it didn't take much to guess what she wanted that word to be about.

'You did not win the scavenger hunt.' She spread the folds of her fan wide, letting them act as a subtle barrier between them and the guests milling with pre-prandial drinks in hand and discussing the day. In that way, his discussion with his mother was probably not much different than theirs.

'No, we had some difficulty with a few of the objects.' That difficulty had been a pleasant two hours talking and napping under a tree amid wildflowers. He'd have liked to have a Constable painting of *that*. If peace looked like anything, it would have been those hours in the meadow.

'Much difficulty, I'd say. You came in nearly last. Only Jack DeBose and Miss Brighton were later. But he's planning to offer for her, I hear.' It was said with all the smugness of a matchmaker celebrating victory, and all the shrewdness of a concerned mother making her point. Her son could not claim the same. He was not to be offering for the girl he'd kept out too late on the scavenger hunt.

'You've no news from Dorset?' He might as well beard the lioness in her den. The sooner this discussion was over, the better. It could not change his feelings. There would soon come a point where he and his mother would reach a fork in their road, and he would have to decide which path he'd follow—his heart or his head.

'Dorset is a long way from here,' she said sharply. 'Although it seems to get closer every day. You are always with *her* and, when you aren't, you're following her every move. People notice and I fear there will be repercussions.' She dropped her voice a notch lower. 'I don't want to see my son hurt. I may be a duchess, but I am a mother, too. I remember the last time a woman led you astray. It left scars. I don't want that for you again.'

Declan stiffened. 'That was eleven years ago. I was young and foolish. I didn't know better.'

'Nevertheless, it affected you.' His mother didn't need to mention those affects. 'You've not trusted anyone since, not been close to anyone.'

'All the more reason I am surprised you're not a champion of Miss Graylin. I feel a true connection there, we've discovered we have much in common. Our love of the outdoors and country living for instance. She's devoted to family, which appeals greatly.'

'A family you would no doubt become responsible for,' his mother pointed out. 'How many sisters did you say she had? Four? She'll expect you to launch them. They'll be underfoot until they're settled.' She let out an exasperated sigh. 'She came out of nowhere and suddenly she has things in common with you. Doesn't that ring warning bells? Does it remind you of someone else who got under your skin? You nearly married her, too, until your father and I got wind of her real intentions and put a stop to it just in time.'

Even now with the perspective of years and adulthood, that remained a dark, embarrassing chapter in his early adulthood. 'I am aware, Mother. I thought we'd agreed not to speak of it again,' he said tersely. Miss Esme Randolph had been a difficult episode, leaving behind a disappointed and disillusioned young man, one who'd not yet had the first-hand experience of being appreciated for his net worth as opposed to his sparkling personality.

'It doesn't feel that way with Miss Graylin,' he said solemnly. 'She is genuine. However, I will continue to give the matter careful thought and, because I appreciate your wisdom and concern, I will not make an offer until you've heard from Dorset.' It was the closest thing to an olive branch he could offer her while still naming his own terms. 'Now, please excuse me.' He turned on his heel and left the drawing room, wanting a moment alone to tamp down his anger, to summon the calm of the day, the images of peace, before going into supper, where he'd be expected to smile and feign interest in girls who had no idea who he was beyond his title.

Declan took refuge in the long gallery that ran the length of the house. In medieval times, the space had been used for winter exercise. Now, since the family used the estate primarily only in the summer as a quick escape from Town, the space was mainly taken up displaying portraits there was no longer room for in the townhouse or at the family seat.

He stopped in front of a painting he liked of his father. It had been done in his father's younger years as the Duke, and in the autumn, his father's favourite time of year. He sat down on the wide, square, velvet ottoman in front of the picture with a sigh. 'She's being stubborn, Father. She's determined I marry one of them.' It wasn't that he didn't know what to do about it. He did know. It would just be difficult.

If anyone had told Declan a week ago that he would *want* the house party to go on another week, or that he'd fall headlong for a woman he'd not met until now, he would have laughed. But it had happened. He'd fallen far enough that he was considering sharing the rest of his life with her. Mother was right—if he did, it would require compromises. A baronet's niece was theoretically acceptable, but not ideal in practice when there were a plethora of earls' daughters on offer. He would have to walk a careful line so as not to offend the *haute ton* outright. But that was for later. His thoughts were getting far ahead of him. He drew a deep breath, letting the dimness and the quiet soothe his busy mind.

'Declan.' There was a soft rustle of skirts. Declan turned to find Cora in the gallery, her bronze gown shimmering in the evening light filtering in through the long windows. 'Are you all right? I saw you leave and I worried it was because of me.' She paused. 'Am I intruding?'

'Not at all.' He rose as he spoke the words. He went

to her, his body knowing before his mind that she was exactly the person he wanted to be with, needed to be with in this moment. He cupped her face with his hands. 'I should have done this earlier today, but I didn't want to overwhelm you,' he murmured, before capturing her mouth with a kiss.

He felt her give the lightest of gasps, felt her arms go about his neck and draw him close with a whisper. 'You could never overwhelm me.'

He could surprise her, shock her, make her burn, awaken feelings in her that had been dormant until now, but not overwhelm her. Overwhelming assumed dominance, submission. There was nothing of that between them. If she was sure of anything here in the dark with him, it was that they were burning together. His hand was at her breast, his palm flat against the silk of her bodice running over the curve of her. Her breasts tightened in want at his touch, and she felt the answering hardness of his own response against her skirts. He tasted of pre-dinner brandy, of sweetness and warmth, and strength and hope…oh, dangerous hope… Did she dare let herself believe…?

'Declan,' she breathed his name in passion, wanting more touches, more kisses—not just his touches, but hers. It was a wicked thought, entirely new. She wanted to touch him, wanted to feel the hardness of him. She reached for him then, her hand pressed to the length of him. A wicked sigh escaped her, a trill of discovery shot through her, hot and victorious at the feel of him. This was what a man felt like, what *Declan* felt like. This was what he felt for her, what she did to him. She slid her hand down until she could cup him, resenting the fabric of his trousers. What must it be like to feel him, all of him, without barriers? What delicious wickedness that would be.

He gave a moan. 'Good heavens, Cora, your touch would tempt a saint, and I am no saint, not at the moment.'

'Neither I am.' She breathed the words, her mouth seeking his, claiming more kisses, hotter kisses, wanting and wanting until wanting obliterated all other thought. She did not want this to stop, and yet it must. It had to. They were here alone, in the dark, there'd be no explaining this if they were caught. He might have started this, but he would not thank her if they were noticed.

His eyes were sapphires, twin flames lit from within, his voice a low, seductive rasp. 'I want you, Cora, make no mistake, let there be no misunderstanding on that.'

Her arms were still about his neck, her fingers playing with his hair where it curled against his nape. 'And I want you, Declan Locke. Make no mistake—but they'll be missing us for supper.'

'Not yet. I want to show you something first.' He took her hand and led her to a portrait, the one he'd been studying when she'd found him.

'Your father?' It was an easy guess. Declan might have the Duchess's eyes, but he had his father's chin, his nose. There was an indefinable quality the artist had captured, and Declan had it, too, that sense of authority and responsibility that spoke of strength, that made a person feel safe. She stared a while longer at this man who'd made such an impression on his son with camping trips and botany lessons. 'You look like him.'

'Do you look like your mother?' Declan asked quietly.

'I have her hair and her eyes. People say I act like my mother, too, and I far prefer that compliment. She was the kindest person I ever knew. She found happiness everywhere, even when there wasn't much of it to go around.' Her throat tightened, the emotions of the moment getting the better of her. 'You have that same quality that your father has. It's not in any single physical characteristic, but it's there. The artist has shown it well.'

She felt Declan's eyes on her, considering. 'That's something only another artist would know. Do you paint, yourself?'

Cora shook her head. 'I used to, but not any more.' Not since there wasn't money for such hobbies. 'Since my mother passed, there's been too much to do.' But enough of that, it was leading them down a path she didn't want to travel with him, a part of her life she didn't want to show him for fear of disappointing him. It wasn't part of the fairy tale, but this moment was. Her past didn't belong here. 'We should go, Declan, or else your mother will send Alex to find you.'

'Is it terrible that I don't want to go back?' Declan slipped her arm through his and they began a slow return to the world beyond the gallery. 'I'm tired of it, Cora. Tired of being hounded.'

'It's just a few more days,' she consoled, 'and then you'll be back in London.' She didn't like thinking of that. For herself, the end of the party was the end of the fairy tale. She'd go back to the circles she belonged in.

Declan would be beyond her then. There would be no chance meetings, especially when he knew the rest of her story. For now it was enough to be the niece of a baronet. But he would learn soon enough she was also the daughter of an impoverished vicar. He would soon be glad their ties were cut. But not tonight. Tonight was for the fairy tale.

'It's not just a few days.' Declan shook his head. 'It's been non-stop since my father died and our "ducal need", as it were, became public. Even at my father's funeral, there were men who came to shake my hand and offer condolences and, before our conversations were done, they mentioned they had daughters. At my father's *funeral*, Cora. They hadn't a scrap of decency. They were too busy using my grief as an opportunity for them to grab the coattails of a dukedom for themselves.'

'I am so sorry, Declan. Grief is hard enough to navigate without worldly concerns creeping in.' She squeezed his arm in commiseration. How odd it was to think that they'd both been mourning the loss of a beloved parent at the same time and yet not known each other. They might inhabit different levels of Society, but they were united on this.

'It might not be on the level with the concerns of a dukedom, but it was that way for us when Mother died. Some people were truly kind and wanted to help, but others saw an opportunity. A few widows made advances towards my father, disguised as apple pies and canned goods. John Arnot made advances towards me, taking advantage of my father's vulnerability to press his own suit. It was indeed a difficult time. It was hard to know who one's friends were. It was like watching crows pick at carrion despite the stakes being much smaller than yours. I would prefer to not relive such a time.'

They finished their walk in silence and she wondered if it had been wrong to tell him. Perhaps he thought it was selfish of her to talk about herself or to put her own experience equal with his. It had not been her intent. At the hall he turned to her, covering her hand with his. 'Thank you for sharing that.' He smiled—a soft determination lit his eyes. 'I've not told anyone about that,' he added. 'But I *knew* you would understand.'

'It's why I told you,' she said solemnly. Because she'd known she would be understood. And in that moment, her heart echoed his words. To her they seemed the most powerful five words in the world. To understand another, and to be understood, was perhaps the greatest gift one could give, greater even than love, and she had three days left of it. She was determined to make them count.

Chapter Fourteen

They were both determined to make the remaining days of the party count, and Cora did not question the reasons for it. She knew her motives, if not his, although she did not want to dwell on them. To do so would be to take herself out of the moment, out of the fairy tale. For now, she wanted to take a page from Declan's own book and focus on what was right in front of her. It seemed he did, too.

He kept their days filled with activity. They rode early in the mornings along quiet bridle paths, strolled the maze and sat at its hidden core in the afternoons, engaged in yard games with the other guests. There were private moments, too—stolen kisses in alcoves, heated glances, hot touches, lingering interludes out of doors, where their privacy might be prolonged and an exploration of her awakened desires might be encouraged at a more leisurely pace, until passion outstripped patience. Soon, it might outstrip even caution. She was less desirous in these moments of holding back than she was of seeing that passion fulfilled. With Declan.

When they were with the others, Cora surreptitiously watched as other matches seemed to be made, Miss Brighton with Jack DeBose among them and, she hoped, her sister with the charming Mr Wade. The one thing she and Declan did not do was discuss the return to Town or what came next. Which was, she well knew, nothing. For them, nothing came next.

She would not be Miss Clara Brighton returning to Town triumphant with a match. When she got in the carriage and drove away from Riverside, that would be it. It had to be. It was the best way she could protect him, keep him from scandal for his choice. He could claim he'd been entirely innocent of any of the damning knowledge that was bound to come out.

Until then, there were just these moments, and Cora meant to savour every one of them. And yet, savouring couldn't stop the sands from slipping out of the hourglass. It was the day of the Fantasia Ball—the final event of the party. All that remained was the ball and then departure. And then a return to reality. It was time to face facts.

Cora took the afternoon to stroll the gardens. Alone. Declan had gone out with some of the men to climb a nearby hill of some renown. Most of the girls had gone to the village for last-minute ribbons and Cora had the place to herself…and her thoughts, which were crowd aplenty. How would she ever find her way to the surface of this wondrous idyll when it was time to leave? More than that, how could she leave *him*? It would be like leaving a part of herself behind. How would she settle for a lesser man?

She knew the answer. Because her family required it. She had to think of Kitty, Melly and even Veronica. Even if Elise married Mr Wade, three young sisters to launch would be a burden to the Wades. Cora needed to do her part. She'd not been brought to London to dally with a duke and have her heart broken. She'd been brought to make a good marriage that all could benefit from.

'I'd offer you a penny for your thoughts, but I think I know them already,' Elise interrupted softly, joining her on the garden path. She'd been so lost in her own thoughts she'd not heard her sister approach. Elise smiled apologetically. 'I saw you from the house and we've had so little time alone lately. I didn't mean to disturb. Shall I go?'

'It's fine, please.' Cora patted the bench beside her. 'Come and sit.' She instantly felt guilty. She'd been much too self-centred. 'Tell me all about Mr Wade. Do you like him, still?'

'Very much so, perhaps even more now that I've had time to know him.' Elise blushed, looking pretty and young in her new yellow afternoon gown. 'I have every expectation that he will call on Uncle George when we return to Town. He must settle some affairs with his father first, but my background should be no impediment. They're quiet people and he may marry for happiness.' Elise paused, worrying her lip, some of her happiness diminished.

'I do have a concern, though, that I thought to address with you. When Mr Wade talks with Uncle, all will be officially revealed. He will be apprised of our financial situation. He will know the dowry comes from Uncle and that our own father was not in a position to provide it. He already guesses it is Uncle who has provided the Season for us.' Cora knew what Elise was delicately hint-ing at. Everyone would know they were the daughters of a poor country vicar, girls with nothing but their looks to recommend them. Elise shrugged. 'Perhaps the Wades would keep silent on that account. There's no need for them to tell anyone, it's just that...'

'Someone else would know,' Cora finished for her. The more people who knew, the harder a secret was to keep.

'I am eager to wed Mr Wade, but I have told him that it may be best to wait until you are wed. I don't want to impede your chances, and it is tradition for the older sister to wed first.' Elise slid her a worried look and Cora clasped her sister's hand in gratitude, her heart squeezing at the thoughtful gesture.

'Do not wait on me, Elise. I am sure Aunt B can help me find a suitable gentleman who will be fine with my antecedents,' Cora smiled to ease her sister's concern, 'especially when my sister is married to a viscount's heir.' She gave Elise a happy hug. 'I'm so pleased for you. It's all we hoped for. You will have love and a good station.' She was happy for Elise, happy enough to ignore the little pain in her heart.

'But what of the Duke?' Elise asked. 'He likes you, Cora. I see the two of you together. He's focused on you to the exclusion of the other girls. Lady Mary Kimber has all but given up after the archery contest, and Clara Brighton has made another match.'

'Declan will not propose,' Cora told her softly but firmly. Saying the words out loud made them real— made her, for a moment, move out of the fairy tale. 'He hasn't Mr Wade's luxury of marrying only for happi-

ness. Even if he disagrees, I cannot allow him to propose and then be laughed at for being swept away by a
vicar's penniless daughter.'

Elise frowned. 'Whyever not if he loves you, Cora,
and you love him?'

'Because, my dear, love is not enough. You are not
marrying Mr Wade on love alone. He has more than affection to offer you.' Elise hadn't needed to choose between the two. She'd been offered both. 'I would bring
scandal to his family. I would diminish him in the eyes
of Society.'

'You could diminish no one, Cora,' Elise insisted.

'He would come to despise me for all I would cost
him. You saw how hardship destroyed Mama and Papa.
I do not want that. I do not want to see his affections for
me die a little more each day.'

Elise grimaced. 'Some men are stronger than Papa.'

'The Duke needs his strength for other responsibilities,' Cora said staunchly. 'I will leave Riverside and
return to my rightful circles, because that is how I can
best protect him when his mother's enquiries turn up
just how straitened our circumstances are.'

'Leaving—disappearing—will hurt him,' Elise argued.

'Leaving will protect him,' Cora said shortly. 'I've
thought it all out, Elise. This is the best way, the only way.'

'What about telling him the truth before the reports
get here? Let him decide.'

Cora shook her head. 'No, if I tell him, he becomes
culpable for knowingly courting someone entirely un-
suitable for his station. This way, he can claim igno-

rance, that he was duped.' There was another reason, too, a more selfish reason. 'And, Elise, I suppose I am afraid to tell him. What if he does feel duped and betrayed? I don't want to face his anger.' She gripped her sister's hand. 'I know it's selfish of me, but I came here because I wanted just one more day, one more moment with him, and I've had more than that. I just don't want the fairy tale to end yet, not before it has to.'

'I am sorry, Cora. I thought...well, I thought there was a chance with the Duke,' Elise said softly.

Cora wrapped her arm about her sister. 'Not for girls like us.' But there was still tonight. She would dance one last time in Declan's arms and let herself be transformed by that blue dress—so it could finish what it started.

By evening, Riverside had been transformed into a Fantasia spectacle of lanterns and lights, of flora and fauna artfully designed and placed. A veritable fairy land awaited Cora when she and Elise came downstairs for the ball. The veranda gardens had been altered into a beautiful fantasy where one might spend a magical evening. The Fantasia Ball, as the Duchess was calling it, was held out of doors, Her Grace of Harlow taking advantage of the fine weather and the opportunity to show the gardens to advantage.

The speed at which the transformation had been accomplished was impressive. A dancing area, large enough to accommodate the twenty-five girls and their partners at any given time, had been constructed beneath rows of colourfully strung paper lanterns. Carefully shaped topiary animals had been positioned throughout the gardens, each in their own inviting alcoves, complete with benches and pots of flowers to make inviting bowers where a couple might linger in plain view of chaperones. 'There's even a unicorn,' Elise whispered excitedly as they moved out on to the veranda with the other guests. 'And look, roving artists to draw pictures.'

'I can scarcely take it all in,' Cora breathed, her eyes going everywhere at once. 'I want to remember every detail so we can tell Melly and Kitty. It's a fairy land come to life.' A place where dreams might come true for a night. Perhaps it was a place where young hearts might be inspired to make promises. If so, the Duchess had planned well for the final night of her party.

'And you are perfectly dressed for all of it,' Elise whispered encouragingly.

Cora fingered the silk of her skirt. 'I *feel* perfect.' She smiled at Elise. 'Look, there's your Mr Wade.' She nodded in Mr Wade's direction. The men had all worn dark evening attire for the occasion—black pantaloons fitted tight at the ankles, and dark coats nipped at the waist, beneath which peeped waistcoats in varying festive colours. 'Mr Wade looks handsome tonight. I see his waistcoat is a pale rose, perhaps to match your gown?' Cora hazarded with a teasing nudge.

'Do you think the Duke will wear blue?' Elise didn't bother to deny the rationale behind Mr Wade's waistcoat choice.

Cora shook her head. 'It would be too much of a declaration. People would read into it. I don't think he can dare.' From the dais set up at one end of the dance floor, the orchestra began to serenade the evening with quiet music before the dancing began, the soft music adding to the magic of the night.

Elise's eyes took on a twinkle, her gaze darting just beyond Cora's shoulder. 'Perhaps he would dare. I think our Duke is a brave man who knows what he wants, Cora.'

'Miss Graylin, Miss Elise, you both look lovely tonight.'

Cora turned at the sound of Declan's voice. 'Lady Graylin, you're as beautiful as always,' he complimented their aunt as he offered them a short bow. But his eyes were for Cora. 'I was hoping you might wear the blue gown.' Beneath his dark evening coat, a pale blue silk waistcoat peeped. Not an exact match of the vibrant cerulean, but certainly a soft complement to it.

'You flatter me,' she replied, her pulse racing, caught up in the sight of him and the magic of the evening, a pulse that refused to think of tomorrow. Only now.

'My mother insists on opening with a waltz to set a tone of romance for the evening. I do think she's hoping for a few more matches to be made.' He held his hand out to Cora, gloved hands meeting, his fingers curling gently but possessively over hers. His mouth was close to her ear as he led her out to the dance floor. 'It's meant to be a night of romance beneath the stars, and I intend to make full use of it.'

'As do I,' Cora whispered with a secret smile, and they laughed together as they took up their place on the dance floor, his hand at her back, her hand at his shoulder, their gazes locked and lingering. She could not help but think how different it was to waltz with him now. 'Not long ago we were strangers dancing together,' she said as the music began.

'Even then, you did not seem a stranger to me.' He smiled the smile that was just for her, a smile she'd not seen him give to another. 'You are certainly more to me now, much more.' He swung them through a quick turn and her skirt belled out. Oh, how she loved dancing with him, loved looking up into his eyes, feeling the strength of his arms. She would miss this.

'What is it, Cora? You seemed sad for a moment.' He carefully manoeuvred them around an overexuberant couple.

'It's only that the night is so beautiful. I hate to think of it being over. Have you ever seen a fairground after the fair?' She laughed at her question. 'Of course not. I have, once. It was one of the saddest things I've ever seen. All the life was sucked from the place. There was nothing but scraps and trampled grass left behind, where the night before it had been full of laughter and fun and lights and dreams. Magic, really.'

He leaned close and she made no secret of breathing him in. She was down to last times. She wanted to memorise the scent of him. 'Then don't think on it, Cora,' he whispered. 'Think of now, think of what is in front of you, of who is in front you.' He picked up the speed of their waltz, perhaps on purpose to ensure they didn't talk, and Cora allowed it. There was so much they needed to talk about, and she was loath to discuss it all. If only tonight could last for ever. He swept her through another turn that left her breathless with the waltzing and the wanting. Of him. Of things impossible. Of things unspoken. Things she dared not hope for.

'I know what you need.' Declan gave a boyish smile

when the dance concluded. 'You need a trip to the wishing fountain.' He gripped her hand and discreetly led her away to the entrance of the maze. He snatched the lantern from its hook and tugged her inside, stealing a kiss as they disappeared from view. 'I've wanted to do that all night,' he whispered. 'From the moment you came down the stairs and stole my breath all over again, just like you did that first night.'

Oh, this was dangerous, to be alone with him and his words in the privacy of the maze. Her blood heated at his kiss, at his touch. The night was not long enough for all the kisses she wanted. They would have to last her a lifetime. They made the centre of the maze and Declan set the lantern down beside the fountain. From here, the strains of the orchestra were still audible. 'Dance with me here, Cora. Let me hold you as I would like to hold you.' He held out his hand, his voice rasping with naked want.

'Yes,' she could barely manage the word, her body going to him, drawn like a magnet. But this was no ordinary waltz. Bodies meshed, breasts pressed to chest, hips moved against hips, mouths joined, hands caressed, until there was no space between them, no place where their bodies did not meet, did not meld. It seemed even their very breath was shared. Want burned, desire kindled, and it was still not enough, not enough of him, not enough of them, of what he made her feel.

She gave a moan of frustration and they swayed in their intimate dance. 'This is everything and it's not enough. There must be more, I want more.' She moved against him at his core, her own core damp and feverish, instinctively knowing he held the key to its cure, its release.

'Cora.' Her name seemed ripped from his throat, a benediction and a plea, both release and torture. There was a wildness in his eyes when she looked at him, perhaps that same wildness was in her own—goodness knew she felt it.

'Please, Declan, help me.' She moved to the stone bench, drawing him with her. 'I want, I want so much. Please... I am begging you.'

She was begging but he was the one on his knees. Declan knelt before her, his hands at the hems of those exquisite blue skirts, pushing them up, revealing the slim length of silk-stocking-encased legs, while desire rocketed through him. He could not fight his want and hers. He was not saint enough to resist what they both wanted. He placed a kiss behind the back of each knee, his mouth and hands working their way upwards, while she sighed above him.

He reached the junction of her thighs, breathed in the musky scent of her want, his pulse ratcheting with his own desire. He whispered her name against her nether curls, her own hands finding their way to his hair and sinking deep, gripping tight as his mouth teased at her seam, his tongue licking its way to her core and its secrets.

He heard her breath catch as he found her hidden nub, his own breath hitching as he teased and tasted. Her thighs clenched, wanting to keep him there. Something within him soared at the notion that she was as lost as he. Her breathing became ragged and he felt her body gather, seeking, reaching for the release he'd pushed it towards, and then it was there, rolling over her, claiming her. He felt her body shudder, heard her sigh with disbelief, with wonder and relief. Her grip slackened, her thighs relaxed.

'Oh, my,' she whispered in awe.

Declan sat back on his haunches and studied her. Oh, my, indeed. His Cinderella looked beautifully ravished and quite content with her lot. He swallowed hard. All he wanted to do was stare at her, to stare at his future. How was he going to get through the rest of the evening? It seemed pointless now that he'd found what he wanted.

Chapter Fifteen

The rest of the evening seemed a pointless blur to Cora. She was never quite sure how she'd got through it—dancing with Lord Fenton, smiling for her sister, laughing at Mr Wade's jokes. Her heart had not been in any of it, it had been with Declan, watching him carry out his duties—dancing with Lady Mary Kimber and Ellen DeBose, who'd had the cattiness enough to toss her a *Look at me dancing with the Duke* smile as she sailed past with Declan.

These were the women he'd move on to after she left him, the choices he'd have. Her heart could not bear it. Even as her body basked in the euphoria of the maze, her mind tussled with reality. Why did she expect it to be different? She'd always known that with great joy came great cost.

Yet, when she lay in bed beside a sleeping Elise, the remaining hours of the night slipping away as the clock chimed one—dancing had ended promptly at midnight out of deference for the departures tomorrow—Cora's thoughts went only to the joy, the pleasure. The feeling of Declan's hands on her, his mouth on her, still echoed. But echoes simply weren't enough for her, and perhaps even for him. She'd seen the look in his eyes in the maze, the fire that had burned there for her. That fire had burned all night—even when he'd done his duty and danced with others, his eyes had sought hers.

She reached for her robe at the end of the bed, emotion riding her hard, obliterating her usual sense of control. But tonight there was no time for rational thought, or perhaps she simply didn't want to embrace it. Perhaps she was tired of being practical. There were just hours before the carriages would pull into the drive and take them all home. They were down to last things, and there was still so much she needed. One last moment, one last conversation, one last touch, one last kiss. That one thought drove her to reckless action, had her flying down the hall barefoot, her plan unclear. What would she say? What would she do when she reached him?

At his door, she gave a soft rap and it opened to reveal Declan in dishabille, wearing only his trousers and shirt. 'You came,' he breathed the words like a prayer, shutting the door behind her and smothering her with kisses. 'I couldn't sleep, I was thinking of you and then you were here.'

'Yes, I'm here.' The heat between them was building, something hot and heady kindling with each kiss. 'I couldn't sleep either, not when all of this will be over tomorrow. It seemed like wasted time to be without you.'

'Heaven forbid we waste time.' He laughed and then sobered, stepping back from her, a pained expression crossing his face. 'I am glad you're here. I *want* you here, but I should warn you, I don't think I can play the gentleman. I want you too badly. I had hoped our interlude in the maze might have assuaged my need, but it has only heightened it. My heart yearns for you, Cora, my body craves you. That will not change if you decide to return to your room. But if you choose to stay...'

Her breath caught. If she chose to stay, they would make love in the big four poster beyond his shoulder. Perhaps a week ago, she would have walked away, bound by the teachings of gentle Society. But she was different now. She was a woman newly awakened to her own passions, of what real communion with a man could be. A man who matched her in heart, soul and mind as well as body, a man who understood the tension between duty and desire as she did, the tug between wants and reality, and ultimately who understood that responsibility required sacrifice.

It was why moments were precious to them both. Dreams that could not be lived elsewhere could be lived inside of moments. She would have her moment. She held his gaze as she undid the ribbon of her nightgown. 'I understand. I didn't come here, Declan, simply to go back to my room.' This was the point of no return. She pulled her nightgown over her head, tossed it away and stepped into the firelight.

'Good God, you're even more beautiful out of your clothes.' Declan swallowed hard, his gaze sweeping her with a rapt appreciation that made her blood heat. No one had ever looked at her thus—it roused all nature of feminine feeling in her. But Declan was not to be outdone. He undid his shirt with great solemnity, revealing the smooth, muscled expanse of his chest, the sculpted sinews of his arms.

'So are you,' she managed, her own throat going dry. Was this how he felt when he looked at her? She felt as if she'd been gifted a god straight from Olympus.

He smiled as if the compliment pleased him. 'But I'm not done yet, perhaps you might want to reserve judgement.' His hands dropped slowly, intentionally, to the waistband of his trousers, working the fastenings with deliberateness, as if he meant to prepare her. He pushed his trousers down over lean hips and stepped out of them, giving her eyes carte blanche of his body. It was an embarrassment of riches. She wasn't sure where to look first, so glorious was the sight of him—the long, muscled legs of a horseman, the lean waist of an athlete, the hard, ruddy core of a man in the full throes of desire.

'I want to touch you,' she whispered, her body taking an involuntary step towards him, unable to help itself.

'And I want to touch you. Come lie down with me.' He took her hand and led her across the room to the big bed. It wasn't until he'd stretched out beside her that she noticed.

'Declan, you're shaking. Are you cold?' Instinctively, she reached to pull up the coverlet.

He laughed. 'Don't you dare. I want to look at you, Cora. If I am shaking, it's because you do this to me.' He took her hand and kissed it. 'I've waited my whole life to find you, and now I can't believe that I have. *That* is how much I want you.'

'Then I shall warm you another way.' She kissed him, mouth, then throat—she traced his chest with her fingertip, running her thumb over the flat of his nipple, rewarded by a groan of appreciation. This was the intimacy her body had craved, to be together with him, skin to skin in the privacy of the darkness where it was just the two of them. No guests, no agendas, no disapproving stares.

He was kissing her now, his hands following his mouth, from her mouth to her neck to her breasts, his actions copying hers, and her body trembled with the knowledge of his touch, her skin hot with the flush of desire. His mouth sucked at her breast and a little moan escaped her. The heat in her was rising as it had in the maze. The sea was coming for her again, ready to sweep her away. She both revelled and rebelled in it, wanting to regain control as much as she wanted to let go of it and allow passion to have its glorious way. She reached her hand between them. If she could touch him, perhaps she could regain control. Or, if not that, perhaps he could give some up. Her hand closed over his phallus, its heat and hardness like a living being in her grip.

'Minx,' he growled at her ear, his eyes going the shade of indigo flame as she gave an experimental stroke of his length. This was so much better than holding him through his trousers. He rolled onto his back, giving her full access. 'I don't know what I like best.' He let out a long breath as if he were trying to keep himself in check. '*Feeling* the pleasure you're bringing me, or *watching* you deliver it. You, Cora Graylin, do not disappoint— beautiful, intelligent, passionate.' He sat up to steal a kiss, his abdominal muscles flexing from the motion. The look in his eyes nearly undid her. How would she ever let him go? Every minute, every moment, made it more difficult to contemplate.

His hand covered hers at the root of his phallus. 'We'd

best stop this. I want to last,' he said meaningfully. 'Much more of this exquisite play and you'll have me spending too early. It's my turn now.' Then, in a fluid movement, he rolled her beneath him. 'Our turn. Together.'

He came up over her, his hands bracketing her, his arms taut with muscle, taking his weight from her, his blue eyes intent with a depth of desire that surpassed any she'd yet seen. She felt cherished in that moment, revered—even honoured by this man. The atmosphere between them changed, and she was acutely aware of the heavy weight of his manhood against her thigh. 'I've never wanted anything as badly as I want you right now.'

'Yes.' Her own reply was hoarse with longing. Her body knew one truth—it required him as surely as it required water, food, air. He was essential. In answer, her body opened to him, welcomed him. Arms entwined about him, inviting him close.

'Cora, there may be some discomfort,' he whispered the warning but she was beyond caring. 'I will try hard to prevent it.' He was using his hand on himself, his fingers spreading a bead of moisture from the head of his phallus over his length, then doing the same for her, his fingers conducting an intimate massage at the entrance of her core that made her catch her breath and her pulse race in anticipation. Her nostrils caught the musky scent of sex, his and hers mingled together.

'I trust you, Declan. It will be all right,' she assured him. 'I want this, I want you.'

Declan had never wanted like this, never been so overwhelmed with desire that it was nearly impossible to keep his own passion on a leash. As he looked into her eyes, felt her legs wrapping about his hips, he felt pushed to the brink of his control. He could not let it slip, not now when she needed his control the most. He refused to hurt her, refused to rush this for his own personal pleasure. He would make it good for both of them. She would have no regrets about having come to him.

Declan gritted his teeth, his breath more shudder than exhalation, and gently pushed himself forward, testing the pliability of her entrance. He sank into her warmth, slow inch by slow inch, his body trembling from the exertion of holding himself at bay. He stopped at intervals, letting her body accustom itself to his presence, letting his own body revel in the snug welcome of her. His body knew what his head tried to deny. He fit here. He fit with her. With her, there was a sense of homecoming, of having arrived at a long sought-after destination.

He gave a sigh of completion when he was fully sheathed in her, his destination deep and reached. 'Cora, you are heaven.' He gave a groan of relief, and looked down into her emerald eyes, seeing his own contentment reflected there. Then he began to move within her, his control tested once more as her hips raised up to join his, instinctively matching his pace, finding his rhythm. All thoughts of being her tutor on this first foray into passion fled in the wake of her response. They were partners in this.

She was exquisite, caught up in passion. Her long neck arched, her dark hair spilling about her, her hips pressed into his. Her legs gripped him, held him close, even deigned to guide his movements, suggesting he get deeper still. He'd not meant for this first time to be rough, but they were beyond sensibility now, both of them urging the other on, mouths ravaging, a bite here, a nip there, his wildness mirrored in her own. His breathing was reduced to ragged pants, hers to begging moans, her dark eyes pleading with him for release.

Release was not far off. She need not plead, need not seek much longer, although her body had enjoyed the seeking. His own body was gathering for the final surge, he felt the tension build deep within him, crawling through him, growing as it came like a wave at sea, cresting as it neared shore. Her eyes were locked on him as he gave a final thrust, determined she achieve the pinnacle of their pleasure before he gave into his own. He saw the moment passion claimed her, saw her eyes go wide with surprise, felt her breath catch with amazement, her body shudder with awe, and then he left her with a guttural cry, letting his own pleasure bury itself in the sheets.

Oh, God, oh, God, oh, God, had anything ever felt as good as these moments? As complete as these moments?

His body heaved with the exertion of leaving her, the power of his release shaking him to his core. His arms felt weak from the effort of keeping his weight from her, and his breathing was laboured as if he'd run miles. He ought to get up and find a cloth for her, but all he wanted to do was draw her close in his arms, hoping that he could hold onto her and the moment for as long as possible.

'Cora, you have undone me,' he whispered into the soft rose scent of her hair.

'That makes two of us, Declan.' She sighed against him, her body fitted to his side, her head nestled in the nook of his shoulder, as if that part of him had been made solely for that purpose. His arm tightened around her. If for ever had a *feeling* he was certain it would feel like this—like *her*.

Chapter Sixteen

This was what goodbye felt like—exquisite happiness wrapped in layers of pain, an ache that could not be numbed with the myriad chores that awaited one upon homecoming. Trunks to unpack, clothes to press, correspondence to be sorted, replies to write.

Cora had pressed her aunt to be one of the first to leave Riverside, even before a full breakfast was laid for the departing guests. She wanted to be gone before Declan woke, before she had to face him again. It wouldn't stop the hurt, but it might ease it for them both. Her aunt had taken one look at her face and agreed. Perhaps Aunt B guessed all of the reason, or at least enough it.

Cora had been silent the whole way home and her aunt and Elise allowed it. Despite the gorgeous travelling weather, her mind was back where she'd left Declan, asleep in bed, the covers riding at his waist, his bare chest on display. She would carry that image of him with her always, along with countless others.

If she thought being home at the townhouse off Curzon would offer relief, or alleviate the pain of heartbreak, she was wrong. Heartbreak knew no borders and did not stop for walls. Even in her chambers, she could not lock it out. She threw herself into unpacking, hoping to find that elusive refuge in work, only to discover she was unpacking more than gowns. Every gown held a memory, and it seemed those memories were unavoidable, imprinted on everything she touched. The ghost of Declan Locke had followed her home.

When she hung up the bronze gown, she thought of the conversation by the Constable painting that first night. When she put the small box containing the golden arrow on her vanity she thought of the archery competition and what had happened afterwards—that had been the first day he'd kissed her. When she put the opal pendant in her jewel case, she thought of the scavenger hunt, of listening to the stories he told about him and his father camping out on the land.

Perhaps that was why she put the blue ball gown away last. No longer was her first thought about their waltzes, but how this was the dress he'd slid his hands beneath on their last night in the maze, giving her a first taste of pleasure. That opened up a floodgate of other memories that had more to do with not wearing clothes, memories of conversations that left their minds as naked as their bodies.

Tears threatened and she wiped them away. There was no reason to cry. She'd made the only choice she could, because there'd been *no* choice. How had Cinderella done it? She fled the Prince with no expectation of seeing him again, despite her heart being engaged. She, too, had known there was no future beyond the moment. But still, how had she reconciled herself? The fairy tale wasn't instructive in that regard.

But reconcile herself she must. While they'd been at Riverside, May had become June and the Season was in full swing, a reminder to Cora that the clock was indeed ticking. She had one less week to find a husband. It was time to set the Duke behind her and focus on the task at hand. She would start by packing away the mystery gowns. She'd wear her own dresses, live in her own skin, starting tonight. For her, the fairy tale was gone.

Cora was gone. From his bed, from his life. It had been a difficult way to start the morning. Declan was still reeling from the discovery as he waved off the last carriage holding Lady Mary Kimber and her parents. The day had not gotten off to the start he'd wanted.

He'd awakened to find the bed empty and cold. He must have slept the sleep of the dead to not hear her slip out. And she'd slipped out early from the feel of the sheets. He'd not panicked initially. He could understand her desire to be back in the chamber she shared with her sister, before her sister awoke and worried, or before her aunt discovered her absence. Still, he would have liked to have walked her back. They'd spent the night making love, which meant there was much they needed to discuss regarding their future.

He needed to speak with her uncle and then her father. The sooner the better. She'd entrusted him with her virtue and he'd taken it. To his mind, it was an implicit contract of marriage and nothing could please him more. He'd gone downstairs, dressed for the day, thinking he might speak with her aunt about his intent to call on Sir Graylin as soon as possible.

But Cora and her aunt hadn't been at breakfast. They'd already gone, Mr Wade informed him over a plate of eggs and kippers—left before a full breakfast was even set. Mr Wade thought that was a grave sin, but he'd seen them off despite their hurry.

That had not sounded like a leave-taking then, Declan thought, but more like a getaway. It had certainly put a different cast on things. It hadn't made sense at the time and still hadn't a few hours later. How could they discuss the future if she wasn't here? His cup had stopped abruptly halfway to his mouth, coffee sloshing, as the first threads of dread had come to him.

Did she not want a future? Had Cora run from him?

The thoughts had made no sense, but were no less insidious for their ridiculousness.

His initial response had been to argue. How could that be true after all they'd shared—their hearts, their minds, their bodies? None of which had been shared lightly. The coffee threatened to curdle in his stomach, proof that something wasn't right.

He'd forced his agitated mind to cool and think. He could do nothing here. Cora would already be back in London. He would go to her uncle's home and speak with her. They would sort this misunderstanding out. Having a plan had made him feel marginally better. He would go to the stables, saddle Samson and ride out immediately.

That plan had been instantly foiled, adding to his growing consternation. His mother had required his assistance in seeing the guests off. So, here he was, smiling politely as he handed young ladies into carriages, fuming inwardly and wondering when would he get to

London. His rational mind groped for perspective. This was just a small setback. Cora was in London. He knew where to find her. He was only delayed a few hours. This was just another example of how personal desire must give way to ducal duty.

He turned to his mother as Lady Mary Kimber's carriage trundled down the drive out of sight. 'Our guests have gone and now I will take my leave. I have a desire to ride back to London, given the good weather. I thought I would set out immediately before the day turned too warm.'

'I've had an early luncheon set out for us on the back veranda,' his mother replied smoothly, undaunted by his attempt to depart. 'Come eat first. There are some people who've just arrived and I'd prefer we speak to them together.' She looped her arm through his, giving him no space for recourse, and strolled through the house.

Damn it. How had the morning deteriorated so quickly? He'd awakened full of joy, thinking of a future with Cora, only to find her gone without explanation, any attempt to reach her delayed by obligations. Those feelings of joy were further tempered at the sight of the two guests waiting on the veranda.

He shot his mother a stern glance of disapproval. 'Guests, Mother? I think the term is a bit liberally used. Since when you have taken luncheon with your solicitors?' He nodded towards them. 'Barnes, Stockton, good day. I trust the weather in Dorset was comfortable,' he said wryly. These were the men his mother had sent to look into Cora's family. 'The roads must have been dry, you've made excellent time.'

Barnes cleared his throat. 'Of course, Your Grace. The matter was urgent. We made all haste possible.' Yes, urgent indeed. His mother was eager to stop her son from making a fool out of himself.

Declan shot his mother a hard stare. He understood the necessity of vetting, but that didn't mean he approved of the methods. These men had gone to spy, to ferret out information by asking around and learning it second-hand. It felt dishonest. He far preferred learning about someone on their own merits. It was what he'd thought he and Cora had spent the week doing—learning one another. He waved an impatient hand. 'Well, get on with it. What did you learn?' He doubted there was anything in that folder he didn't already know. To think there was would be to doubt Cora.

Barnes pushed a folder forward and summarised the contents. 'It's all written down here. Miss Cora Graylin lives near Wimborne Minster. She is the eldest daughter of Vicar Graylin who has served the parish since acquiring the living in 1802.' This was both new and not new. The Bible scholar father was a vicar. There was no lie per se. What was a man to do with that? If Cora had omitted that detail in order to hide the fact, that was problematic. But if she'd thought the fact was of no consequence, then it was an honest omission. She'd made no secret that her father was a biblical scholar. Perhaps she assumed his occupation was obvious.

Barnes continued. 'The vicar lost his wife two years ago and, according to neighbours, it sent him into a deep depression. Miss Graylin runs things at the house now, for herself and her four sisters.'

'We know this.' Declan let out an impatient sigh. Cora had told him that. 'I even know the names of her sisters,' he said, partly to make a mockery of the report, and also to demonstrate how little there was of it.

'She's a *vicar's* daughter,' his mother snapped. 'A *country* vicar's daughter. That's different than being the daughter of a celebrated biblical scholar. Her father is gentry at best, just as I thought. No wonder no one has heard of her.'

'She's not a liar,' Declan chastised. His mother could not accuse her of that.

'She's a social climber, that's what she is,' his mother snapped. 'What better way to elevate herself than to make a titled marriage. You are beyond her wildest expectations.' Then why flee when such success was all but assured? Declan's mind chased the arguments around with no answers.

Stockton spoke up. 'While Barnes was investigating the family, I investigated the finances. There wasn't much to see, positively speaking. Their outlook is bleak. The family has very little money. No dowry for any of the girls.'

'Sir Graylin must be providing for the girls, then,' his mother commented shrewdly. 'Lady Graylin said the girls each had a modest four figure sum.'

Stockton nodded. 'If they do, their uncle is indeed providing it. The father has nothing to his name. But the uncle can afford it, although bringing out all five girls would tax him.' That, too, seemed plausible, based on what Cora had shared about having only the one Season and her need to marry swiftly. Declan started to relax. So far, so good. There was little for his mother to dispute other than Cora's antecedents. His mother had wanted a grand scandal hidden in Cora's closets, but there was nothing.

'I don't care about her money,' Declan said when Stockton finished.

Stockton gave him a steely stare. 'You may not care about funds, but you should care about the family debt. He has no land of his, the vicarage belongs to the living not to him, although that, too, is need of repair. The roof leaks, windows need replacing and there's no savings to speak of to do the work. There are also no servants. There's no money for them beyond a woman of all work who cooks and cleans, so it's up to him and the girls to keep everything else going.'

Up to Cora. Declan rephrased the sentence in his mind. He was in new territory now and it was his fault. What the men described was indeed a new and different image of Cora's life in Dorset than the one he'd created, full of summer picnics on the river, fishing for trout for the luxury of sport instead of fishing to eat.

We had plenty of suppers from that river.

Declan drummed his fingers on the tabletop, his lunch untouched. How had the family afforded her ball gowns? And why? Such expensive gowns could not come from a family living in genteel poverty. He did not like to imagine what had been sold or sacrificed. The landowner in him didn't like the idea of taking on debt in order to pay for them, instead of seeing to the roof. He'd not been impressed with her father when she'd spoken of him. Perhaps he was as frivolous as he was depressed. Perhaps the uncle was frivolous as well, only better able to afford some luxuries on occasion. Again, something niggled at him. Again came the feeling that something wasn't right. The puzzle pieces didn't fit smoothly.

'Gentlemen, thank you, you may go,' his mother dismissed them when Declan remained silent, too busy mulling it all over to be concerned with Stockton and Barnes. She waited until they were gone before delivering her verdict. 'Well, that's done with, and just in time,' she said briskly, tackling her own plate of cheese and cold meats. 'No one will blame you, although the papers may take a bit fun at your expense. The facts are clear. She's obfuscated the realities of her life, leading you to think circumstances were different than they were.'

'That's not true. She's lied about nothing.'

'Omissions are lies of a sort, Declan.' His mother set down her fork. 'She is a poor gentleman's daughter and a coattail relative of a baronet, hunting a title and fortune with her looks.'

'You don't know that she's a fortune hunter.' The claim seemed too harsh. Declan knew better. 'She does not hunger for the expensive luxuries of Town. She loves the simplicity of the countryside, of being close to her family, of riding horses and fishing in rivers.'

Perhaps she was not hunting a title, but that does not preclude hunting a fortune, his conscience nudged. *There are signs if you look close enough. She told you love wasn't enough. What else is there but money?*

'Because *you* love those things, Declan. Are you that naïve? Perhaps you are. Men don't see what's beyond their noses. Have you considered those dresses? What is a financially challenged vicar's daughter doing with them if not casting about for a wealthy man? Did you notice the sister had nothing their equal? The family invested, sent the eldest fishing for a prize larger than the sort she was going to find in the Baronet's circle. One does not need cerulean silk to catch a steady barrister,' she said shrewdly. 'Women understand these things. Miss Graylin's gowns were well above her station, because she wanted a man who was well above her station. But you—you only saw how lovely she was.'

His mother gave a brief smile. 'Well, as I said, we've caught it just in time. We know her for what she is, and you can avoid any public entanglements back in Town. We've received a note from the Duke of Colby, inviting us to the private reception he's holding for Turner when we return. It will be the perfect outing for spending time with Lady Elizabeth at last, and showing the gossips that you've moved on, that they've misunderstood the situation with the Graylin chit.'

'It will take more than a little news about her finances to overcome my feelings for Cora, Mother,' Declan answered with terse authority. 'We understand each other. She looks at me and sees a person, a man—not a duke.'

His mother scoffed. 'You have always had a fanciful side. What she sees are pound notes, a life of security for her and all of her sisters. She doesn't care about the scandal she'll bring to you. The Society pages will eat it up if you pursue her. This will all come out, and the gossips will tear her to shreds. She will be a money-grabber and you will be a fool. Whatever happiness you think you've found with her cannot survive in such a climate, Wash your hands of her and move on.'

She paused, a look of horror washing over her face. 'You can do that can't you? You haven't slept with her? Does she worry she might be with child?' She slapped down her linen napkin as if slapping a gauntlet. 'It's the oldest trick in the book, and you've fallen for it. Give a man good sex and he'll follow you anywhere, even right down the street into scandal and up the road to the altar.'

'Mother, I must insist you cease,' Declan bristled.

'No, *I* must insist, and if your father was here he would insist as well. You know your duty. It can come as no surprise to you.'

'I know my duty and I have done it day in and day out since Father died. I dedicated myself to learning that duty in my youth, never once have I contested my obligations or resented them. Now, I want one thing of my own. I want to choose my bride. I owe myself a duty as well.' Declan set aside his napkin and rose. 'I'm off to London to get answers.'

'You have answers, you just don't like them,' his mother protested.

'Those answers do not make sense. If she was after my title and my fortune, why did she run this morning when victory was assured?'

It was the one thought that sustained him on the ride to London. Something had spooked her. Surely, Cora had not come to his bed without caring for him, surely the week had not been a lie, had not been a grand effort to manipulate him into a proposal. He'd given her his heart. He'd believed she was the one person who wasn't out to capture him like a matrimonial prize. The alternative was unthinkable. He couldn't be wrong in love…again.

Chapter Seventeen

Love had proven its limitations once again. The protections she'd put in place had not been enough. Despite her best efforts, part of her had hoped that somehow the fairy tale might end differently. Cora had not realised how deeply embedded that hope was, hidden behind the rationale that leaving Declan was her only answer. She'd known it couldn't be different, but she'd wished it was, more vehemently than she'd realised. Because she loved him, and love couldn't change anything, couldn't make anything better. Once more, it simply wasn't enough. She'd had to protect him, and leaving was the only way she could do that.

She fingered the opal at her neck and stared unseeing at the blank page in front of her, which was supposed to be a letter to Kitty. The necklace was the one piece from the house party she'd been unable to bring herself to stow away. The dresses were at the back of the wardrobe, but the necklace had lain on her bureau until the temptation was too great and she had put it on. Had it only been a day since they'd come home from Richmond? Had it only been one morning since she'd risen from his bed, her body still warm from his lovemaking? It seemed an eternity since her body had felt his touch. Only the freshness of her pain proved the newness of her loss.

'Cora.' Elise opened the door to her chamber, a little breathless, her colour high as if she'd run up the stairs. 'The Duke is here. Harlow is here and he's downstairs with Uncle, asking for you.'

Declan. It took a moment to register that he was here. Harlow was the Duke, and Declan had not been the Duke to her, except for perhaps a fleeting moment when he'd claimed her hand that first fateful night. 'Do you know why he's here?' Cora's hand went to the opal, clutching at it for strength, for balance.

'No.' Elise closed the door. 'Oh, Cora, isn't it exciting? Do you think he's here to ask for your hand?'

Cora rose from the writing desk and went to the mirror, checking her hair and pinching her cheeks. She was so pale and she hadn't slept well. 'I doubt it.' She smoothed the skirts of her green day dress, there was no time to change. It would have to do. 'We have unfinished business.'

Elise's eyes were sharp. 'Does that business have to do with why you were out of bed half the night after the Fantasia Ball?'

Cora frowned at Elise. 'I can't talk about it now.' It was either that or he'd come to exact retribution because he knew her secrets. Neither prospect boded well. Yet the thrill that he managed to raise in her was still there, as she brushed past Elise and headed to the stairs. Even under dubious circumstances, her body, her heart, *wanted* to see him.

He was waiting for her at the bottom of the stairs, dressed for Town in half boots and grey trousers for summer, with a charcoal grey frock coat and white waistcoat with a shawl collar, embroidered with blue forget-me-nots. He looked fresh and vibrant, where she felt sluggish and pale, not fresh in the least. 'Miss Graylin, it's good of you to receive me.' He smiled up at her, but his eyes were solemn and searching, taking her in, guessing her secrets. 'I do apologise for coming by unannounced, but I hoped that we might talk. Your aunt suggested we use the front parlour.'

'Of course, Your Grace.' Great. He had allies in her own home. There would be no help from that quarter. But they didn't know what she knew. Perhaps they would feel differently about letting her be alone with him if they knew where she'd spent the last night of the house party.

'Shut the door, Cora,' Declan said in a low, authoritative tone when they reached the parlour, with its bay windows and sunlight. 'I'm not sure you want the rest of the house to hear our discussion. And it's Declan when we're alone. I don't want you to call me "Your Grace" ever. That's not who we are to each other.'

But it would be, she thought, should they ever meet again after they wrapped up these last few loose ends. Cora sat on the jonquil settee, body tensed for his revelations. He made her wait as he paced the length of the mantel, making her eyes appreciate the sight of him as he gathered his thoughts, marshalled his control. He was unnerved, she realised. She was not the only one who was undone by this visit.

He turned to face her, an arm propped on the mantelpiece. 'Why did you leave me, Cora?' There was real anguish in his gaze. 'Do you know what it was like to wake up without you, to discover you were gone without a goodbye?' He swallowed hard against emotion. 'I was ready to plan our future and you were gone.'

She'd hurt him. She'd not considered that, not thought it possible that the Duke of Harlow—that the strength of Declan Locke—could be breached. Guilt swept her. She loved him, she had not meant to hurt him. It took a moment for her to respond. 'I was protecting you, Declan. We had a week, but we have no future.'

'You don't get to decide for me, alone. That is something we should have talked about.' Anger crept into his angst.

'There's nothing to talk about, Declan, and you know that. When your mother finishes vetting me, you know I'll be found wanting. You know it already. My father is a gentleman of no particular means. I am here on my uncle's benevolence. I am no match for you and the whole of Society knows it. Your mother's vetting will confirm it.' She paused as something shifted in his eyes. 'You do know it. A report has already come back.' She felt her own temper rise. How dare he come here and ask questions that didn't matter, when he knew everything.

Declan gave a short nod. 'It came the last morning. It's why I wasn't right behind you on the road to London. Even then, I would have called yesterday afternoon, which was my intent, but Samson threw a shoe halfway here and I was delayed further. By the time I arrived, it was too late to call.'

A dangerous rill of elation shot through her at the re-alisation. He *knew* and he'd come after her anyway. But realism quickly chased the joy away. What did it matter? It changed nothing. 'Then you know that my father is a vicar without funds for anything beyond essentials. I can offer you nothing but disappointment, Declan. I have no money, no connections, no rank. I am a country gentleman's daughter from Dorset, nothing more.'

'As if any of that matters to me. You *are* Cora Graylin, the woman who understands me, who knows my thoughts before I think them, who loves the country, who values family, who appreciates the dilemma between duty and desire, because she struggles with it, too. Cora, how can you say you offer me nothing? You offer me everything that has any worth to it—your heart, your mind, your body—and I will take all of them gladly.'

His blue eyes were in earnest. He was laying himself out for her, and the enormity of it pierced her. 'When you came to me, I thought we were agreed that we would be married, Cora. I would not have taken you to bed otherwise. I love you. And you love me, I am as sure of it as I am that the sun rises in the east.'

She would not bother to deny that. She did love him, but it was worth little in the fights they would face. All along, she'd thought to protect him from her, but how did she protect him from himself? From his honest, decent heart that deserved so much more? 'I will bring scandal to the Dukedom, Declan. Love isn't nearly enough for what we'd be up against.'

Declan gave an exasperated sigh, frustration in his gaze. 'You're not making sense, Cora. You fled my bed because you love me. It's counterintuitive. We stay where we are loved.'

'No, Declan. We don't hurt the people we love. And

I will hurt you, far worse than you're hurting now. I've seen it happen. Hard times erode that love until there's nothing left.' Mama and Papa's love had not survived the pressures and disappointments of life. She had to make him see reason. *Now.* 'Will you listen to me?'

She was beseeching him with her emerald eyes, desperation welling up from within, and it tore at his heart that she believed her position so fervently—that love failed, that it was weak. What had happened in her life to prove such a point? He'd promised himself he wouldn't touch her, but the temptation proved too much when she sat there in such obvious need of comfort. He left his position at the fireplace and went to her, sitting beside her on the jonquil sofa. He took her hand. 'Tell me how you know such a thing, Cora.'

'My parents. I saw their love disintegrate first-hand over the constant battering of years. They married for love. My aunt tells stories of their wedding day, how my father had the world by the tail. He had all that he wanted when my mother walked down the aisle. And he had hopes of what the future would hold—children, sons. Those hopes were not unrealistic. But the sons never came and, after a while, each daughter became a disappointment.' She sighed as if she, too, carried some of that disappointment. 'The world is not a kind place for men without sons. The world pities them. But it reviles women that do not produce sons.'

'No one could regret a daughter such as you,' Declan offered. He would adore a horde of daughters if they looked like Cora, lived and loved like Cora.

'Year after year, daughter after daughter, their love slipped away, even though they tried to hold on to it. There was a cycle of hope at the beginning of each pregnancy, that this time it would be different. They would talk at dinner about names for our new baby brother. They would smile and laugh and everything would seem right again. In some ways, each later pregnancy—Kitty, Melly, Veronica—was met with increasing amounts of hope. Surely, *this* time it would be a boy. After all, the odds must certainly be in their favour after two, three, then four girls.' She shook her head, her eyes sad. 'But the higher the hopes the more easily are they shattered. Each time, disappointment lingered longer.'

Declan stroked her arm idly, thinking through what he knew of her family. 'Why did it matter when your father had healthy, lovely daughters? He has no title to pass on and the living is not hereditary.' Perhaps her father, who'd not impressed him much already, should have readjusted his hopes. Five healthy children was a blessing, when so many children died in infancy.

'As I grew older, I came to understand that my uncle hoped for a nephew. Between the two of them, Uncle George and my father had always thought they'd manage at least one boy who could inherit. Now, unless my father remarries and has a child late in life, which seems highly unlikely, the title will pass to a distant relative, *if* we can find one, or it will revert to the Crown upon my uncle's death.'

She fixed him with a stare of weary victory. She'd made her point. 'You see, love could not conquer that burden. Perhaps it even made it worse. Then, he lost my mother. She took ill and never recovered. But their love had suffered for years before that, the light dimming in their eyes with each failure. Perhaps they blamed each other. After the baby died, they withdrew into their grief. Their moment of happiness, their reward for long-suffering years, had been snatched from them just as they reached for victory.'

She shook her head. 'They told me that love conquered all. God's love for his children and a family's love for each other. But it didn't. Reality will always outpace it. Love is a hot flame that burns bright and hard and fast and, when it's gone, there is only emptiness. The power of love is a myth. It is not strong. It may be beautiful and fine but it is also fragile, breakable, and it is not enough, Declan.'

Good God, the scars she carried ran deep. No wonder she'd fled his bed. She was scared. He saw that plain as day now. What could he tell her to allay her fear? He cast about his mind and came up with…his parents, who were quite the opposite of hers in both their beginning and their end.

'My mother told me there was no such thing as love at first sight, at least not for a duke. A duke must never think about such things.' He gave a light laugh. 'But then I saw you, and I *knew* she was wrong. Sometimes, I think she's angrier about being wrong than she is that I have chosen someone not on her list of approved candidates. My mother likes to be right. Her marriage to my father was arranged, and it was a grand success. The ball and the house party are an homage to that success. She is certain history will repeat itself. And in a way it has, because I have found you.'

He shifted, leaning close to her in his earnestness. 'What I am saying is this. If your parents are proof that love doesn't last, and my parents are proof that love can indeed grow from nothing, deepening over time into something strong and enduring, who is right? Perhaps it means that we should chart our own course, make a clean break with the past. Cora, if you will give me a chance, I want to show you that love need not fail.'

'I do not think the outcome will be different. We cannot change Society and hundreds of years of tradition,' Cora began.

'You think too much, you look around too much, Cora. Do you remember what I told you that night at the ball? To focus on what is right in front of you, to forget about all else. And we waltzed divinely, didn't we? I am asking you to do the same now. To just look at me, to focus on what is in the moment, and all else takes care of itself.' He could see her wavering, could feel it. His own hope soared at the encouragement. 'You're wearing the opal, so I suspect you don't truly want to give up on us. You only feel you have to. I'm here to say that you don't. Will you try? Will you fight for us?'

'Hope and love, these are dangerous things, Declan.'

'No, they're not. Trust me. We'll take it day by day.' He would show her love was enough, that wishes made in midnight fountains came true, that she could follow her heart and that her heart led straight to him. She would see that a duke and a vicar's daughter could take on the world.

Chapter Eighteen

If the house party week had been the most exciting week of her life, the following three weeks certainly came in a close second. It would be a June to remember. Declan squired her everywhere, showing her possibilities brought to life. He had Magic brought up from Richmond for her. They rode in the park in the mornings. Drove in the park in the afternoons and ate ices at Gunther's. There were picnics and rowing on the Serpentine, an evening at Vauxhall, complete with fireworks, a night at the theatre and trips to Hatchard's.

Each day, she fell further in love with him, and each day hope grew within her that she was wrong. Love *could* survive. They were surviving, weren't they? The gossip columns might remark on them, but there was no scandal. Perhaps Declan was right—they simply needed to chart their own course. Perhaps it was safe enough at last to give herself permission to seize the joy he was offering, without always looking over her shoulder out of fear of having it taken away. Things *were* going well. Elise had announced her engagement to Mr Wade a few days ago, and Declan was taking her driving this afternoon. She'd not seen him yesterday and she'd missed him.

When he pulled up at the kerb she could hardly contain her delight long enough to let him call for her before racing down the steps. 'You brought the phaeton,' Cora exclaimed. 'I've heard about them but I've never ridden on one.' He did spoil her with treat after treat.

'Then today you shall. Put your foot on the wheel and take my hand.' He helped her to the seat and went around to climb up.

'I can see the whole world from up here,' she crowed. 'What an advantage you have on the traffic.' They moved gently into that traffic, Declan slowly giving the horses their head. 'We are up so high. It's a little unnerving,' she laughed. 'It will take some getting used to.' She slid her hand through the crook of his arm. 'That's better. I missed you yesterday. Alex was at Lady Orton's Venetian breakfast so that was something at least. How was the art reception?' The Duke of Colby had invited Declan to a gathering for Joseph Turner and she was admittedly envious. But Colby had been explicit Declan and the Duchess were to attend alone.

'Interesting and the art was enjoyable.' He slid her a warm look. 'You would have loved seeing it. Turner showed some brand-new works that have yet to be widely viewed. You could have helped me appreciate the brushstrokes and techniques. I am sorry I could not get you invited.'

'I would have made it more difficult for Lady Elizabeth to cling to your arm all afternoon.' Since the return to Town, Lady Elizabeth had been making up for lost time, now her wardrobe difficulties had apparently been sorted out. She'd been in constant appearance at every event Declan attended, and had managed to find her way on to his dance card—as had Lady Mary Kimber, whose parents had not given up hope. But lately, it was the Duke of Colby who had become tenaciously persistent putting his daughter forward. 'How was Lady Elizabeth?' she asked.

'The usual. Obsessed with talking about others, half of whom I don't even know.' He flashed her a smile as they approached the Grosvenor Gate entrance off Park Lane. 'She reminds me why I appreciate you so much.' He sobered meaningfully. 'Every day I am reminded tenfold how lucky I am to have found you. You're worth the wait.'

He turned the horses and wove them through the crowd of pedestrians, carriages and riders at the gate. 'I thought we'd take the north-western path towards the enclosure. You've not seen it yet, and we can have some privacy there. Ah, there's Fenton.' Declan nodded to an approaching rider, but didn't stop as Alex tipped his hat and rode past.

It was a ritual they repeated several times on the way to the enclosure, nodding and passing but never stopping. 'I am all yours today,' Declan murmured. 'If I stop to talk, we're done for, and I have bigger plans for this afternoon than making small talk on the park paths.' He gave a secret grin for her alone, and Cora felt the usual trill run through her. He was surrounded by the finest women London had to offer and he chose her, again and again, further proof that perhaps just maybe love was enough indeed. Each day it became easier to believe that.

'Here we are.' Declan pulled the phaeton to a halt. 'There are no carriages allowed in the enclosure, so we go on foot from here.' He jumped down and came around to help her, giving instructions to his tiger. He set his hands about her waist and swung her down. 'Your maid can wait here, too, in the shade with the horses. We'll just walk a bit inside and sample the water.' That last was said for the maid's benefit, she thought.

'Is that all we're going to do? Sample the water?' Cora whispered under her breath as they walked through the gates.

'Sampling the water might be a metaphor, one never knows.' He laughed, low at her ear.

Cora decided almost immediately that this was quite the most pleasant place she'd visited in London. Open only to foot traffic, the enclosure was quiet. The rumble of carriages and the clomp of horse hooves faded away entirely as did the crowds. They walked past the woman selling glasses of mineral water inside the gate. Declan explained how people would come to drink the water of one spring for their health, and use the water of the other for their eyes.

'Does it work?' Cora asked, caught up in his stories and the luxury of private time with him.

'It must. People have been coming back for centuries.' He gave a jerk of his head towards a limestone, white-washed two-storey building. 'Over there is the keeper's cottage.'

They stopped to admire it from their vantage point, a cow lowing in the distance. 'This reminds me of home, all of this verdure.' Cora gave an appreciative sigh. 'It's a marvel to think this place exists in the middle of such a bustling city. I wonder what it feels like to be the keeper of the park and to live here every day, the city just beyond your walls?'

'I would say he's a lucky man to have the best of both worlds, as I do in this moment. Right now, it feels as if we're the only two people in existence. Adam and Eve and our very own Eden right here.'

The wistfulness in his tone caused her to look up at him. She caught his gaze on her, his soul in his eyes, and she trembled at the intensity of it, the knowledge that it was all for her. She was still getting used to accepting that, trusting that it meant something enduring. She leaned in and their mouths met in silent communion, sending a little shock of desire flicking through her.

'I can't stop wanting you, Cora,' he murmured. 'I thought of nothing else yesterday.' He broke the kiss but kept her arm tucked close in his. They began to walk in unhurried steps deeper into the enclosure. 'I want to kiss you without worrying who might see. There's only one way I can think of to have all of that.' He slanted her a look both serious and playful. 'I want today to be the day I ask you, Cora. Have you seen enough over the past three weeks to believe me? That what you and I have together is enough to take on whatever the world hurls at us?'

His words had her stopping in her tracks—freezing.

Declan's stomach went cold. Why did she always look like that when he brought up a more permanent future? Well, he knew why—those darned disappointed parents of hers. He did understand. Truly, it was an enormous leap for them both. But he was ready to leap. More than ready. He wanted her back in his bed, and in his life full-time. He wanted the Lady Marys, Lady Elizabeths and their pushy parents retired to the sidelines. He was done with the game and ready for life with the woman he loved, the woman he chose. But what if she wouldn't choose him after all this?

'We can have a good life, Cora,' he said simply. He'd fought Society, and he would continue to fight Society if they did not care for his choice. The more difficult fight was fighting her. 'Yet I sense that you will not come into that life simply because I ask. So, today is the day I want to vanquish your dragons once and for all.' They would not be a united front until then.

Her eyes softened to the shade of spring grass. 'Oh, Declan, there is no argument you can make. In the end, you will still and always be a duke.'

He gave a dry laugh. 'Most people don't hold that against me.' But Cora was not most people. It was what he loved about her. She saw beyond the moment, for better or worse. He took her hands as they were out of view now, deep in a group of trees. 'Why does it matter so much to you, Cora? You, who doesn't want people to be judged by their titles alone. When you looked at me that first night, you saw that I was a man first, a duke second. So why does it matter now?'

'Because now this is not a fairy tale. I can't pretend you're not the Duke. You will have responsibilities and a lifestyle that you must adhere to.' She faltered here. 'Maybe I don't want everything that comes with you. I want you. Just you, Declan. I want walks in the woods, camp outs by the river. I want children who will know their father, who will grow up in one place.'

Declan drew a deep breath. 'Those are things I want, too. All of them. We can work on building that life together. Isn't that the point of marriage? To build something together? There will be compromises. I would be lying if I said we could have all of that all the time. I can't promise it. But we can choose to have that *most* of the time.' Did she see what it cost him to tell her the truth? It would be so much easier if he made promises he knew he couldn't keep—if he could tell her what he thought she wanted to hear.

They stopped beneath an oak. 'Dream with me a moment, Cora. Let me paint you a picture of our life, of what I've been thinking about since the moment you came to my room. We will find a place in Wimborne Minster to rent or purchase for now. Over time, we'll build a home of our own. We will live close to your family. Your younger sisters can visit as much as they like. They can continue their lessons with you, or we'll hire tutors until they're ready to come out. We'll bring them to London if they wish, or help them begin adulthood on their own terms. I can run the other properties from there. I have good stewards, they can take on more responsibility for the other estates and send reports. We can turn our property into whatever we like. Perhaps you'd like to start a school for other girls, not just your sisters? Or perhaps we could have a small horse operation. Maybe both.'

He could see those ideas pleased her. His Cora could not sit idle for long, and neither could he.

'Of course, London must be a compromise for us. I

must vote my seat. But perhaps it will seem a small sacrifice for the other nine months a year.' He gave a boyish smile. 'Besides, you don't entirely hate London. You love the theatres and the shopping and the arts.'

'I do like London.' She answered his smile with a slow tentative smile of her own. He could see the battle in her. The girl who believed love wasn't enough to sustain a dream wanted to believe in this dream, in him.

'Cora, this is absolutely everything I can offer—my heart, my dreams, my life, my hopes, my love. That will not change in three more weeks or three months. What I can give you today is all I will ever be able to give you. I desperately want all of me to be enough for you. Tell me that it is.'

The past weeks had been both terrific and terrifying, knowing that he could lose her. At any point, she might decide the life of a duchess, of being *his* duchess, was not something she could do. If she could not, he owed it to them both to set her free to find the life she'd needed, and for him to find a way to somehow move on. His mind, his heart, could not take much more of this limbo. If she could not consent to marry him today, his heart knew that would not change with more time. Cora was nothing if not constant.

He danced her against the trunk of the tree, drawing her close as he whispered the only question that mattered. 'Will you be my wife?' Not his duchess. His *wife*.

Her eyes searched his face at the words, her gaze so full of love it made his heart ache. 'It's a big leap, Declan, and I am…afraid.' She held his gaze, letting him see how hard it was for her to confess that.

'That's why we're leaping together, Cora. I won't let you fall.' That was the moment he knew she was his. The resistance fell from her gaze, replaced by misty tears. He had won for both of them. 'Cora, don't cry, my love. The fight is over.'

She pressed against him then, seeking sanctuary in his arms, and he wrapped her in his embrace, needing the sanctuary of her as well. He understood those tears. His own relief was pounding through him until his body was filled with it. The uncertainty, the worry, the edge that had underlain the past weeks was gone now, leaving only joy in its wake. She was his and he was hers. If they were together, nothing could stand between them.

Gently, he untied the ribbons of her hat and tossed it aside, taking her face in both his hands. 'I can kiss you properly now. Those hats make it deuced difficult on a man.' He gave a deep chuckle. 'I suppose that's half their purpose.' But he'd had enough difficulty to suit him for a while.

The kiss that followed was no laughing matter. It was long, and deep, and all-consuming, the first kiss of the rest of their lives together. 'Our happiness matters, Cora.'

'Perhaps you might consider making me happy, right here.' She nipped at his ear, her hips pressed to his. Dear Heavens, she was burning him alive with such suggestions.

'As you wish, my love.' His hand slid beneath her skirts, over a stocking clad leg, finding her core with unerring accuracy. He breathed her in, this woman he knew body and soul. She gave a long moan as his fingers worked their magic. Her body pushed against him, attempting to cajole release from his hand on her terms, on her time.

'Not yet my sweet.' He kissed her neck and felt her pulse race. 'This is no less than how I feel every time you walk into a room, when you waltz in my arms, when you awake in my bed. The way you burn now, is how I burn for you. Always.'

'Then join me in the fire.' Her beautiful neck arched against the tree as pleasure teased her. What a sight she was! The only thing better than watching her claim that pleasure in full would be to join her in it, finding that pleasure together, until all else was obliterated—responsibility and reality with it.

In his haste, he fumbled with the fastenings of his trousers, so greatly did the idea appeal—making love out of doors, just the two of them, where no one would see, would know, would even guess.

'This feels deliciously wicked,' she murmured against his mouth. 'Doing something so decadent with so many clothes on.'

'Wicked and right. Wrap your legs about me.' He lifted her then, balanced her between the tree and him, meeting his body with hers—legs about his hips, arms about his neck, her core offering him unfettered access, which he claimed with alacrity, the fit tight and perfect as if there wasn't an inch to spare and his body revelled in this...*homecoming*. This was where he belonged. With this woman, under the skies. He began to move, hips grinding against her, his own fevered need matching hers. This would be fast and fulfilling, a potent reminder of all they would be together.

He thrust once more, feeling her body gather with his. 'Let go with me, Cora.' He wanted her there with him at the end. It wouldn't be long now. He watched the pleasure take her even as his own release surged through him. He saw the moment she let ecstasy spiral about her, let it take her, let her moans fill the early summer air because there was no one to hear.

They held one another in the privacy of the trees for a long while after. Listening to the silence around them, listening to the thudding of one another's heartbeat within them as they slowed. 'I'm afraid, too, Cora.' He whispered his confession into her hair. 'These past weeks I've been afraid of losing you, of never feeling this way again with another if I did.'

She laid her head on his shoulder and let out a long exhalation. 'You won't lose me, Declan.' Those were exactly the words he needed to hear.

'With your permission, I will speak to your uncle, this afternoon,' he said quietly after a time. 'I'll write to your father. I'll send an announcement to *The Times* for the morning edition. I want to announce our engagement tonight at Cowden's ball. He was married just a couple of years ago. He'll appreciate the romance of it. We can sort the rest out later.' He wanted the rest of the Season with her, to show her London without being swarmed by women, with time to plan their life together. Such plans had never felt better.

He could feel her smile against him. 'You've got it all worked out. Is there anything left for me to do?'

'Would you wear the blue dress tonight?' Blue was the colour of hope, and it seemed the perfect bookend to this courtship.

'Yes.'

He took her hand and they walked quietly out of the enclosure, each of them filled with a joyous solemnity. By this evening, all of London would know the Duke had found his Cinderella.

Chapter Nineteen

First, he needed to tell his mother. Declan climbed the steps to Harlow House, knowing full well this news would not be received as joyously as it had been at Graylin House. There'd been champagne in the drawing room, hugs and kisses and feminine excitement over having two weddings to plan. He loved watching Cora with her family. Soon that family would be his as well.

He found his mother in her private sitting room, her head bent industriously to a letter she was writing. Declan took a moment to study her when she wasn't *en garde*. She looked…older. There were new grey hairs at her temples, and the late afternoon light caught the creases at her eyes. He was not the only one the past two years had taken a toll on. If she allowed it, his news could ease her worry. He cleared his throat and stepped fully into the room. 'Mother, I have some news that I hope you will be happy to hear.'

She looked up, once more *en garde*, the Duchess fully in command. They were alike that way, he and his mother, always on duty. Cora was like that, too, if his mother would let herself see it.

'I have news, too.'

Declan was immediately concerned. Her news didn't sound…happy.

'But you first.' She rose from the desk and took a seat in one of the leather Chesterfields before the cold fire. 'How was the Turner reception yesterday? You finally had a chance to spend time with Lady Elizabeth Cleeves. I understand Lady Mary Kimber was there as well. It was a good chance to see them side by side.'

Declan took the other chair. 'Lady Mary is polite enough but Lady Elizabeth has a shrew's tongue. I will not tolerate a wife who puts down others in order to promote herself. Or simply for the pleasure of it.'

'She is young and hasn't honed her skills yet. You can teach her,' his mother interrupted before he could steer the conversation towards his news. 'She's lovely, the Season's Diamond of the First Water.'

'A moniker she's done nothing to earn,' Declan countered with equal sharpness, watching his mother's intent gaze. She was on edge, as if something else was at work here, something he didn't quite grasp. 'Out of curiosity's sake, what were you and Colby discussing yesterday? You spent a fair amount of time together.' And they were not usually comrades.

She hesitated for only a fraction of a second but Declan caught it. 'His daughter of course. He is eager to put her forward. Colby is disappointed that his daughter didn't attend the house party or the ball, and he perceives that she is somehow behind in your consideration.' There were volumes wrapped in that, none of the layers friendly, all of them condemning.'

'That's in part what I want to share. I'll not be pursuing either Lady Mary or Lady Elizabeth. I've offered for Miss Graylin. She has accepted and we celebrated with her uncle this afternoon. An announcement will be printed tomorrow.' Declan smiled. 'I'll need your help with the wedding. I was thinking September, in the fall—Father's favourite season.'

His mother's gaze turned hard. She was entrenching and suddenly he felt as if this was the last battle. There would be no retreat on her part. She had no ground left give. Neither did he. 'This is disappointing, indeed, Declan. She was not on my list. She has no experience with Society. She brings nothing of merit with her. I thought our discussion at Riverside made that clear.'

'She loves me. She is more to me than a hostess. She's actually a lot like you if you'd get to know her. She's interested in starting a school for girls.' Declan waited but his mother said nothing. 'You're being stubborn, Mother,' Declan said with quiet sternness.

'You are being stubborn. I am being realistic, and it's time you were, too. Perhaps the fault is mine in thinking that I should give you more choice, more time.' She shook her head. 'Too much choice has muddied the waters instead of clearing them. I should have decided for you. I should have told you it was Elizabeth or Mary and that would have been the end of it.'

'And be damned to what your son wants? Is my happiness of no import?' He'd never felt so much like a stallion to be bought, sold and bred than he did right now in his own home.

'No profanity,' she snapped. 'When my son isn't thinking with his brain, what he wants is not a consideration. It can't be about *you*, Declan. Have I taught you nothing?'

Declan narrowed his gaze. 'Perhaps you'd better explain that. Does this have to do with the Turner invitation and your conversation with Colby?' He racked his brain trying to think of what Colby might attempt.

His mother shifted in her seat. 'Colby asked when he could entertain a call from you. He said the sooner the better, since he was eager to champion your application to the Prometheus Club.' But it was the reverse of that statement that held the real threat. If he did not marry Elizabeth, he would be denied entrance into the elite club.

'Unbelievable. He thinks to pressure me into asking for Elizabeth. That's blackmail.' And it was no small thing. Colby carried weight in the club. To block his membership meant to block his access to investments and reliable financial growth for the Dukedom. The Prometheus Club was a new organisation of like-minded noblemen who believed in the responsibility of economically securing their families' well-being, and thus England's well-being, through investments abroad. It was headed by the Duke of Cowden and had already made extraordinary strides forward. Declan needed the Prometheus Club to move the Dukedom into a more modern era.

'He'll argue you show bad judgement. That you're rash. People will listen to him,' his mother warned. 'I know how much you are counting on the club.'

'But could Colby actually make good on that threat?' Declan mused. 'I wonder if he could actually turn the members against me? Cowden is somewhat newly wed, as is Creighton. If the club is open to Creighton, surely it would be open to me.' Not that he wanted to argue it that way, nor did he want to be the cause of a rift in the club. There were traditionalists that would side with Colby, and Cowden wouldn't thank him for any in-fighting. But it did seem to him that Colby might not have as strong a hand as he thought. And what choice did he have but to withdraw his application or call Colby's bluff?

His mother's brow knit. 'We've not had a breath of scandal on this Dukedom for centuries, and now you're looking to court two with an unorthodox marriage and making trouble over the Prometheus Club. Colby will not like having his nose tweaked. He will entrench,' she pointed out. 'If it's not the Prometheus Club, it will be something else. Push him far enough and he'll want revenge. Think of how it will look from his perspective, and Lord Carys is on his side, wanting his piece of revenge for Lady Mary.'

Declan nodded. 'Carys wants a duke for Lady Mary.' He thought of the references Lady Mary had made at the house party. Carys had lost face to see his daughter overlooked by two dukes in two years. Together, Colby and Carys were two desperate men. Desperate men did desperate things. As did their wives. They could make Cora's introduction into Society highly unpleasant. 'But I don't hold with blackmail and that's what this is. Perhaps I should talk with him, let him know that blackmailing the Dukedom is not likely to get the results he wants, but rather the opposite.'

If he didn't stand up for himself now, he'd spend the

rest of his life giving in, of always compromising, and that ultimately undermined a man's duty and honour. He rose and excused himself. 'I appreciate the information. I need to go up and change now. I still intend to announce my engagement at the Cowden Ball tonight. I hope you'll be there to support me as you've always been.'

He bent to kiss his mother's cheek. He would not let his decisions be driven by the likes of Lords Colby and Carys. Did Colby really think he'd enter into a marriage where his father-in-law thought he could be bullied into submission? That set the wrong precedent. He would begin his first steps into married life tonight as he meant to go on—on firm footing. The life he wanted with Cora couldn't be built on shifting sand.

Dresses changed lives. Cora was proof of it as she stepped out of her uncle's carriage at Cowden house, the skirts of her blue ball gown susurrating gently as she climbed the stairs to where Declan was waiting to take her and her family through the receiving line.

It had only been a handful of hours since he'd left her in her uncle's drawing room, but already she was eager to see him again—hungry to see him again. He looked handsome and commanding tonight, every inch the Duke. It sent a certain thrill through her. She liked both the Duke and the country man in him. Tonight, his dark hair was brushed back, his jaw clean-shaven, his evening clothes immaculate, including a new blue waistcoat—this one matching her dress exactly.

'We may start a trend,' Cora commented wryly as they waited patiently for the chance to greet their hosts.

They'd certainly already started tongues wagging. She'd only been there a few minutes and already glances were being thrown their way, some of them speculative—would tonight be the night the Duke made his choice official? How had an unknown girl managed to capture a duke? Other glances were more critical. It was the second time she'd worn that dress in London, possibly more if she'd worn it at the house party, a sore spot for those who hadn't been invited. What did it say when a girl wore a dress that often? Some matrons did not bother to lower their voices as they made their guesses.

'Let them have their petty jealousies. At the end of the night, they will understand,' Declan said in low tones. 'As for me, I love that dress. You can wear it every evening if you want to.' He bent low to her ear. 'I like you in it as well as out of it.'

That made her blush. 'You shouldn't say such things in public,' she chided. 'Someone might overhear. Aunt B and Uncle George are right behind us.'

Declan's eyes twinkled. 'Let them hear. I want everyone to know that I am in love with my betrothed. It might do them all a bit of good to know that a man *should* love his wife, that marriage should be more than a financial transaction.'

Love. Again. That beautiful fragile thing that floated on the whims of hope's wind. Today, they'd spoken of taking a leap of faith—that all would work out, that they had the strength and fortitude to ensure things worked out. She let out a breath and pressed a hand to her stomach to settle the butterflies there. They were certainly jumping tonight. It was still new and a little unsettling, but leaps of faith were like that. She slid a look at Declan, so handsome and strong and hers. He'd made her believe in the impossible again. She was trusting he was right—that as long as they stood together, obstacles could be overcome. Love would not prevent the obstacles, it would just help deal with them.

They reached the Duke of Cowden and his wife. Cora was surprised to see how young they both were. Declan had told her Cowden had recently married, but she'd assumed he was an older man. That was not the case. Cowden was tall and dark-haired with sharp eyes, a sharp nose and only a few years over thirty. Cora could see why Declan liked him. He had a way of putting people at ease even for the short time spent greeting the reception line. 'Harlow, it is good of you to come.' He shook Declan's hand. 'Allow me to present my bride, Her Grace the Duchess of Cowden.'

His bride. He still called her that after two years of marriage, and a child already. Cora hoped Declan would refer to her as his 'bride' with such affection. But she doubted the Duchess of Cowden had brought even a whiff of scandal to her engagement, and she probably hadn't been a vicar's daughter from Dorset.

'We are honoured you want to make your announcement here tonight.' The Duchess smiled at Cora. 'Enjoy this evening, my dear Miss Graylin. You'll be a celebrity tomorrow. Everyone will want a piece of you until you walk up the aisle.' She gave a sly smile. 'If you want my advice, get a special licence and be done with it so you can get on with your life. People will retreat if there's nothing to see.'

'It is good advice, Your Grace, if it were only up to me.' Declan slipped Cora a private look and covered her hand with his—a gentle gesture that sent the usual jolt of warm heat through her. 'But this is Cora's first time in London. I want her to enjoy the Season before I rush her down the aisle.'

'Go on into the ballroom, the dancing will start shortly.' Cowden gestured to the room just beyond them, where Cora could see chandeliers glittering. 'Perhaps you and I can talk later, Harlow. I hear you have some business with Lord Carys and Colby. Perhaps I can be of help.'

Declan nodded, suddenly looking serious. What was that about?

Before she could ask they were through the door and she was distracted by the sight before her. The ballroom was awe-inspiring. Not one but three glittering chandeliers hung the length of the dance floor, each crystal sparkling. 'It's Venetian glass. All three of them were imported from Italy by Cowden's father,' Declan explained.

'Like your wishing fountains? It's a wonder there's anything left in Italy,' Cora teased. But inside, some of the elation she'd allowed herself to feel throughout the afternoon—as Declan talked with her uncle and drank champagne at her side, toasting their engagement—began to fade, replaced by the old concerns. She knew nothing of this life, where people ordered enormous chandeliers and fountains from Italian villas, shipping them across a continent for the mere pleasure of decorating homes that were five times the size of the vicarage she'd grown up in. 'I cannot imagine myself ordering glass from Italy,' she whispered.

'You can't imagine *yet*,' Declan assured her. 'We can honeymoon in Italy if you like. Although, I don't think we need Italian glass in our home in Wimborne. I was hoping for a cosier décor. Perhaps I can persuade you?' He flashed a smile that put her worry back to bed. 'There's Fenton, Cora. Let's go say hello. I want to be sure he hears our news from me first, since he's one of my oldest and best friends.'

Alex Fenton was standing with a group of people who were now quite familiar to Cora. She recognised them all—Ellen and Jack DeBose with his new fiancée on his arm, Lady Mary Kimber and the sharp-tongued but elegant Lady Elizabeth Cleeves. This was another sign of how much things had changed for her. A few weeks prior, she had known no one, and now her circle of friends included the daughters of a viscount and an earl, and a viscount's heir.

But perhaps friend was too liberal of a term. They weren't really her friends. Merely acquaintances. She would not feel comfortable confiding in any of them. The only friend here was Fenton, and that was out of loyalty to Declan. Her hand tightened on Declan's arm. Suddenly she felt very lonely. Was this how Declan felt all the time? No wonder he'd come looking for her. She wished Elise were with her, but Elise was off already with Mr Wade.

Declan raised his voice slightly to command the attention of the group. 'I am happy to see you all together. Miss Graylin and I have something to share with you, something I wanted you to hear personally from us first. Very shortly, before the dancing begins, I've asked the

Duke of Cowden if I might make an announcement. This afternoon I asked Miss Graylin to be my wife, and she has generously accepted.'

Cora couldn't help but smile as Declan said the words, her thoughts going back to the afternoon at the enclosure, but her smile soon froze. Lady Elizabeth Cleeves was staring at her with the oddest expression, something between recognition, realisation and hatred. Hatred? That seemed a bit intense for someone she hardly knew.

'Why, you conniving little witch,' Lady Elizabeth Cleeves said in an aghast tone—hardly the expected response to an engagement announcement. 'I remember you now. You were at Madame Dumont's. And that's *my* dress, the gown I was supposed to wear to the Harlow Ball, but it never arrived.' She pointed a well-manicured finger at Cora. '*You* stole my dress. I saw you that day in the shop, eyeing the fabrics meant for me.' She flashed a stormy gaze at Declan and then back at Cora. 'And then you stole my duke. He never would have noticed you if you hadn't worn my dress.' Her voice had risen, shrill and clear, attracting attention to their group. 'You have schemed for him from the start, pretending to be an innocent miss.'

'It wasn't like that, it's not like that,' Cora replied, disbelief rocketing through her. Lady Elizabeth seemed nearly unhinged, but Cora knew better. Pieces were starting to fit in all the wrong ways. 'I didn't mean to take your dress. I didn't know it was yours. It showed up in my order by accident,' she protested with the distinct impression she was babbling. People were staring at them. Her world was reeling, everything having become surreal—being here in this ballroom, with this woman accusing her of stealing a gown.

'But you knew it was certainly not yours!' Lady Elizabeth railed. 'You knew you hadn't ordered it but you kept it and you wore it while I had to stay home because I had no dress. Meanwhile, you were dancing in *my* dress with *my* duke!' she raged. 'And now he thinks he's going to marry *you*.' She stamped her slippered foot before sliding Declan a look. 'Or maybe not. What do you think of her now, Your Grace? This little *liar* who stole another girl's dress to crash a ball she wasn't even invited to.'

'No, I was invited, I was Lady Isley's guest...' Cora protested, only to be overridden by Lady Elizabeth's ire.

'You weren't a *real* guest. You were not hand-picked by the Duchess herself. You are nothing but an opportunistic hanger-on. No one even knows who you are, not even the Duke, apparently. You have stolen him, trapped him. But now you're the one who is trapped.'

Cora looked at Declan. He was ashen, a thousand horrors running through his blue eyes as he stared back, as if seeing her for the first time. 'Perhaps we should go somewhere and talk,' Cora suggested quietly, aware that he was no longer touching her, that the arm that she'd held all night was absent from beneath her hand.

'It's not quite like that,' she said in low tones for Declan only, her own outrage growing. Not at Lady Elizabeth, but at him. Just this afternoon he'd declared how much he disliked Lady Elizabeth for her cattiness, and now he was willing to take her side, her word. So much for the idea that love was enough. Pangs of regret shot through her, hard and stabbing. She didn't want to be right. She didn't want love to be delicate and fragile, easily broken, after all.

'I don't want to talk, Miss Graylin,' Declan said grimly, and she felt her last hopes fade. What did it say about love if the merest whiff of trouble could blow it away? That it had barely endured a handful of hours?

'As for you, Lady Elizabeth, you should watch your tongue and think about when and how you employ it.' Declan delivered the scold with full ducal authority, but it brought Cora no pleasure. The man she loved had dismissed her publicly.

'I *do* watch my tongue. I speak the truth, Your Grace.' Lady Elizabeth did not back down. 'Your fiancée is a fraud and you've gone after her like a stag in rut, shunning decent young women. You have insulted all of us. My father will have you denied entrance to a certain club because of that insult.' She tossed a smug smirk Cora's direction that said she knew full well, between her rather graphic words and her raised voice, *she* was commanding the direct attention of all those around them, and indirectly commanding the ballroom—those who could hear the exchange whispered to others. She would not apologise to the Duke. But she'd make sure the Duke apologised to *her*. Such was the power of a woman raised to be a duchess.

Cora wanted to disappear into the floor. People were openly staring now. The daughter of a duke had just publicly called her a woman of loose morals and she could not deny it technically. Declan looked at her, as if willing her to say something to Lady Elizabeth, to refute the claims. But it was all true. The dress wasn't hers, she'd not really been invited to the ball the way the other girls had been, and she'd slept with him. Not to coerce him into marriage but who would believe that? All of London's finest were staring at her as if she stood there naked. Part of her thought she might as well be—her pride and honour were in tatters on the ground, along with her love, her trust and her hope.

She cast a look at Declan. It was the sight of him that undid her more thoroughly than Lady Elizabeth's condemnation. His eyes held anger and sadness, not only for her but for himself, and disbelief that he had been duped. That cut deep—the idea that he thought she'd used him, lied to him. It was the message in his blue eyes that slayed the last of her strength.

How could you do this to me? I thought you were someone I could love. I thought you were someone who could love me. I thought what we had was honest.

She gave a little cry of despair, picked up her skirts and ran from the ballroom before the hurt overwhelmed her.

Chapter Twenty

'Cora!' Declan stirred from his angry stupor too late, her blue skirts passing through the ballroom doors and into the foyer. He pushed through the crowd of gaping onlookers, determined to make an effort. He'd hurt her, with his words and then with his silence. He'd hurt her and humiliated her with his public choices. He'd chosen his anger over action, over protection. He'd been stunned of course. Everything Alex and his mother had warned him about had come to pass; that Cora was too good to be true, that she had somehow manufactured the connection he felt with her.

His response was understandable given the shock, given the events of the evening—the blackmail from Colby, his mother's resistance to the match. He'd been fighting for Cora, for *them*, for so long only to encounter one more fight. He'd not been ready for it and his reaction had hardly been chivalrous.

He gained the foyer, catching sight of her skirts on the stairs as she entered the carriage at the kerb. He was too late.

Alex was beside him, a hand at his shoulder. 'Come on, let's get you home and talk it through.'

'I appreciate it, Alex, but I think I'd rather not talk just now.' He wanted to hide, wanted to think through what had happened, how this one thing had been the straw that had broken the proverbial camel's back.

Alex clapped him on the shoulder. 'If you're sure? I'll see that your mother gets home and I'll call on you tomorrow, then.' Because tomorrow would be worse. By then, this whole debacle would be public. Everyone would know.

Know what? Declan climbed into the carriage and gave directions to Harlow House. That Cora had duped him? That she'd stolen another girl's dresses? Was any of that true? It did seem like there was a nugget of truth to it at least. Cora had not denied Elizabeth's claim of theft. But did it even matter if it was true? Truth was what people wanted to believe. Now that these things had been said they couldn't be unsaid.

It took so little to start a scandal. Lady Elizabeth's words had been like a match to dry tinder. At its touch everything had gone up in flames. How did he move forward? With Cora? Was that salvageable after his reaction tonight? This was the second time she'd run from him. Should he salvage it?

This scandal would stick. If he managed to marry her, it would always be there between them, and it would be out there in Society, ready to be unearthed at leisure. Lady Elizabeth had let loose a hydra tonight. He pushed a hand through his hair, something akin to grief swamping him. He felt as if he'd lost a part of himself. He'd lost Cora and all he thought that relationship had stood for, all he thought it had proved possible. Lady Elizabeth's accusations had raised issues deeper than the dresses.

His mind was full of questions. Who was Cora Graylin really and why had she done this? Most of all, if she was indeed a manipulator, why did his heart feel as if it had been shattered in a million pieces? Surely he should have been able to detect a fraud?

The carriage rolled to a stop and he got out, looking up at the townhouse with a sinking heart. He'd left here a few hours ago feeling like a man victorious. He was returning very much a man defeated. Even though he loved Cora, things had still fallen apart. Did that make Cora right? Did it prove love really wasn't enough?

It was thought enough to keep Declan up all night. He was still grappling with those ideas when the sun came up, when breakfast was served, when his solicitor called to go over the dividends on the ducal investments, and when Alex Fenton called shortly after two o'clock. The only thing Declan had changed in the long hours since returning home was his location. He'd managed to move from the impersonal drawing room to the comparative comfort of his estate office. If anyone noticed he'd not changed his clothes, no one dared say any differently.

'The papers were brutal this morning. I assume you've seen? Or maybe not?' Alex set down a stack of papers and took a seat in the empty Chesterfield.

Declan picked the top paper up with a sigh. 'I suppose I'd rather face them with you than with my mother.' His mother had considerately left him alone since the ball.

He'd best get it over with. He couldn't help himself if

he wasn't informed. He grimaced at the first headline: *Duke Duped by Debutante.*

'Ouch.'

The rest were similar in tone, reporting a Lady E's outburst at the Duke of C's ball the prior evening, which resulted in accusing Miss G of stealing the Duke of H under false pretences.

Declan set the papers down. 'All things considered, it could have been worse.' There was no mention of why or how the Duke had supposedly been 'stolen' from Lady E. Neither had there been mentions of any dresses.

Alex crossed a leg over one knee. 'You're a duke. No one wants to risk offending you by saying too much, and no one wants to risk offending the Duke of Colby by calling his daughter a liar—if that should turn out to be the case.' The last was asked almost as a question. Alex wanted to know. How much truth was there to Lady Elizabeth's accusations?

'Cora didn't deny it, did she?' This was what had haunted him. Last night, when Cora could have denied it, she'd merely said she could explain. Her answer implied extenuating circumstances, but it also implied quite heavily that lady Elizabeth was right—the gowns were not Cora's. 'I think,' Declan said slowly, 'the gowns were not Cora's, that they came into her possession somehow and she made use of them.' He paused. Mother had warned him to consider those gowns and the reasons behind them, especially with Barnes and Stockton's report staring him in the face. He'd forged ahead anyway in spite of his mother's caution.

'God, it's just like Esme all over again.' That was the

salt in the wound. He'd been fooled by her, too, only Cora had played a much deeper game with his heart. Esme had never been interested in that.

'You don't know, you're just guessing. Everyone knows Lady Elizabeth is a jealous cat.'

Declan shook his head. 'I do know, Alex. The pieces are all there. I received a report from Dorset at the end of the house party—' which seemed a life time ago. 'She is one of five daughters born to an impoverished vicar. Apparently, their standard of living has declined severely since her mother died. The vicarage is crowded and in desperate need of repair. She and her sister are here to make advantageous matches this Season in a gamble to restore the family. I just didn't think she was using me. I thought it was all for real.'

He made a fist of his hand on the armrest, his anger rising afresh. 'The thing is, Alex, I can't sort through my feelings. I am still so furious. She stood there last night and didn't deny a single thing. I feel betrayed. I feel lied to. I *hate* that Lady Elizabeth was right.' He glanced at his friend. 'I loved her. She was my hope. I saw my future with her. And she turned out to be worse than all the other girls. The other girls didn't pretend to be anything other than what they were—innocent, empty-headed dolls eager to marry for a title. And she pretended to be otherwise—that the title didn't matter to her, only me, only the man. The harder I pursued her, the faster she ran, and I ran after her until she *let* me catch her.' What a chase she'd led, what a deep game she'd played. 'I thought I'd won a significant victory, that I'd convinced her it was all right to marry a duke. But she'd wanted that all along.'

In the dark of the night and in the depths of his anger, that was what was his mind had sorted out. 'I should hate her for that. My heart should not be open to such a woman.' It made him feel weak and vulnerable that he had indeed been duped. Even when the facts were staring him in the face, he didn't want to accept them. 'Maybe this is why I've not allowed myself to be smitten since Esme.' He sighed. 'If this is what it feels like, I can do without it. Perhaps I should call on the Earl of Carys and ask for Lady Mary Kimber's hand and be done with it.' He would not give Colby the satisfaction. But he could do Mary Kimber a favour and he could get on with a tepid life of duty, respect and friendship, forget about passion and the wild reckless dreams Cora inspired in him.

'You will do no such thing,' Alex scolded. 'At least not until you're thinking straight, which you definitely are not. Right now, you are reeling from a significant shock.' He went to the console and poured two drinks. 'You can't just stop loving someone overnight, no matter what they did. It's going to hurt for a while.'

Declan took the offered tumbler and stared into it. 'I can't believe I fell for it.'

Alex was silent a long time. 'I can, because I'm not sure you fell for anything. Are you really so certain none of it was real? I see how Cora looks at you, how the two of you are together.'

'No, I'm not sure,' Declan said slowly. 'That's what eats at me.' Those kisses, the lovemaking—he'd unequivocally been her first—the passion was honest and true. The conversations, the rides, the walks. There was real connection there that his heart said could not be fabricated, no matter how his mind argued to the contrary. She'd seen his mother's treasure hunt list for what it was—the hopes for a good marriage. Cora had heart.

'Here's a wild suggestion,' Alex said with a hint of facetiousness. 'Talk to her. Go to her. If this is real, she's reeling, too. I saw her face last night. Lady Elizabeth rattled her.'

'Because the accusations were true.' Declan speared Alex with a stare. 'What could she say that didn't make her more of a liar?'

Alex interrupted. 'Don't you want to know *why* she did it? She had to know there was risk of discovery. I won't countenance a lie in general, but I do think motive matters. If she did it for her family, if they are as bad off as you say…think about it, man, what would you do for your nieces and nephews, for your sisters, for your mother?'

'I have sworn them the protection of my name. I would do anything for them,' Declan admitted, giving his brandy a swirl. 'But that doesn't change the fact that she used me. She made me believe…things.' Lots of things—that he could find love, that a *duke* could *have* love, that there was a woman who could be his partner, not simply an empty vessel waiting for him to fill her with his opinions and heirs. He knew better. Life didn't work that way simply because he wished it did. He'd conveniently forgotten that for a few weeks. 'I don't know that talking with her does any good or solves anything.'

Except drag him back in again. Perhaps what he needed was distance.

Alex fidgeted, re-crossing his leg. 'So you mean to break the engagement?'

'It was never official.' But, oh, they'd been so close. A few moments later and the ballroom would have known. A few hours later and the announcement would have run in *The Times*. Some would say he'd had a narrow escape.

'You will cast her to the vultures then?' Alex quizzed.

'She will appreciate it could have gone worse for her. You saw the articles, you know there was some protection there.' What was Alex getting at?

'You will weather this. You are the wronged party,' Alex said sternly. 'Everyone is on your side, everyone is always on a duke's side. But her Season is done. Innocent of Lady Elizabeth's claims or not, no one will countenance her. They do not need to. She was an interloper from the start. You made her decent for a time and now that you've dropped her, she will be the interloper once more, an upstart niece of a baronet.'

Declan sat with that knowledge in silence. People would say it was his revenge of course, and his right to ruin her after she'd ruined him. Only, he wasn't truly ruined. The matchmaking mamas would redouble their efforts, thankful for the reprieve, with still weeks to go in the Season and the Duke's need to marry still pressing.

Lord Carys would be overjoyed, His Grace the Duke of Colby would be breathing easier now that his daughter was the hero of the hour, for all the good it would do him. For Declan, the hounding would start all over again. For Cora...disgrace, exile, a chance for a decent match gone. Perhaps for her sister, too. Would this affect Elise and her newly announced engagement to Mr Wade? He hoped not. The family would need that marriage more than ever now that Mr Wade would be the family's sole source of hope in evading perpetual hardship.

'Blast it.' He pounded the armrest with his fist. 'I'll write to Wade and encourage him to go through with the wedding, tell him that this need not reflect on him.' He could do that much.

Alex shifted again in his seat. 'And Cora? Are you really going to let her go?'

'I don't see how I can do any differently.' That was all ruined. There was a breach between them that could never be truly mended. Trust had been shattered by both parties.

'She needs protection. Ruination doesn't deal with women well. You know she won't survive it.'

He knew. But what could he do without sacrificing himself? If he did, he'd be no good to any of the others counting on him—tenants, the people he did business with. His credibility must be intact. No one could respect a man whose fiancée had lied to him and he married her anyway.

Alex nodded and met his gaze evenly. 'If she cannot have the protection of your name, perhaps she will take the protection of mine.'

Declan felt the announcement like a blow to the stomach. 'You mean to marry her?'

'You know I'm fond of her. We got on famously at the house party and at the ball, too, that first night. We are good friends and I think quality marriages are built on much less. We'll both be going into this with our eyes wide open, no surprises.'

Yes, he did know Alex was 'fond of her'. He'd felt the prick of envy at the archery contest seeing them together. He'd been jealous of all the time Alex could spend with her that he couldn't, because she did seem to enjoy Alex's company. She'd smiled for him, laughed for him. Now, she would kiss him, she would… No, he wouldn't think of those things Alex would get to do with her, things he would have to pretend he knew nothing about for the rest of his life. How hard it would be to see Alex in the clubs and know…

'It's the right thing to do,' Alex argued patiently. 'We cannot allow her to be ruined. I understand your position and I respect it. You are my oldest friend. I do not want this to come between us. You cannot save her, but I can. I came by to see how you were doing and to tell you. Now that I have, I am off to Graylin House to put my offer to her.'

Declan sat still and silent, his drink untouched for a long while after Alex left. So that was how the story would end. Cora would marry Alex. She had no choice and he was not a bad choice. Alex was in fact a very good choice. There would be a country life for her and the attentions of a loyal and doting husband that would inevitably result in children. She would have her family. And what would he have? Nothing. Once more the Duke stood alone.

Chapter Twenty-One

Cora stood alone at the window of her bedchamber looking out over the townhouse garden. She was utterly ruined and all by her own doing, an Icarus of her own making. She had flown too close to the sun and now the wax of her wings had most thoroughly melted. She would not be received anywhere. The papers had been full of her disgrace. Aunt Benedicta had been beside herself last night and again this morning, which had only made it worse. Cora would not deliberately choose to repay her aunt and uncle's generosity in this way.

'It will pass,' Uncle George had said kindly at breakfast, once the papers had been dissected. 'These people are not our people anyway.' But she knew he had gone out this morning as soon as possible to visit Mr Wade's father to ensure Elise's marriage went through.

Elise had been comfort itself, staying with her last night and never once worrying over how this might impact her own newfound happiness. She'd even offered to pack up her things and go home to Dorset with her. 'No, you must stay, you need to shop for your trousseau,' Cora had told her in earnest. If Elise could survive this, she must stay and take full advantage of the city. She would not have her sister suffer, too.

Aunt Benedicta had tried to offer absolution by taking the blame on herself, saying she should not have allowed Cora to wear the blue dress in the first place. She'd been a poor chaperone to allow such a thing. But Cora could not permit someone else to take the blame for her. She was a firm believer that no one could *make* someone else do anything. Ultimately, we each decided what we did or did not do.

She could have protested. She could have refused to wear the dress or go to the ball. This was a cautionary tale against vanity. She'd had her head turned by those fabrics in the dress shop. It was a disaster of her own making. And Declan's, although she tried not to think of him. The only thing that had got her through so far was thinking about those around her: Elise, Aunt B and Uncle George. It excused not thinking about Declan, about the shock and the hurt.

There was a knock at her door. It would be the maid to help her with packing. The sooner she was back home in Dorset, the sooner she could start recovering, putting herself back together and moving, always moving forward. 'Come in,' she called. 'I'm ready to pack.'

'Oh, miss, it's not that, begging your pardon,' the maid said awkwardly. 'There's a caller for you downstairs, a gentleman. Shall I tell him you're at home?'

Her pulse raced. Dammit. She didn't want her pulse to skitter at the mere mention of Declan's presence, and yet her body quickened with hope and desire. He'd come. He was ready to listen to an explanation. Together, they would find a way to make this right. She was sorry, so sorry for this. She had tried to tell him, although she acknowledged that she'd waited too long. She smoothed her skirts. 'I'll be down shortly.'

She took a moment to check her appearance. The puffiness around her eyes had gone down from crying. She pinched her cheeks for colour, but she could do nothing about the dark circles that betrayed her sleeplessness. It won't matter to him, she told herself, as she came down the stairs and headed towards the drawing room, which had been the scene of such happiness yesterday. He had come. He was ready to make rapprochement.

Cora fixed a smile on her face—was that the right expression for such a meeting?—and entered the drawing room, her expression freezing. 'Lord Fenton.' She hesitated, recovering herself, her heart sinking. She tried to stay positive. Still, perhaps this was good. Perhaps Declan had sent him as an emissary.

Alex bent over her hand. 'Miss Graylin, it is good to see you. I am sorry I'm not who you expected.'

'Please, pay me no attention. I am always happy to see you,' she apologised. 'My manners are atrocious today.'

'It is understandable. Last night was…difficult.' Alex was so gracious, and she was grateful for his courtesy.

'Come and sit. I will ring for a tray.' She gestured to the settee and chairs set near the cold fireplace.

He sat and for the first time she notice how he was dressed, not for riding or driving in the park but more formally. He was not merely here because he was in the neighbourhood. She wanted to ask if he'd seen Declan but she didn't dare. It would seem desperate, and she wanted to hear why Alex was here. Had he come on Declan's account or on hers?

He cleared his throat. 'I've come because I have something to ask you, Cora, and I hope you will hear me out.' He seemed nervous as he ran his palms over the knees of his trousers—that made *her* nervous.

'You can ask me anything,' she encouraged, trying to put him at ease. He'd been a good friend to her, and that he was here now while she was in disgrace was proof of that.

He gave a winning smile. 'I want to ask you, Cora Graylin, will you marry me?'

Cora stared. Speechless. There was a time not so long ago when she would have said yes with relief if not abject joy. Not so long ago, this moment would have been the pinnacle of her hopes and even beyond—a peer's son proposing to her, a man who'd shown himself to be a friend, to be kind and interesting. Lord Alex Fenton would be a catch for any girl. But not for her, not now. She shook her head. 'I am flattered, but I must refuse, for both our sakes.' Surely, he understood that?

He sat back in his chair, his eyes solemn. 'That was quicker than I thought it would be. I am refused before the tea tray even arrives. I thought you might think about it just a little while before turning me down.' He did not say the words in hurt so much as he said them for instruction. 'We have always been able to speak plainly with one another, it is one of the many things I admire about you, and I think we must speak plainly now.'

The tea tray rattled in, China clinking as the servants set it down and departed. He continued as Cora poured out. 'A great social calamity has occurred. It is just beginning. It is likely to get worse before it gets better. How soon it gets better and goes away depends on how we choose to manage it and ourselves. We have a small window in which to respond.'

Cora poured a splash of cream into his cup and passed it to him. 'I am responding to it. I am leaving for Dorset in the morning. My maid is upstairs packing even as we speak.'

'I did not think you were the leaving type,' Fenton admonished.

'I am the protecting type,' Cora replied. 'Leaving is the best way for London to forget about me, for Declan to move on and for my sister to continue enjoying her engagement. The longer I stay, the longer people will be reminded of what happened.'

Fenton took a sip of tea, mulling over her words. 'Leaving is running and it's tantamount to saying you're guilty of all Lady Elizabeth charged you with.' He gave her a strong look. 'I don't simply mean the dresses. From a man's perspective, who cares about the dresses? It's the rest of it—the idea that you manipulated a good man, that you "stole" him from rightfully deserving girls. She paints you as a whore, do forgive my frankness.' He paused. 'If you leave now, you cannot come back.'

Cora gave a lift of one shoulder. 'Why should I stay? I shall not be invited anywhere. The Season is over for me either way.'

'But your life is not,' Lord Fenton protested. 'You are new to London's ways. Do not be so stubborn as to ignore good advice from someone who does know. A good marriage has resurrected many reputations. Marry me. We'll come back next Season and start over. Give it two years and no one will care in any significant way.'

Cora took a long, slow swallow of her tea. A reasonable girl would see the advantage of that. Once, she'd been a reasonable girl, ready to do her duty. She was still ready to do her duty, but not like this.

'Why would you sacrifice yourself like this for me?' What Lord Fenton offered was extraordinary, she did recognise that. In her darkest hour, he had come with a way out. Not just a way out, a way forward, a way to snatch victory from devastating defeat. What a coup it would be to see Lady Elizabeth Cleeves' face when the engagement was announced. But it was also petty.

Fenton smiled winningly. 'It is no sacrifice to marry you, Cora Graylin. I have often envied Declan for having seen you first. I wonder if I might have stood a better chance if it had just been you and I that night at the Harlow Ball.'

Cora played with a piece of shortbread. 'The papers will say the same things about you as they are saying about Declan, perhaps worse because you'll be taking his leftovers, a girl with a scandal.'

'It will all blow over and I am willing to wait for it because I believe in the life we can build.' He leaned forward in earnest. 'We can be happy together, Cora.' Hadn't Declan said those words just two days ago to her?

She could not let him tell himself that lie. Declan would always come between them. 'Your selflessness and gallantry humble me, but I cannot let you do such a thing. You deserve better. But I thank you, as a friend.'

He nodded slowly, weighing his words. 'I do not say this out of spite or disappointment, Cora, but I do not think Declan will come. If you're waiting for him, if you're hoping for him, I think that hope is misplaced. I saw him this morning. He is reeling. He feels betrayed, confused. He is full of self-recrimination. But he remains determined to do his duty for the Dukedom.' A duty she'd now made harder. 'I am told there is some additional difficulty with Lord Colby. The man has threatened to block Declan's membership in the Prometheus Club, a business investment club run by the Duke of Cowden. Membership is highly coveted.'

Cora stilled at the news, the shortbread forgotten. 'I suppose an engagement to Lady Elizabeth Cleeves would erase the threat. All the better that I am soon to be gone from the city then.' She rose, making it clear that the news did not change her mind regarding Fenton's proposal. Perhaps she *had* held out some hope in the depths of her heart that Declan would come, that he would want to listen to an explanation, to *her* account of events, that all could be repaired.

Lord Fenton stood and handed her his card. 'Call on me, any time before you leave, if there's anything I can do.' Or if she changed her mind, she was sure.

'Thank you, I will.' She said it out of politeness only. His chivalry deserved no less. But she would not see him again. She would not change her mind, although she saw misguided hope still lingering in his eyes that she would. She would leave tomorrow for Dorset and not look back. Ever.

Cora was gone and London acted as if she'd never existed. It had only taken three weeks and a handful of minor scandals to erase her presence. Lady Elizabeth

Cleeves in her newly acquired 'second' wardrobe which had been the cause of her missing early entertainments was the talk of the Town as the Season headed towards its frenzied zenith. Parliament was busy at work, keeping him up at all hours to meet and discuss legislation. Balls were in full force, as were the matchmaking mamas, who were closely watching their calendars. They'd barely drawn breath from Cora's departure when they'd been back at him again. Papas, too, this time, Declan noted.

All of it made him irrationally angry as he sought a moment's peace in a corner chair at White's, away from the low rumble of conversation on a late, lazy, summer afternoon. He ought to be glad Cora's name wasn't being dragged through the social mud. But he was irate over her being forgotten. Everyone carried on as if she'd never been here, which was of course in their best interest. But for him, it was as if she'd died. He was mourning her.

There was an emptiness in him that could not be filled, no matter how many hours he devoted to Parliament and entertainments. He wanted to escape, but how could he? He could not go to Riverside. The place, the grounds, would be full of memories of her. He could not drive in the park without thinking of her, could not walk in the enclosure without remembering their glorious afternoon, could not attend a ball without thinking of that first ball, could not pass a fountain without thinking about their wishes, about their talk that first morning at Riverside.

Declan pushed a hand through his hair. He'd been a bear to be around these past weeks. No one understood. His mother thought he was overreacting about a girl he'd only known a few weeks. Even Alex had not been his usual empathetic self, but perhaps that was because Alex was licking his own wounds where Cora was concerned. In his own words, Alex had reported she'd turned him down flat without even thinking about it. Out loud, Declan had said 'perhaps it's for the best', but inside part of him had rejoiced, even as he genuinely commiserated with his friend. It would have been too difficult to watch them together.

'May I join you?'

Declan looked up to see Alex approach. He could wave him off and he knew Alex would understand that. Sometimes a man just needed to be alone. 'Please, join me, although I can't ensure the company is worth it.' He signalled for the waiter to bring another drink.

'Still brooding, I see.' Alex settled in comfortably in the spare chair. 'Want to tell me about it?'

Declan gave a grim grin. 'Do you want to hear about it? Goodness knows you've borne the brunt of my dissembling these past weeks.'

Alex took the drink from the waiter's tray. 'That's what friends are for. Cheers.'

Declan waited until he'd had a sip of the brandy. 'I can't get over her. I know it's for the best that London has moved on, but then I get angry that it has. Because I can't. The truth is, I don't want to. I like remembering her. I replay our...conversations—' he had to choose his words carefully here, remembering that his friend had also been willing to marry her '—looking for clues as to what was real and what was not. What was betrayal, what was the lie, what was the truth? It's all mixed up in my head.'

He tapped his fingers on the chair arm. 'I think I might have made a mistake, letting her go without talking to her. I was so quick that night to dismiss her and then I was too stubborn. Now she's gone.' Had been gone for quite some time. The townhouse was closed. He'd gone by only to learn from a servant that Cora was gone and her aunt and uncle and her sister had accompanied Mr Wade to his family seat to celebrate their engagement *en famille*. To his credit, Mr Wade had not needed any encouragement from Declan to maintain the match. It had been a relief to him, and no doubt to Cora, to know that Elise's marriage would go forward.

'Does talking change anything at this point?' Alex enquired, taking a longer swallow of his drink.

What a good question that was. Distance, something he'd thought would serve him, help him heal, had not worked. What did he want from a conversation with her? Did he want an apology? Did he want an explanation after all? 'Perhaps I want closure. Perhaps hearing an explanation is the only way I can truly put her behind me.' Had he come to the same conclusion Alex had reached weeks ago, that perhaps not all lies and betrayal were equal, that there were some that might be understood, tolerated and forgiven so that people could start anew? If that was so, did he mean this conversation as a chance to mend their bridges?

Alex gave him a considering look. 'She might want closure, too. She is owed an apology, as well. You're not the only wronged party here.' It was something only a best friend could say to another. Not many people were willing to tell a duke he needed to say he was sorry.

Declan gave a wry smile. 'You always keep me humble, Alex.'

Alex grinned. 'Someone has to. Cora does.'

Declan nodded. Yes, she did. It was one of her many charms. She was not afraid to speak her mind and yet she did so unobtrusively, not like Lady Elizabeth Cleeves.

Alex studied his drink. 'Would you rethink your engagement if the two of you could settle things?' Because closure implied endings, but also the opportunity for new beginnings.

'Maybe. I don't know.' Something akin to nerves fluttered in Declan's stomach. It was not a feeling he was used to. Dukes weren't nervous. Everything was a foregone conclusion. But not with Cora, nothing had been assumed. She'd made him work. 'We might get closure. We might be able to heal our wounds, but I am not sure that means we could get to a place where we could try again.' He hesitated, not wanting to say the words out loud for fear of making them real. But they were real, and they deserved to be spoken. 'The damage might be too great.' They had betrayed each other that fateful night in Cowden's ballroom. One gust of scandalous wind had been enough to blow them down. He regretted that.

'What of Lord Colby's threat?' Alex asked. 'That will still exist.'

'Cowden has handled him for me. As of this morning, I am a full investing partner in the club.' Declan smiled. It was the first bit of good news he'd had in a long while, and it had pleased him mightily. This membership was about the future, about the legacy he would hand down, God willing, to his sons, to his daughters' dowries and sons-in-law. It was for a family he didn't have yet.

Alex grinned and finished off his drink. 'Then all you have to do is shop and pack. We'll have you off to Dorset in no time.'

'Shop?' Declan furrowed his brow. Alex's statement had caught him by surprise. He supposed he was off to Dorset. That's where all of this was leading, although he hadn't actually said the words. But how else was he to speak with her?

'She has sisters, you dolt. Ladies respond well to gifts, they respond even better when gentlemen show kindness to their little sisters. Hasn't anyone ever told you that the true judge of a man is how he treats family, dogs and the elderly?'

'What about horses?' He didn't know if Cora had a dog but she did have a horse, Delilah.

'I'm sure horses count, too.' Alex clapped him on the shoulder. 'Come on, let's go pick out gifts and then we'll pack your trunk.'

'Nothing too big, I think I'll take Samson and not the coach. The weather is good for a long road trip on horseback and I'll make better time.' The last thing he wanted was to spend days cooped up in a coach with nothing to do but think about Cora and his regrets, what he might have said instead that awful night, and what he might do when he got to Dorset. He'd be second guessing himself before the first day was over.

Chapter Twenty-Two

Cora had been second guessing her decision since the day she arrived home. Not because home seemed that much shabbier after the luxuries of the Graylin town-house and London, but because she was not used to running from a fight. Nearly a month later, here she was, hanging out laundry and replaying her choices yet again. Should she have stayed in London? Should she have stormed Harlow House and demanded he see her? Demanded she be allowed the courtesy of an explanation? But it wasn't just about the explanation. It was what the explanation stood for. Love hadn't been enough to see them through.

Cora flapped a wet sheet to loosen the sodden folds, then reached for another wooden pin to fasten it to the line. Had leaving been selfish? She'd told Lord Fenton she was leaving to save face for others, but privately she knew she had also left to save face for herself. To be shunned by Declan again would have been too much to bear. To be in Town and know he was choosing not to see her—to watch his engagement to Lady Mary Kimber be announced after a decent interval—would have required more strength than she had.

She'd given him her heart, among other things. She'd trusted him with her hope. Stupid, stupid girl that she was. She knew better and she'd let herself be talked into something different, simply because she'd wanted it to be true. Wanting didn't make it so. It wasn't just her heart that was broken, it was her hope.

She reached for a chemise from the basket and hung it up. It had been a relief to be home, otherwise. She was needed here. She could see to the garden, see to the menus for Cook, she could see to the house and the parishioners. Kitty and Melly had done their best, but they were still young and more successful with parish duties when they could follow her on rounds instead of going alone. She smiled at the thought of her sisters. Kitty and Melly had loved the rolls of pink ribbon. The three of them had spent enjoyable evenings trimming hats and summer dresses with it. Even Veronica had trimmed a dress. She was developing a very neat stitch.

Between the parish, her sisters and the house, there was plenty to keep her busy. But she was fast learning being busy wasn't enough to fill the hole inside her left by Declan's absence. Or perhaps it wasn't Declan but the hurt? It was hard to tell. Declan and hurt seemed inseparable these days.

A little reminder nudged at her: *It means you loved him. If one did not love in the first place, one could not hurt in the second.*

She fingered the opal necklace she wore beneath her work dress. It had become habit. What was Declan doing right now? It was not quite mid-afternoon. Perhaps he was at his clubs, talking with Alex. Or maybe he was still doing estate work and meeting with his solicitor. Or, maybe, he was taking Lady Mary Kimber for a drive in Hyde Park, showing her how to handle his phaeton. Maybe they'd pulled over to the verge and were talking to a group of friends. Maybe later tonight, he'd waltz with her at a ball—the papers would report on how well they looked together, how well he'd recovered from the upset earlier in the Season, how the world had righted itself, all people back in their places as July careened towards August and the end of the Season.

This was a game she played too often when she was alone with her thoughts, the 'What was he doing now and who was he doing it with?' game. It was a special kind of torture, but it served as a reminder that things were over between them. Ducal lives didn't mesh with parish lives. She understood that better now. The fairy tale had become a cautionary tale with a strong moral at the end, like the Russian folk tale of the bun her mother had once told them. The bun had tried to escape his fate by running away, but buns are meant to be eaten, and so he was.

Cora picked up the laundry basket and settled it against her hip, wiping a hand across her forehead. It was warm today. The clothes would dry quickly, thank goodness. She'd been a bit late getting them hung out. She ran through the remaining chores in her head. There were sugar snap peas to pick in the garden, weeding to be done, Veronica's lessons to plan for the next day and…

She shielded her eyes and looked down the road. A cloud of dust was forming, a sure sign of a carriage or a horse and rider. Cora gave a grumpy sigh. Had her father invited someone to supper again and forgotten to tell her? It had happened last week and she'd had to improvise something above the usual fare on short notice. Her mind was already going through the larder. There was a ham they could use, and potatoes to go with the fresh snap peas. She squinted hard. It was a rider on a big chestnut horse.

Her pulse sped—it was silliness really. Just because it was a chestnut horse didn't mean it was Samson. Just because the rider was dark-haired, didn't mean it was Declan. Dorset was a long way from London. And yet, the closer they drew, the surer she became.

He was here.

A thousand thoughts went through her mind, not a single one of them about ham or snap peas. All of them about him and what he'd come for. Had he come for her? For an explanation? Or had he come to tell her in person that he and Lady Mary Kimber were to be wed?

He pulled the horse up in front of her and swung down, the casually elegant dismount of a man born to the saddle. 'Hello, Cora.'

'Declan.' Was that a hint of reticence she heard in his voice? Uncertainty over his reception? Or, horror of horrors, the thought coming too late to her, the unpleasant surprise of seeing her in a work dress and damp apron splotched from the laundry, a kerchief on her head. It was a far cry from the high fashion she wore in London. 'Were you just out for a ride? Just in the neighbourhood?' She tried for a joke. How long did it take to ride from London to Dorset? It was at least ninety miles. The journey had taken her and Elise almost three days by coach in the opposite direction.

'I heard there was good fishing,' he joked back, and it helped to ease the surprise and the tension. Then he sobered. 'I wanted to see you.' He reached for her empty basket. 'Let me take this. Were you going inside?'

'Yes.' She wasn't sure she wanted him inside, though. The house was a mess due to it being laundry day, and the girls were there. They'd be wild with the prospect of a handsome guest and there would be explaining to do. And there was his horse to consider. If he was waiting for a groom to come out to take Samson, he'd be standing here the rest of the day. 'Perhaps we should stop by the barn first and take care of Samson.'

In the barn, she studied Declan over Samson's back as she brushed the horse's coat. He didn't seem to mind doing his own work. He'd made himself right at home, stopping to pet Delilah before stripping out of his riding jacket, grabbing a pitchfork and preparing the empty stall for Samson. His muscles seemed to know what to do, heaving forkfuls of hay effortlessly, and her eyes clearly hadn't forgotten how to watch him. That was a bad sign. She needed to be rational with him, stand her ground. This was her home, her territory. She needed to be strong here. She could not forget he'd hurt her, and she'd hurt him, just because it was entrancing to watch him toss hay.

Once they'd settled Samson, Declan put his saddlebags and valise in the basket—she could put off going to the house no longer. But another concern cropped up. 'How long are you here? Do you need a place to stay?' There were no spare rooms. She could give him her room though. She could move in with Melly and Kitty since Elise was gone.

He offered a tender smile that had her stomach doing flips. 'It's all right. You needn't discommode yourself. I have rooms at the George and Dragon on Corn Market.' He lowered his voice, leaning closer in that way of his that implied intimacy. 'I remembered what you said about the house being crowded.'

'I appreciate the thoughtfulness.' She wished he wouldn't be so considerate, though—it was hard to maintain resolve. 'You will stay for dinner? There's always room for people at the table. It won't be fancy,' she warned.

'I would love to stay for dinner and I've had enough of "fancy" to last me a while.' He halted before they reached the door. 'A word please, before we go in. Make no mistake why I am here, Cora. We have much that is unresolved between us, and I've been in error thinking that it could be ignored. I thought distance would be the answer. I was wrong. You and I must talk, later. These last weeks have been tumultuous for me. Nothing has been clear without you and I am at a loss as to how to go on. But for now, I've had a long ride and I want to enjoy meeting your family, and simply being with you. If that is not possible, tell me. I will fetch Samson and be on my way. I don't wish to bother you and I don't wish to cause you further hurt.'

It was a pretty speech and it mirrored much of what was in her heart. Distance had not solved anything. The wound was still open. It was a salve to her own hurt to know that she'd not been hurting alone. That he'd missed her as she'd missed him. But that resolved nothing. The issue was still there.

She swallowed against the tightness in her throat. She

needed to be careful not to assume this was an apology or a resolution. It wasn't. She smiled. 'Please stay.' Then she slid him a sly, playful look as she pushed open the door. 'But brace yourself, and don't say I didn't warn you.'

The three girls were at the long dining room table, finishing lessons. They looked up at the intrusion, mouths dropping, eyes going wide. 'Girls, I'd like you to meet—' Cora began, wanting to get at least a few words in before her sisters started squealing, but Declan interrupted.

'I'm Declan Locke, a friend of your sister's from Town,' he said swiftly, shooting her a look. There would be no Duke here tonight. His Grace the Duke of Harlow had been left in London. He reached into his saddlebags. 'You must be Miss Melisandre, and you, Miss Katherine, and you must be Miss Veronica.' He passed each of them a small, prettily wrapped box of bonbons from Gunther's. They remembered their manners, but just barely, Cora noted.

'I've brought a larger box for dessert this evening.' He handed a final box to her, a secret look passing between them.

'I'll have our cook arrange them on a plate, they'll look too pretty to eat. You are too thoughtful to think of the girls.' They had so few luxuries. Cora thought Declan couldn't possibly know how much they'd appreciate the little gift. 'We'll leave them to savour the treat. Come through, if you don't mind the mess. We'll leave the chocolate in the kitchen and head into the garden. I have snap peas to pick and it's cooler out there.' It was more private, too, for whatever they had to say to one another.

The kitchen was a crowded, warm space, the worktable filled with Cook's dinner preparations and fresh vegetables. There were introductions to make. Cook was charmed by Declan but all Cora could see was the mess, the shabbiness. She grabbed a bowl for the peas, bumping into Declan in the tight space. 'Oops, sorry. Tight quarters.'

Declan turned her around and ushered her towards the back door. 'What are you apologising for, Cora? Stop it.' It was better outside, the afternoon starting to cool.

'The house is a mess.' There was a blanket draped on the settee that hadn't been folded, the girls' school papers were strewn on the table and the vase on the mantel was empty with no fresh flowers.

'It's cosy,' Declan assured her. 'And if anyone should apologise, it's me. I've shown up unexpectedly and disrupted the day.'

She laughed. 'But you've brought chocolate, so all is forgiven.' Cora let out a sigh and felt the weight release from her shoulders. She shouldn't give in so easily, shouldn't let go of her wariness. 'You are sure you don't mind? It's a far cry from Harlow House.' She set the bowl down between them and began picking. 'We don't have Italian glass and Roman fountains.'

'If I wanted Harlow House, Cora, I would still be in London.' His gaze lingered on her, forcing her to meet his eyes, to see all that statement entailed. It wasn't just Harlow House but all that Harlow House stood for. 'I had thought we'd talk later after dinner, but I find I can't wait. My heart is full at seeing you again.'

He gave a humble smile that rocked her foundations.

Her resolve was slipping away rapidly. 'On the journey, I convinced myself that I was coming so that you could give me an explanation. But that was rather arrogant of me, to think I was doing you the favour of my presence. Now that I am here, I want more than anything to offer you *my* apology. I had sworn to you that my love would be enough, just that afternoon, and I broke that promise hours later. I allowed you to be vilified when you are the most precious thing in my world.'

His voice broke a little and Cora reached for his hands. 'I was not strong at the crucial moment, Cora. I had come from Harlow House and a difficult discussion with my mother. I learned that the Duke of Colby had a blackmail scheme to entice me to offer for Lady Elizabeth, which put the future economic health of the Dukedom at risk should I fail to comply.' And he'd spent his strength that afternoon fighting her, too, Cora thought, convincing her that they could have a life together.

He'd had to be strong for both of them, fighting for them on all fronts, all those days and weeks. It was no wonder Lady Elizabeth's claims had broken him. His fight had been for nothing. His efforts had been betrayed.

'No, Declan. You were always the strong one.' If she'd been braver, told him everything, trusted him, they could have been a united front, he could have used his energies better. In her own way, with her own fears, she'd weakened him even as she thought to protect him.

'Cora, let me say this.' His eyes pleaded for patience, for silence. 'You are precious to me. Not your dresses. Not your house or your social standing. None of that matters. I am not myself without you, my real self. I don't think I've been my real self for a very long time.'

His hands closed tightly around hers, squeezing hard. 'Blue is the colour of hope, did you know that? That first night at the Harlow Ball, I'd nearly given up hope. I'd decided to waltz with Lady Mary because there was no hope left. I had to concede. Then you walked in and you were my hope and my life started again, or perhaps for the first time. And then I stupidly threw that hope away. The way I treated you at the Cowden Ball was despicable. I cannot apologise enough. You gave me your trust that afternoon, and I proved unworthy of it almost immediately. That remains true even if we've mismanaged the aftermath between us.'

'You are not alone. You gave me your trust, too, and I was not a good steward of it either, because I didn't believe in it and, without intending to, perhaps I treated it cheaply,' Cora said softly. She'd not expected this. 'I could have told you from the start I was a vicar's daughter with no money or prospects. That first night in the garden, when you asked why you hadn't met me before, I could have told you then. But I was so wrapped up in the moment, in the fairy tale of you.'

Her voice struggled against the wave of emotion that swept her. 'I thought it didn't matter, that I wouldn't see you again, that I could go home and put away the dress, the memories, put away you. Then you asked me to the house party. I should have said no, I should have warned you so that you knew what you were getting into. But I didn't. There were so many chances to tell you and I didn't take them. I didn't trust you with them. I didn't trust myself with you. I wasn't supposed to fall, I was just supposed to enjoy the fairy tale. I tried to convince myself I would only be hurting me when it ended, but I was hurting you, too. At first, I thought ignorance would protect you. Then, after Lady Elizabeth, I thought distance would protect you.'

She drew a deep breath. 'She was right about the dresses. I didn't order them. We tried to return them and, when we couldn't determine the dressmaker, we tried to pay for them, but Madame Dumont was out of Town and her assistant wouldn't take the money. They're not real, as in they're not really mine. The love was always real, though. What hurt the most about Lady Elizabeth's accusations wasn't the dresses. I deserved that. The worst was that you thought I had manipulated you, lied to you about my feelings.' After weeks of thinking through what she wanted to tell him, wanted to explain to him, all that really mattered was that. The love was real.

'It's still real. It's still there, Cora,' he whispered, 'if you want it.' His blue eyes glittered like gems as he pressed her hand to his heart.

'*Is* it that easy, Declan?' Oh, how she wanted it to be. Standing here in the garden, every pulse of her wanted it to be true. 'What about Colby and the Prometheus Club? It's just the beginning of doors that might be shut against you.'

He pressed a finger to her lips. She'd rather have his mouth. 'Cowden has taken our side. No one challenges dukes, it will all be fine eventually. In the meanwhile, we have our own relationship to mend. I *do* want to mend it. You keep me honest and humble, and I desperately need that.' Declan smiled.

'What about your mother?' She felt obliged to bring up all of the obstacles before she let hope run away with her. 'Family is important to both you and I, and your family includes her.'

'She will come around. Just give her time.' He gave her a look. 'What about *your* father? Do you think he'll approve of me? May I speak with him tonight?'

He was leaving their future up to her. She'd been given a second chance and she was going to take it. This last month had shown her that perhaps they were both right. Love was indeed precious and fragile, but if used correctly, it could be applied to great things. 'Yes, speak to him as soon as he gets home.'

She was in his arms then, mouths and bodies meeting, a dam of emotion and absence let loose. There, amid the rows of snap peas, she could not get enough of him. A month apart had been too long. 'Don't worry, Cora, I am not going anywhere. Not ever again,' he whispered between kisses.

She laughed. 'Well, you haven't had dinner with the whole family yet.'

He took her hand firmly and smiled, his blue eyes dancing. 'Then let's go in and get it over with.' But he laughed as he said it, and Cora thought the future suddenly seemed as bright as his eyes.

Chapter Twenty-Three

Her family did not disappoint. When Cora and Declan returned inside with a bowl full of peas, the house she'd worried over had been tidied, courtesy of Kitty, and the table set with the best dishes and a fresh bouquet of wildflowers at its centre, courtesy of Melly and Veronica. Cook outdid herself on the meal, filling the house with delicious aromas. By the time food was on the table and Declan and her father disappeared into the study, a trill of anticipation was already running through the house. Perhaps it might have been the simple rare treat of having company for supper, or perhaps her sisters sensed something more important was in the air.

Melly offered to do her hair, and Kitty urged her to put on one of her London dresses from Aunt B. 'The blue one with the white flowers,' Kitty suggested as Melly threaded a ribbon through her hair.

'Are you two playing matchmaker?' Cora laughed. Her stomach was aflutter with nerves, with wanting to be downstairs in Father's office with Declan.

The two girls exchanged sly looks. 'We think the match has already been made.' They giggled. 'Oh, Cora, how did you meet him? He's so tall and so handsome,' they gushed.

'It's a long story,' Cora told them, 'too long for right now. We are needed downstairs. Cook can't get supper on by herself.' Declan or no Declan, there were still chores to do.

He was waiting for her at the bottom of the stairs, looking at ease in his surroundings. He'd borrowed her father's room to wash up and change his shirt. He wore a fresh waistcoat embroidered with flowers, and he'd made a good effort at brushing his jacket. 'I see you've mastered the look of country gentleman,' Cora complimented, sliding her arm through his.

'As have you. The country becomes you. I like you this way, in your natural habitat, although you look good in London, too.' He always made her feel like a queen with his manners and attention. Perhaps it didn't matter if they were at the vicarage or a fine townhouse. Perhaps it only mattered that they were together.

'I trust all went well with my father?' Would Declan see beyond the brokenness to the man he might still be? The father he'd once been?

Declan drew her aside before they went into the dining room, his gaze softening. 'He cares for you. He asked me if *you* approved the match, and he asked if I loved you. He was very adamant that this not be a marriage of convenience, but of love. He didn't want you throwing yourself away out of some notion of sacrifice for the family.' He chuckled, his eyes warm blue pools as they rested on her. 'I'm glad I only have to do that once. It was very lowering to be cut down to size.'

'Thank you.' Cora kissed his cheek.

He tugged her hand. 'Come, let's go make this official.'

Inside the dining room, her sisters and father were gathered around the table, the platters of food already on, a rare bottle of wine beside her father's place. Cora's heart soared after her father gave the blessing. It was to be a party of sorts. Declan held her chair, and as she sat he cleared his throat and took her hand.

'Before we eat, I would like to share that Cora has consented to marry me.' There was immediate commotion around the table, her sisters gasping and sighing. Declan waited for the excitement to die down. 'When I left London, I took the advice of a good friend. I procured a special licence. If it is all right with Cora, I'd like to be married as soon as possible, next week, at the church here in Wimborne.'

'My church?' her father said, surprised and perhaps a bit awed.

'Your church, Sir, and, if you please, by yourself performing the service. I do ask for a week's time so that my mother can make the journey, and so that the rest of your family can attend.' Cora's heart squeezed. He'd thought of Elise and Aunt B and Uncle George, who were currently visiting the Wades.

'And we must plan!' Melly put in. 'There are flowers to decide, and a wedding breakfast, and a gown. Oh, dear, what will we do for a gown? There's no time to make anything.'

Cora laughed. 'I have plenty of dresses from London that will work fine. You can help me pick one.'

'Or you can wear Mother's,' Kitty put in, exercising

her newfound authority. She might not be ready to take over parish duties, but she'd made great strides in running the house. 'I know where it is.'

'We'll decide that later,' Cora put a gentle lid on the excitement. 'Tonight, we should celebrate.' She looked around the table at the beaming faces of her family. She felt the press of Declan's hand on hers beneath the table, the discreet brush of his thigh against her skirts. Her heart was full. So this was love, and she was surrounded by it on all sides.

So this was love. It was heady and chaotic, and full of laughter and hope. After a week of being surrounded by feminine frivolity and girlish giggles, as Cora's sisters put a wedding celebration together, Declan finally stood at the front of St Cuthburga, the great stone church of Wimborne Minster—Alex on one side, his bride's father dressed in his ecclesiastical robes on the other, the common book of worship in his hand.

In the front pew on the groom's side sat his mother, the Dowager Duchess of Harlow, wearing an enormous purple hat. Her posture was perfectly straight. But Declan thought he detected a distinct sparkle to his mother's eye when she'd seen him standing there, ready to take the next step into full adulthood. His father had once told him age didn't make a man. A man wasn't truly a man until he had a wife and a family of his own. Today, he'd take one step closer to that, and hopefully the rest would follow soon.

On the bride's side sat his soon to be new in-laws, Viscount Graves and his wife, their son, and Mr Wade,

Cora's sisters, Aunt B and Uncle George. Most of the parish had turned out, from merchants to the squire, to a few of the more prosperous sheep farmers minus one John Arnot, Declan was glad to note. Others would come for the wedding breakfast. The only arrival that mattered now was the bride.

Declan drew a breath and closed his eyes, letting his mind travel the route she would take in an open carriage with Elise beside her as her maid of honour. They would make a brief circle through the village so that those who weren't attending could see the bride in her finery, and then they would stop outside the church. The big door at the back began to open and Declan opened his eyes. She was here.

Elise came first, looking summer-fresh in a dress of white muslin with yellow flowers. There would be those who'd remark on how lovely she looked, but Declan, as he had the night of the Harlow Ball, was already looking past her. This time, though, he knew what he would find. Cora Graylin, the woman he loved, the woman he needed and wanted as a partner for the life ahead, a woman who looked at him and saw the man he was.

She was radiant today. Some would say it was the gown—in the end she'd worn her mother's dress of white linen with the embroidered flower hem—that accounted for the radiance, but Declan disagreed. He thought it was the love that made her shine. He sought her gaze and held it as she began the slow walk towards him, sending up a prayer that he be worthy of her. That his love be worthy of her. That she never have cause to doubt him again.

She reached him and he took her hand, surety and

hope filling him as Vicar Graylin began the service that would bind them together for life. In the summer of 1824, Declan Locke, Duke of Harlow, knew this one truth to be self-evident. Love was enough. Best of all, his wife believed it, too.

Epilogue

Autumn, Wimborne Minster,
1830

'Hold your pole steady…that's right, son. Now, reel it in nice and slowly.' Declan stood behind his five-year-old son Andrew, coaching him through his first catch, a net at the ready. 'You're doing well. Mama and the baby will have a good supper. Look at that! A nice big one.'

He treasured moments like these, of being with Andrew, of doing with him all the things his father had done with him. He had once only dreamed, only hoped of times like these. Now they were his in abundance, and he did not take them for granted.

Declan got the net around the fish. 'Let's show Mama. She'll be so proud.' They tromped through the summer shallows of the river. At the shore Declan paused, putting a hand on his son's shoulder. 'Take a moment and look at that. What do you see?'

Drew turned dark eyes on him that were so like Cora's. 'I see Mama and baby sister on the blanket. I see a campfire burning. Our tent set up for the night. The horses grazing.'

'Make a memory picture, Drew. It won't make sense now, but it will later, my boy, when you're grown up. This is what love looks like, what family looks like. Hold it in your heart so you don't forget.'

The sun was setting, turning the early autumn sky pink and purple by turn. The sight of Cora playing with their eight-month-old daughter stirred an emotion so strong it could not be named. It had been a hard birth, much harder than Drew, who had been born nine and a half months after their wedding after an indecently short labour. Perhaps that was why Alexandra Catherine, named for Cora's mother, was all the more precious to him.

Cora spied them and gave a wave, her face breaking into a smile as he held up the net. He loved her more now than when he'd married her, and even then he'd thought his heart would break from loving her. They'd managed the compromise of ducal life well. He'd made good on his promise to build her a home in Wimborne Minster that was both cosy and stately and sans Italian glass. He did travel occasionally to his other estates, but this was home, where everything he loved abided.

Everything she loved was here with her, beneath the stars. She treasured these family camp outs. Cora looked about her as the fish roasted on the spit. Andrew was rolling a ball to his baby sister who was almost able to roll it back. Little Alexandra adored her brother—anything Andrew did made her giggle. Cora would never tire of the sound of her children laughing together.

Declan stretched out beside her, reaching for her hand. 'Are you glad to be home?' This was the first camp out since returning from London. The session had run slightly longer than usual, and they'd made a trip to Somerset to see Elise and her new baby. Alexandra would have a cousin her age to grow up with.

'So glad. Just look at the sky. And you? Are you glad to be back?' She hardly needed to ask. She'd seen his face in the river with Andrew. He'd lived for the moment his son caught his first fish. Just as he lived for the days he gave Andrew riding lessons in the round pen, Andrew trotting around on his wondrously patient and fat pony. Declan had been born a duke, but he was *meant* for fatherhood.

He raised her hand to his lips and kissed her knuckles. 'I was thinking of expanding the school this year, perhaps building living quarters so that girls could come from further away. Kitty has shown an aptitude for teaching and organising. I was wondering what you thought about making her headmistress?'

Cora beamed. 'I like that idea very much.' The school had been one of their first passion projects. She'd overseen much of it, but, with two children of her own now, she wanted to spend more time with them and take on a supervisory role that was less focused on the day-to-day operations of the school. 'I'll ask her on Sunday after church and see what she thinks.'

'I promised your father I'd look over his books after Sunday dinner. He's making progress, Cora.' Declan gave her a wink.

'All thanks to you. You put his finances back into order and gave him very useful suggestions.' Declan's efforts with her father had eased all their burdens and allowed them to reclaim their lives. Melisandre was spending the year with Aunt B and Uncle George preparing for her debut next spring, and Veronica was thriving with the other young girls at the school, having discovered her own passion for biblical studies, which pleased Cora's father. It had, in fact, done a world of good for his spirits. He had taken over his parish duties now, making visits with Veronica at his side, which had been a relief to Cora, who had her own home to run. She owed this man beside her so much. He'd made her whole again.

Declan stole a kiss. 'How's the fairy tale going, my dear?'

'Well.' She laughed softly, holding his gaze.

'What do you think the chances are of us living happily ever after?' he murmured at her ear.

'Quite good, actually.'

And so they did.

* * * * *

If you enjoyed this story, be sure to read
Bronwyn Scott's previous Historical romances

The Captain Who Saved Christmas
The Art of Catching a Duke

And why not check out the author's
Enterprising Widows miniseries?

A Deal with the Rebellious Marquess
Alliance with the Notorious Lord
Liaison with the Champagne Count

Reader Service

Enjoyed your book?

Try the perfect subscription for Romance readers and get more great books like this delivered right to your door.

See why over 10+ million readers have tried Harlequin Reader Service.

Start with a Free Welcome Collection with free books and a gift—valued over $20.

Choose any series in print or ebook. See website for details and order today:

TryReaderService.com/subscriptions

RSBPA24R